Also by Nancy Coco

All Fudged Up

TO FUDGE
OR NOT
TO FUDGE

Nancy Coco

KENSINGTON PUBLISHING CORP.
http://www.kensingtonbooks.com

KENSINGTON BOOKS are published by

Kensington Publishing Corp.
119 West 40th Street
New York, NY 10018

All Kensington Titles, Imprints, and Distributed Lines are available at special quantity discounts for bulk purchases for sales
promotions, premiums, fund-raising, and educational or institu-
tional use. Special book excerpts or customized printings can
also be created to fit specific needs. For details, write or phone
the office of the Kensington special sales manager: Kensington
Publishing Corp., 119 West 40th Street, New York, NY 10018,
attn: Special Sales Department, Phone: 1-800-221-2647.

Kensington and the K logo Reg. U.S. Pat & TM Off.

ISBN-13: 978-0-7582-8712-0
ISBN-10: 0-7582-8712-7
First Kensington Mass Market Edition: September 2014

eISBN-13: 978-0-7582-8713-7
eISBN-10: 0-7582-8713-5
First Kensington Electronic Edition: September 2014

10 9 8 7 6 5 4 3 2 1

Printed in the United States of America

For my sister Kathi,
who understands about puppies, chocolate, and murder.
Thanks for a lifetime of listening to my stories.

CHAPTER 1

"A lilac by any other name still smells as sweet."

"Mal, get out from under that lilac bush," I called. It was almost time for the Lilac Festival, and my bichon/poodle puppy Marshmallow had fallen in love with the thick mulch that was spread under the lilacs. For some reason she found the bushes next to the *Town Crier,* Mackinac Island's newspaper, to be the most enticing.

I tugged on her leash. Mal dug in her heels and refused to budge. Like a fisherman fighting a hook, I reeled in the leash. This served to pull on her pink harness and drag one stubborn doggie out from under the bush one inch at a time. "Come on, Mal, let's at least pretend I'm in charge," I muttered and pulled harder.

As the proud yet harried owner of a 121-year-old hotel and fudge shop, I'd walked down to the newspaper to place a want ad for a part-time maid to help fill in during the busy times. Mackinac Island was known for its quaint Victorian feel. There were no cars. In fact, they were banned from the island. Only bicycles and horse-drawn carriages filled the streets.

Mal was a gift from my dear friend and reservation manager, Frances Wentworth. The puppy was supposed to keep me safe from evildoers. She had done her job well last month when I found myself investigating my grandfather's best friend's murder. I kind of had to as he had been murdered in my utility closet.

Still, on the days when she wasn't protecting me, Mal had a tendency to boss me about. Especially when it came to doing things she was interested in doing . . . like sniffing under lilac bushes—instead of what I was supposed to be doing . . . placing an ad in the paper.

"Come on, Mal, I need to get this errand done before noon." I yanked on the leash. Suddenly she popped out from under the bushes with a bone in her mouth.

I did a double take. Was that a sock hanging from that bone?

Surely not, but on close inspection it had an argyle pattern like a sock. It was knitted like a sock. Okay, so there was a huge hole in what appeared to be a heel like a sock. But then Mal loved socks. Maybe other dogs did too. Maybe, just maybe, some dog buried their bone in their favorite sock. It could happen, right?

I mean, what were the chances that the sock belonged to the bone? Slim to none. Right?

Mal proudly dropped the sock-wrapped bone at my feet and nudged it as if to show me what she found. Her little stubby tail wagged.

"I sure hope that's not what I think it is." I poked it with my white Keds. There was no way I was going to pick it up.

She pushed the bone toward me, wagged her bobbed tail, and darted back under the lilac bush. "Mal, come on, I have work to do." I yanked on her harness only for her to prance out from under the bush. This time she had what looked like part of a shoe in her mouth. She shook the shoe as if to kill it. Dirt and mulch went flying, along with hard pieces that hit my legs with a *thump, thud, thump*.

Those hard pieces had toenails painted a neon orange.

The spit dried up in my mouth. Adrenaline washed through me. I did what any sane person would do. I scooped up my dog, yanked the shoe out of her mouth, dropped it next to the sock bone, and ran straight into the *Town Crier*.

There was no way I was going to be alone outside with portions of a dead person. I mean really, what if whoever it had been had been attacked by a wild animal and dragged under the bush to be saved for a later meal? Or worse. What if the animal was a rabid creature using the remains as bait? It could be true. There was no way I was going to hang around and find out.

"Dogs aren't allowed in here," said an older gentleman with a white beard, a balding head, and reading glasses perched at the edge of his nose.

"Right." I faced him and held the door closed with my body. Mal leapt out of my arms and sat down to stare at the old guy as if to dare him to kick her out.

He stared at me. "The dog . . ."

I found my voice. "Just dug up remains from under your lilac bush."

He drew his bushy white brows together over his dark brown eyes. "Excuse me?"

I swallowed and cleared my throat as I fumbled for my phone. "Call 9-1-1. I think there's a dead guy under your lilac bush."

"A dead . . . what?" He stood and took a step away from me, using his desk as a shield between him and the crazy woman at his door. It would have been funny if I weren't the crazy woman.

"Person," I said. "Well, not a whole person. A part of a person who wears argyle socks and leather shoes . . . oh, and paints their toenails orange."

He picked up the phone and hit a single button. "Hi, Charlene," he said. "Get Officer Manning over here, will ya? There's a crazy woman in my office. No, she doesn't appear to have a weapon, just a small white dog. Um, hmm, hold on. Are you the McMurphy girl?"

"Yes," I said, my hands fumbling with my phone. After last month's trouble I had Officer Rex Manning's number on speed dial; I hit the button.

"The one who found Joe Jessop dead in a utility closet?"

"Yes." I put the phone up to my ear and listened to it ring.

"It's the same crazy woman," the man said into his phone. "Right. Okay. Bye." He hung up the phone and sat down slowly, watching me with narrowed eyes as the ringing on my phone dropped me into Rex's voice mail.

"Hey, hi," I said into my cell phone. "I hope you're on your way to the *Town Crier.* I'm pretty sure Mal dug up a dead person."

I hit the END CALL button. The old man studied me, and I studied him. He reached into his desk drawer and pulled something out. Then he slapped it down in front of him. It was a rabbit's foot. Ew. Okay, I'd seen enough disembodied feet for one day, thank you very much.

"What is that?"

He raised his right bushy eyebrow. "If you don't know I bet the dog could tell ya."

I sighed and crossed my arms. "It's a rabbit's foot. I know what it is. I wanted to know why you got it out."

"Because I don't know how to make an evil eye." He tipped back in his chair, and it squeaked.

"An evil eye?" I shook my head, dazed. "I don't get it."

"It wards off bad omens and such," he said and reached over to adjust his placement, ensuring the rabbit's foot sat square between him and me.

"Um, okay. I'd join you behind your rabbit's foot, but I'm currently busy making sure the door stays closed."

"Now why would you be doing that?"

"Because there is a killer out there. It might be a wild animal. It might be a serial murderer. Either way, there is going to be a door between me and it." I hated to sound smug, but really, a strong wooden door was a lot better at keeping a rabid animal away than a rabbit's foot.

"Well, there, see, that's where we disagree."

"We do?" I scrunched up my eyebrows.

"As far as I can tell the bad luck is already inside with me."

"What? Where?" I glanced around, but there were only three of us inside: me, him, and Mal.

"I'm looking at it." His gaze was steady on me.

"You mean me?" I pointed to my pink polo shirt.

"You're the only one in this room that finds old men dead and seeing as how I'm an old man . . ."

"But you're not dead," I tried to reason with him.

"Thus the rabbit's foot."

"Okay, seriously, I don't know what you heard, but I did not murder anyone."

"I didn't say you did."

"But you just said . . ."

"That you have been known to be alone when you find old men dead." He shrugged. "I'm hedging my bets."

I didn't know what to say to that, so I simply glared at him. He glared back. Mal sneezed and we both jumped.

"Does the dog bite?" The man finally broke the silence.

"Mal? No, she's a puppy." I picked her up and decided to play nice. I stuck out my hand. "I didn't properly introduce myself. I'm Allie. I run the McMurphy."

"I know." He sat back carefully, still wary. "Charlene told me."

"Right." I pulled my empty hand back.

"Besides, I'm a reporter, not much escapes my notice." He crossed his arms over his wide chest.

"Except a dead body under your bushes."

"I thought you said it was a sock and shoe."

"With bones and toenails." I hugged Mal until she squeaked.

"Orange painted toenails." He pursed his mouth. "Yep, you told me that part, Ms. McMurphy."

"I'm not crazy," I said in my own defense.

"There are people on this island who would disagree with that." He watched me from over the top of his eyeglasses.

"There are people on this island who think we should allow cars. Everything people think is not always right."

"Well, you have me there." He leaned back. "I'm Angus MacElroy."

"I'd say it's very nice to meet you, but right now I'm not so sure." Mal wiggled, but I held her tight. Her fluffy fur was a comfort.

"Why'd you come here, Ms. McMurphy?" Angus asked.

"I came over to place a want ad, but instead it seems I've uncovered a dead body or possibly a murder victim." I tilted my head and studied him as if he were the perfect suspect. For all I knew, he was. "Being a reporter, you probably have seen a million dead bodies."

"Only ten and they were open-casket funerals," he admitted, his brown eyes twinkling. "A murder victim? Isn't that jumping to conclusions?" he asked in a calm manner—too calm, if you ask me.

"It looks like murder to me unless you purposefully buried someone under your lilac bushes."

He leaned back, and the squeak of his chair reverberated round the room. "I didn't bury anyone under the lilacs. There's a law against that, you know."

"Grandpa, are you scaring away customers?" A woman about my age stepped out of the back room. She had dark brown hair, a heart-shaped face, and soft blue eyes. She wore cargo pants and boots and a pale blue tank top under a red, white, and blue plaid shirt.

"She's not a customer," he glanced at me. "She's a crazy woman who won't leave the door. She has some ridiculous notion that holding the door will keep a wild animal from bursting in and killing us."

"Don't be silly." She bussed a kiss on his grizzled cheek. "It's more likely she's afraid to get near you." She stepped around the desk. "Hi, I'm Elizabeth MacElroy. Everyone calls me Liz."

I shook her hand. She had a nice firm grip. "Allie."

"Hi, Allie, who's this sweet puppy?" She leaned in, and Mal jumped into her arms and kissed her. Liz laughed and stood holding Mal. "Aren't you the sweetest?"

"Oh, no." I tried not to panic. "Don't let her kiss you."

"Why not? I love doggies." Her blue eyes twinkled in delight as Mal proceeded to wash her face.

I winced. "She may have dead-body breath."

"What?" Liz froze.

"That's what I told you." Angus leaned back with a smug smile. "Ms. McMurphy seems to think she found a murder victim hidden in the lilacs. Anyone you know missing?"

Grandma's Million-Dollar Fudge

4½ cups of sugar
1 can of evaporated milk
½ cup butter
4 large (4½ ounce) chocolate bars
2 packages of chocolate chips (semi-sweet)
1 pint marshmallow crème
2 cups nuts

Butter an 8" x 8" x 2" pan, then line with wax paper or parchment.

Boil together sugar, milk, and butter for approximately 8 minutes, stirring constantly. Place candy bars and chocolate chips in a large bowl and pour sugar mixture over candy. Beat well. Add marshmallow crème and nuts. Beat until cool. Spread in pan. Let cool and cut into squares.

CHAPTER 2

"Ewww." Liz held Mal out at arm's length.

"Sorry." I scooped up the pup. "This is Marshmallow. She sniffed out a bone from under the lilacs. I wouldn't think that much of it, but it had a sock attached."

"Oh." She wiped the back of her hand across her lovely mouth. Her gaze sparkled, and she laughed. "Joke's on me then."

"We called the cops," Angus said.

"Well, what are you doing sitting here?" Liz put her hands on her hips. "Let's go out and contaminate the crime scene like any good reporter would." She opened the door, and I followed her out. There was supposed to be safety in numbers, right?

Officer Rex Manning walked up to us. The police station was practically across the street. "Liz, Allie." He nodded his greeting. "What's this about a dead body?" Rex was a stocky man with wide shoulders and biceps to match. He looked good in fresh starched blues. His baby blue gaze was serious. He wore his trooper hat over his shaved head. Rex was all no-nonsense and efficient movement with competent hands.

I had a bit of a crush on him. It was hard to think beyond the flutter I felt every time I saw him. "Mal dug up the evidence," I said. The words came out breathless, and Liz glanced at me a little too aware. I told myself not to blush or I would give everything away. For someone as pale skinned as me, not blushing was as difficult as not sneezing.

Luckily Mal barked and jumped out of my hands, distracting everyone from my hideous attempt to hide my emotion.

I loved Mal—for a puppy she was brilliant at keeping me safe. She went over and sat next to the sock-covered bone. A single bark, and she put her white paw on it.

"What's this, little girl?" Rex squatted down next to her and examined the bone. He took out a pen, and using his cell phone, took a photo.

Liz kept an arm's distance back but also squatted to get a better look. "Is that argyle?"

"That's what I thought." I got down next to Liz.

"What made you think it was human?" Rex asked behind his camera. "Besides the fabric?"

As if on cue, Mal jumped up, grabbed the tattered bit of shoe, and shook it. A bit of bone flew out and hit Rex in the face.

"Ow." He rubbed his cheek then grabbed the shoe from Mal. At least I thought of it as a shoe. It was actually only the shredded toe of a shoe.

"Is that a toe?" Liz looked at once horrified and fascinated.

I picked up a twig and pushed at the bits that had flown out earlier and hit my shin. They were scattered in a small arc. "Yes," I said. "I don't know of any wild animal that paints its nails orange." I pointed at the flakes of polish, not wanting to get any closer than necessary.

"Cool." Liz pulled a digital camera out of her cargo pants pocket and snapped a photo.

"Stop." Rex covered her lens with his hand.

"Hey." Liz glared at him.

"I'm declaring this an official crime scene. That means it's closed to photographs."

"I don't think so." Liz lifted her camera and snapped a photo of Rex, momentarily blinding him. He did what anyone would do: put his hand across his eyes to block it.

She was fast. I watched with amazement as she snapped a couple more pictures of the bits of toe and of Mal sitting proudly next to the sock-covered bone.

Rex swore something dark and dangerous under his breath and reached for the camera. Liz ducked out of his way and rushed back inside the newspaper office.

I watched while Rex debated whether it was more important to follow her or to stay with the evidence. Tilting my head, I smiled. "It seems I'm not the only troublemaker on the island."

"Reporters," Rex mumbled and went back to his investigation.

It was then I noticed that Mal had disappeared back under the lilac bush. "Oh, no," I said and stepped forward to get her.

Rex stopped me with a hand on my arm. "Don't move. You're not trained in crime-scene investigation."

"Neither is Mal and she seems to be doing fine." I crossed my arms over my chest. Mal popped back out with another bit of bone in her mouth. She dropped it at his feet and gave a short bark before running back to the bush.

"I'll get her," he strode to the bush and got down and pulled Mal out from under the bush. She rewarded him with a lick on the cheek.

"Ha!" Liz said, coming out of the *Crier* sans camera. "Someone else getting dead-body kisses."

"Don't wipe it off," I warned him with a grin. "It could be evidence."

"It's not evidence," he grumbled and raised his hand to swipe it off.

"It could be DNA evidence," I said, holding up my hand in a stop motion. "Or soil evidence. Do you really want to take the chance of ruining microscopic clues?"

"Oh, for the love . . ." He strode my way, his sexy eyes stormy. My heartbeat picked up, but I stood my ground. "Here," he said and handed me Mal, his cheek clearly dirt-smeared from her kiss.

"This is definitely nail polish on this toenail," Liz said as she studied the bit of bone. "These must be female bones."

"How do you figure that?" Rex asked.

"Do you know any men who paint their toenails?" Her blue gaze teased as she raised one winged eyebrow.

"You can't assume anything," Angus said as he strolled over to her. "Huh, it does look like a toe. Came out of the shredded shoe, you said?" He shoved his hands in his brown corduroy pants. He tilted his head and studied the bits.

Mal squirmed in my arms and gave a short bark. I jumped. It still startled me when she barked out of the blue.

"Dog says yes." Angus nodded. "So, Manning, looks

like there's a body under the lilacs. What are you going to do about it?"

"First thing I'm going to do is get everyone off my crime scene." He narrowed his eyes and put his hands on his hips, emphasizing his gun belt.

"Hey, only looking, boy." Angus pulled his hands out in surrender. "Come on, Liz. Let's take a step back."

"Don't worry, Rex won't do anything. He knows we'd put a big article on the front page of the paper complaining of police brutality." Liz put her hands on her hips and stuck her chin out.

"Um, guys . . ." I pointed. A Saint Bernard had come around the corner while they fought. I didn't think much of it until he got closer to the bone with the sock. Then I felt like it was my duty to warn them that he was there.

Rex spun on his heels to see the giant dog delicately pick up the bone and slowly back away as if we wouldn't notice him taking it. "Ah, crap," Rex said.

"Daisy!" Liz shouted. "Leave it! Leeeeave it—"

For a brief moment it looked as if Daisy planned to obey. Then just as suddenly, she changed her mind and took off down the street.

Mal barked and barked. I held on to her tightly. "That dog could sniff you up her nose if she wanted to," I chided Mal. I put my hand around her nose. Her little growl vibrated up my hand.

In the meantime, Rex and Liz took off after Daisy. It was kind of comical to see a cop and a reporter chasing after a dog with a bone.

"Are you going after her?" Angus asked me, his eyes sparkling.

"No." I shook my head. "Someone has to stay here and keep the crime scene safe." We stood side by side and watched Daisy disappear around the corner in the direction of the Grand Hotel. Rex could run pretty fast in his uniform. Liz was an arm's length behind him. They both called after Daisy to stop.

"Is Daisy Liz's dog?" I asked.

Angus shook his head. "No, that scruffy Saint Bernard belongs to Mrs. Finch. She summers on the island in a home that has been in her family for a century. Unfortunately she's one of those owners who opens the door and lets the dog out without a leash or a keeper. The old bat says it's good for a dog to roam. Besides, she can't go far. It's an island and all the porters know not to let Daisy on the ferry."

"I suppose Mackinac is safer than most summer places. I mean, it's not like Daisy is going to get hit by a car here on island."

"If she doesn't watch it she may end up with buckshot in her rear end. Some of the old-timers don't take kindly to marauding dogs."

Mal snuggled up in my arms and closed her eyes. Her soft fur brushed against my cheek. It was pretty clear she felt that her work here was done. I glanced at the bits of bone and nail polish on the ground. "How long do you think those bits have been there?" I asked. "Doesn't it take a while for bodies to decay to the point of mostly bone?"

"Depends on the weather." Angus walked over to the shoe and studied it. His hands behind his back, he looked through the glasses perched on his nose. "It could take only a few weeks or a few months. I highly doubt these pieces have been here long."

"What makes you say that?"

"Because this bit of shoe, or rather boot, looks familiar."

He sighed and straightened. "See how rounded the toe is?" He picked up a stick and pointed out the edges. "This looks like part of a seam. Possibly from steel-toed shoes. There is one person I know who wears argyle socks and brown steel-toed boots."

I took a deep breath and blew it out slow. "Please tell me it's not a loved one."

"It's not," he confirmed. "I just don't know how to explain the nail polish."

"Why? Didn't she paint her nails?"

"As far as I know, he never did." Angus looked at the top of the bush as if it could tell him exactly what happened.

"He?"

"Steven Karus," Angus said. He turned his steady gaze on me. "The stable manager."

CHAPTER 3

"Do you think Angus is right? That this boot toe might belong to Steven Karus?" I asked.

"It's too difficult to tell who it is based on the toe of a shoe," Shane Carpenter, the St. Ignace crime-scene technician, said as he gathered bits of bone in a washtub. He picked up the toe section with his crime-scene-gloved hands. "We could run a trace on the polish. It could be a special kind." He plopped the bone bit into the washing tub. "More likely it will belong to an everyday ordinary drugstore kind of polish." He shrugged. "Real life is not as clean-cut as a crime show."

"What about the gender?" I had to ask. "Can you tell gender based on toe bones? I mean, I would have figured toenail polish belonged to a woman, but Angus thinks the socks are a man's."

"I think it's best not to make any assumptions based on what little information we have here." He picked up another bit and dropped it in the washtub

Rex had called Officer Brent Polaski over to help him out. Brent was a few inches taller than Rex. He looked to be somewhere in his early thirties, with short, dark hair and brilliant blue eyes. While Rex had that older, in-control sexy thing going on, Officer Polaski had that I-can-do-push-ups-with-one-hand kind of look.

I watched from the edge of the crime-scene tape as the two officers put a black plastic tarp down on the ground and carefully shoveled the mulch onto it. So far they had found nearly an entire foot. Who knew there were so many bones in a foot?

I suppose a doctor would know or a podiatrist.

"Can you tell how long the body has been in the ground?" I asked. Shane worked with the medical examiner. I'm sure he could give me more information than Angus had.

"Depends on a lot of factors." Shane picked through the mulch. "There are five stages of decay—fresh, bloat, active decay, advanced decay, and dry remains."

"These are dry remains, right?" I asked.

"Right."

"Good thing." Angus wandered over beside me. "I don't care for the idea of Daisy snacking on the meat of someone's foot."

Angus had brought out a denim-covered director's chair. It was low to the ground and was one of those people brought to local softball games and soccer when they didn't want to sit on the ground. He popped it out and settled down in its sagging bottom. His dark gaze watched the CSI tech with intent, his hands folded on the top of a mahogany cane. "Any sign of what killed the poor fellow?"

"Hard to tell." Shane picked another small bone out of the debris and studied it in the light. "Looks like the body wasn't too exposed. No sign of animal foraging. Not on these bits, anyway."

A crowd had formed around the yellow crime-scene tape. My best friend and now coworker, Jennifer, waved and worked her way through the crowd toward me. "Hi, Allie."

"Hi," I replied. "How's the McMurphy?"

"We need you to make a few batches of fudge," she said, her attention on the officers working. The men had taken off their jackets and rolled up their sleeves. "The dark chocolate cherry rum fudge is flying off the shelves. Besides, a girl stopped by, she wondered if we needed a candy maker. I told her to come back at 2 PM. That gives you thirty minutes." Jennifer's gaze never left the officers. "Nice eye candy."

"I'm not here for the eye candy." I tried not to blush. It was a losing proposition. I distracted her with a flick of my wrist. "The crime tech was telling us that these are dried remains. So far there isn't any sign of animal activity."

"Besides Mal's teeth marks, right?" Jennifer asked.

Just then the re-enactors at Fort Mackinac fired the cannon. It was a daily occurrence, and island regulars were so used to it we barely noticed. I noticed this time because the tourists in the crowd all reacted as one and looked over their shoulders, spooked by the noise.

"Whoever it is had to be buried at some point," Jennifer said and raised a black eyebrow. "Or you would have smelled them decaying. Right?"

The air currently smelled of fresh mulch, sweet lilacs, and hints of dirt.

"True," Shane said. I noticed that his hazel gaze had moved from his work to Jennifer and stayed there. "Do you study taphonomy?"

"What?"

"Decay of living organisms," Angus said.

"Oh, gosh, no," Jennifer laughed and waved her hands delicately. "Do I look like someone who studies decomposition?" She showed off her lilac nail art. "No, no, I watch those crime shows where they do all that lab work. Some of them are interesting."

"Not much of that is true." Shane pushed his dark-framed glasses up on his nose. His brilliant eyes sparkled behind them. "It takes weeks—sometimes months—to properly analyze a crime scene. By then most murders are cold cases. All that science you see on television is rarely funded. Which brings us back to old-fashioned police work and investigation." He went back to screening the mulch.

"But you do send evidence to a lab, right?" Jennifer pouted, batting her eyelashes at the loss of his attention.

"Yes." He studied the bark carefully. "But usually the science merely strengthens the case—rarely does it solve it."

Angus took a camera out of his pocket and snapped pictures of the crowd from where he sat.

"What are you doing?" I asked, stepping out of his viewfinder's range.

"Taking shots of the crowd in case the murderer has joined in with the onlookers."

"Who would be that stupid?" I asked.

"Most serial killers," Jennifer answered. "They say that there's a good chance the killer is in the crowd or otherwise tries to insert themselves into the investigation."

"Just like you," Angus said and took a fast shot of my face.

"Or you," I pointed out.

"Or me." He nodded, his dark eyes twinkling. "I can't remember the last time I saw Karus. I know I saw him supervising the horses when they moved in for the season."

"That would have been in April, right?"

Angus nodded.

I studied the crowd. The tourists who stopped and watched were tugged back by their impatient kids, who begged for fudge or ice cream from Main Street.

"Here." Jennifer handed me her cell phone.

"What's this for?" I took the phone.

"Call Trent Jessop. He owns the stables. He'd know if Karus is missing." Her eyes twinkled. "I know you know his number."

"Good idea," Angus said as he continued to take pictures of the crowd. "Jessop would know."

I narrowed my eyes at Jennifer. Trent Jessop was the gorgeous grandson of my father's dear friend. The friend who had been murdered in my utility closet. The entire town had been convinced that there was a feud between the McMurphys and the Jessops. So much so that they had started wearing ribbons to let everyone know whose side they were on.

Trent had stifled the feud idea in a rather unusual way. Ever since, I've been nervous in his presence. There was a certain level of sexy that a girl like me didn't dare get involved with—it never turned out for the best. Now someone like Jennifer . . . that was a different story. But she was having none of my protests.

"Call him," Jenn pushed.

I shot her a dirty look, and she winked at me. I glanced at Rex, his broad capable shoulders straining against his fitted uniform as he tossed shovels of dirt and mulch onto the black plastic.

There wasn't a lot of free time in my life for things like dating and relationships. That didn't mean I didn't have a rich fantasy life.

"Do you want me to do it?" Jenn whispered near my ear.

"I'll do it." I punched in the numbers and walked as far from the crime-scene crowd as I could.

"This is Jessop." Trent's rich, deep voice brought shivers down my back.

"Hi, Trent, this is Allie McMurphy."

"What can I do for you, Allie?"

Now that was a loaded question. "Trent, does Steven Karus work for you?"

"Karus? No, he works for the Jacobs' stables. Why?"

"Have you seen him lately?"

"Sure, I saw him yesterday. He stopped in to look at our new gelding."

"He did? Are you sure?" I glanced at Angus.

"Of course I'm sure. I've known Karus since I was a kid. What's this all about?"

"I don't know that I'm able to say just yet," I hedged. "But I'm glad to hear Mr. Karus was alive yesterday."

"Allie . . ."

"Thanks for the info, Trent," I cut him off. "Stop by sometime and I'll get you some fudge and coffee—on the house." I hung up the phone before he could say anything else. Trent was pretty wired into the community hotline. I figured he'd figure things out on his own pretty quickly.

"Steven's alive." Angus studied me.

"Yes, Trent saw him yesterday."

"That shoots my theory down." Angus scowled, then

pursed his lips. "Too bad, I was kind of looking forward to figuring out why he had his toenails painted orange."

I handed the phone back to Jenn. "Maybe we should be checking to see who isn't in the crowd," I said. "These bones could belong to a local who died this spring or even someone who died last fall and has been buried in snow."

"Oh, like the iceman they found in Switzerland." Jenn tucked the cell phone back into her pocket. My best friend was tall, curvy, and elegant. Her long, black hair and fine features made her a perfect candidate for modeling. Cameras loved her hair. In contrast my own mop of dark brown hair, which refused to reflect any sort of light, always looked dull in pictures and videos.

Today Jenn wore a flowery sundress with a buttery-yellow background and a long, blue sweater. Her heels were white cotton espadrilles that had four-inch plat-forms and made her over six feet tall and all elegant arms and legs.

Jenn was not only a good friend, but an excellent event planner. She came to Mackinac to help me with my first season. In the short month she had been here, she had been hired to plan two weddings. The woman was a genius when it came to organizing. She made me feel rumpled in my pink "McMurphy" polo shirt and black pants—standard uniform for retail workers. My uniform matched the pink stripes of the McMurphy's lobby inte-rior. It was an old-fashioned theme meant to remind people of their stay whenever they saw one of my pink and white striped boxes.

On my feet were cushiony athletic shoes meant to be more practical than attractive. A good candy maker was on her feet most of the day. Four-inch platform shoes were useless when moving a copper kettle filled with boiling fudge.

While Jennifer's hair floated in soft curls around her shoulders, mine was pulled back in my attempt for a low ponytail—most of it was in the ponytail. I ignored the wild curls that had slipped out of their confines and flew about my face.

"Allie, what's going on?" Trent pushed his way toward us through the crowd. He wore jeans and a pale blue chambray shirt with the sleeves rolled up. Like me he was a small-business owner. His family had run the island stables for over one hundred years. "You have to know you can't call me like that and not expect me to follow up."

"How'd you know we were here?" I asked as he bussed a kiss on my cheek. I kissed his cheek as well. It was a nothing kiss, really. He turned to Jenn and kissed her as well, then stood between us.

"I didn't. I was headed toward the McMurphy when I saw the crowd and the crime-scene tape. It didn't take long to put two and two together."

"What does that mean?" I put my hands on my hips.

He chuckled. "It means that where there's a crime scene, you are usually somewhere close by."

"I'm sure there were plenty of crime scenes before I got on island."

He raised one dark eyebrow and gave me a look that clearly said I was wrong.

"Mal dug up a bone," Jenn said. "Allie got suspicious when there was a bit of argyle sock hanging off of it."

"The boot part filled with toe bones was also a big clue." I hugged myself.

"Where's Mal now?" Trent asked, looking around.

"Frances came and got her. Officer Manning was afraid she would disturb the rest of the crime scene."

"You do realize,"—he tilted his head and looked at me—"there weren't any murders until you moved onto the island."

"That you know of." I scowled at him. "Besides, Shane says these are dry remains. They could be too old for me to have been on island when the body was buried."

"Then why call me about Karus?" Trent said. "Everyone saw him supervising when the horses came home."

"There's a possibility the body decomposed in the last month or so depending on conditions," Shane interjected.

"Angus thought the argyle socks and steel toe of the boot might have belonged to Steven. But since it isn't him, then the person must have died before I got on island. Right, Angus?"

Angus raised a bushy brow. "Don't bring me in on this. I'm still carrying my rabbit's foot." He winked at me and pulled the white paw out of his pocket.

"I don't get it," Jenn said. "Why do you need a rabbit's foot? That's not real, right?" She wrinkled her nose in disgust.

"Angus thinks I'm bad luck for old men." I shook my head. "He's afraid if he gets too close he'll end up dead."

"Well . . ." Trent said with a chuckle.

I gasped at his inference and pushed him. The man was a slab of muscle and barely budged. So I gave him the squinty eye. My expression only made him laugh harder, showing off white, even teeth in his tanned face. "I've got fudge to make." I huffed off. Really, a girl didn't want a reputation as a man killer. It sort of ruined any dating life. Not that I had time for dates.

"Hey, Allie." Mrs. Renkle waved at me from her front porch. She had a broom in her hand and swept the dust off the porch.

"Hi, Mrs. Renkle." I waved back. "How are you today?"

"Terrible. Got a crick in my neck and my lucky knee says there's a storm coming."

I tried not to smile. Mrs. Renkle was always terrible and loved telling anyone who would listen about her ailments. "I'll bring some fudge by," I offered. "Chocolate is good for what ails you."

"That's not what I heard," she muttered and continued to sweep.

"I'll bring it by later this afternoon, say around three?"

"I'll be taking a nap," she grumbled back.

"Perfect." I wagged my fingers at her. "See you then."

"Not if I die first."

The crowds picked up along Main Street as the ferry boats came in with their fresh load of tourists. *Fudgies,* they were called by the locals. I loved watching them file off the ferries. Sometimes they looked a bit dazed and uncertain—the regulars come off with confidence, certain in where they are going. Others spoke with the porters and were happily surprised when young men on bicycles biked their suitcases to their hotels. The McMurphy was only two blocks from the dock, so my guests usually wheeled their own suitcases over.

On occasion I paid Oliver Crumbley, my neighbor's son, to porter—especially when I knew a large party was coming in for the weekend. Today was Monday, usually a slow day, which is why I had time to run to the *Crier* and place a want ad. At least I thought I had time.

"Hey, Allie." Mary Evans came up behind me. She

was about five foot two inches talll, with a gray pony tail, and big blue eyes. Mary was seventy if she was a day old, but, like many senior citizens on the island, she kept trim with her twice-daily walks. Today she wore a pastel green velour tracksuit and had two-pound weights in her hands. She lifted the weights one at a time over her head as she stopped to talk. "What's this I hear you're burying people under lilac bushes?"

"I am not burying people." I took a step back as she switched her weight training from the overhead move to straight out in front of her, nearly punching me in the chest. I noted that a fine mist formed on her forehead. It was a bright day out and the temperature was mild enough to wear a sweater, but if you worked as hard as Mary, you'd break into a sweat. "Mal uncovered bits of a body—bones really. Shane Carpenter thinks they may have been there a while. Anyone you know go missing this winter?"

"No, all my friends are accounted for." Mary frowned. "I'll ask around. Was it a male or a female?"

"I couldn't really tell." I shuddered. "We found bones mostly. There was the toe of a shoe, but again, hard to tell at this point whether it was a man's or a woman's shoe. It was pretty degraded."

Mary pursed her thin lips. "They might be Indigenous bones," she shook her head. "You'll be in a heap of trouble if they are. The Indigenous don't like anyone messing with their ancestors."

"Oh, I'm sure they aren't." I kept on walking. "They were under the lilac bushes. Whoever planted the lilacs would have found them first if they were Indigenous."

Mary marched a circle around me, dodging tourists in

T-shirts, shorts, and Windbreakers. "Maybe Irene Raiser knows something. Keep me posted."

"I will if you do the same," I said and watched as she waved her hand and took off down the street. Mary owned a jewelry store on Main. It was the next block down from mine. Her son, Doug, ran the store these days, but Mary still kept her eyes on her community. I could only hope that when I was seventy I had half as much energy and interest in the community.

I opened the front door and stepped into the turn-of-the-1900s décor of the historic McMurphy Hotel and Fudge Shoppe. It was noon, and everyone who checked out had already left.

Frances Wentworth, my Papa Liam's front desk clerk and now my hotel manager, sat behind the reservation desk. She had blue, cat-eye glasses, with rhinestones on the corners, perched on the bridge of her nose as she stared through them at the flat screen of a computer.

"We are finally full up for the Lilac Festival," she said as she clutched the mouse and scrolled through her program. "The Santimores are taking rooms 210 and 212."

"Yay, now we can afford the payroll." I took my baker's white coat off the hook just inside the fudge shop area of the lobby. I slipped my arms in, buttoned the length of it, and rolled up the sleeves. I liked the thickness of the coat and had a handful embroidered with the McMurphy logo as a uniform. People liked their candy makers to wear white. It looked clean. "Where's Mal?"

I looked around for my errant puppy. She came running out from the back of the reservation counter. Her feet skidded on the polished hardwood floor until she banged up against me. I laughed and picked her up.

She had learned that she could slide fairly far and, like a little kid in socks, loved to see if she could angle herself into things.

"Hi, baby," I said as she licked my face, her little behind wiggling. "How is my big girl?" I didn't mind picking up Mal with my white chef's coat on. She was a white, shed-free dog. As long as I kept her groomed and I washed up after handling her, I'd make health codes.

"So, Mal discovered a body this morning." Frances slid her glasses onto the top of her head. "How'd that happen?"

"I think the scent caught her interest. She dug under the lilac bushes and pulled out bones."

"How did you know they were human bones?" Frances asked.

"The big bone was wrapped in a sock and the others had toenail polish."

"Others?"

"She didn't find a body per se, she found body parts." I held Mal away from my face after I remembered what she had been chewing on just a few hours ago. "Remind me to brush her teeth."

Frances chuckled as I put Mal on the floor. I headed to the reservation desk in the far left corner in front of the left staircase. The McMurphy was built in the 1800s. The lobby consisted of a wide, open area. The fudge shop was in the front right of the lobby when you entered. I had replaced the walls with wood beams and glass half walls, giving the illusion of a wide-open space. To the back were twin sweeping staircases that went to the second and third floor. In the center was a single elevator with a 1920s grill. To the left of the foyer was a brick fireplace and couches.

Welcoming was the vibe I was going for. We wanted to invite people into the McMurphy, which was why the reservation desk was near the back.

Anyone could come in from off the street and rest their bones (I don't mean that literally) in the soft couches and overstuffed chairs. I had installed Wi-Fi for their smart phones and hoped that the sights and smells of the fudge shop would ensure they bought at least a taster pound before they left. So far it was a big hit with the fudgies.

Mal poked me with her nose as I walked. It was her way of herding me toward the desk where there was a glass candy dish filled with tiny dog snacks. The snacks were there so that anyone could give her one to help break the ice. Mal had decided early on that anyone coming in the door was going to get her a treat. Unfortunately she was right.

I reached into the candy dish and took out the smallest treat. "I happen to know this is your third—"

"Fourth," Frances interjected.

I blew out a long breath. "Fourth treat. You have to do your tricks for this one. Sit."

Mal sat and watched me, her dark button eyes intent on the treat in my hand. "Shake." She held out her paw, and I shook it. "Up . . . twirl." I raised my hand, and Mal popped up on her back legs and did a pirouette. "Good. Sit."

She sat.

"Down." She went down and spread out on her tummy. "Roll over." She rolled and I smiled. "Good girl." I gave her the treat. She snatched it from my fingers. "Ow!"

"You're going to have to teach her to take it easy," Frances warned me.

I frowned and stood. "No kidding."

"Tell me about the body."

I leaned against the dark, polished wood of the registration counter. "So far all they've found are bits of a leg and a foot. Do you have any idea how many bones are in our feet?"

Frances shook her head. She had chin-length hair that was brown streaked with gray. Recently she'd taken to getting it dyed light brown. It framed her face well. Her big brown eyes were wide set, and her nose was thin and straight. She had an elegant look for a woman in her seventies. She had been a contemporary of my Grammy Alice. They had grown up on island together and both had gone to school in St. Ignace before coming back to work on island. "A lot, then?" Frances guessed.

"A lot of bones." I drew my eyebrows together. "These were all scattered and some were cut on angles as if someone had taken a sharp knife to them."

"Another murder, then?" Frances tilted her head in thought.

"I don't know," I said. "You can't really prove anything with only a leg and foot bones."

"Hmm, I heard Angus is writing quite the exposé for the *Crier*."

I surveyed my domain. "As long as he keeps me off the suspect list I don't care what kind of story he writes."

I noticed that the glass candy counter that separated the fudge shop from the foyer was two-thirds empty. "We must have had a rush on the fudge while I was gone."

"Not really," Frances said, following me. "Some guy came in and bought twenty pounds."

"Twenty pounds of fudge! What was he going to do

with that? Did he say?" I put my hands on my hips. Who buys that much fudge?

Frances shrugged. Today she wore a lavender sweater set and a flowing spring-green skirt with lavender flower sprigs on it. "He said he was shipping it back home. He also said something about using it as an example of the best in candy making."

"Okay . . . weird." I made my way behind the counter that separated the candy-making area from the rest of the lobby and pulled out my copper pot. I always started with a quick wipe down of all surfaces, so I grabbed a clean dishcloth and wiped it out. "What did he look like?"

"Younger man," Frances said. "Round face, short black hair."

"That description does not help me since everyone under seventy is younger to you," I teased and pulled down my sugar.

"That's true." She chuckled. "Everyone under fifty looks young to me, but I do have another clue to his identity."

I stopped pulling out ingredients and turned. "Are you holding out on me?"

Her dark eyes twinkled. "He gave me his card." In her hand was a white business card that displayed my graduate-school logo.

"Oh, my goodness," I gasped at the name on the card. "What is he doing here?"

CHAPTER 4

"Peter Thomas is here?" I couldn't help the excitement in my voice as I held out the business card and read the name. Flipping it over, I saw that he had scrawled out his cell-phone number.

"He's on island," Frances said, "but he's not staying here. Who is he?"

"Only the finest chocolatier in the U.S. He taught a semester at my culinary school," I said, staring at the card. "The competition was tough to even get into the class. We were all hand selected. I was so excited to be one of twenty students given the privilege of working with him." I smiled at the memory and my own naïveté. "He was so tough on me. I went home crying every night but determined to stick it out."

"He sounds like a bully." Frances crossed her arms. "And a pompous so-and-so to boot."

"That's what I thought at first." I finished measuring out the ingredients. "He was one of those people you start out hating but then learn to love because they bring out the best in you."

"Love?" Frances raised an eyebrow.

"Yes, love," I said and tried to remain calm. "He's also my father's age, married with a daughter my age."

"Oh, that kind of love." Frances turned on her heel and headed toward her station. "In that case, he's staying at the Grand this month. They are offering candy-making classes in their summer kitchen."

"He'll be on island an entire month?" The tone of my voice rose in excitement. If I was to be honest, I was not only happy and excited to see my favorite mentor, but a little nervous. Would my current list of fudges meet his expectations?

"That's what he said." Frances went back to her computer. Mal played with a stuffed lamb near the front desk.

I pulled out my cell phone and dialed his number. It went straight to voice mail. "Chef Thomas. Leave your number." I suppressed a giggle. The message was so typical of the man I knew. Always an economy of words.

"Hi, Chef, Allie McMurphy. Are you free for dinner? You have my number." I pressed the END CALL button and stared at my phone for a moment before slipping it in the pocket of my baker's coat. I turned to my ingredients and the list of fudges I had scheduled for the week. Somehow what was exciting and new last week seemed dull and boring.

I needed new fudge recipes, and I needed them now. A quick glance back at my nearly empty candy counter, and I blew my wayward hair out of my eyes. First things first—I would make a batch of McMurphy special-recipe fudge. I could do that practically in my sleep. I went to work, letting my mind run free for ideas of fudge that would knock Chef Thomas's socks off.

* * *

Early the next day tourists gathered at the window and milled about inside as the scent of sugar and chocolate wafted through the air. I stirred the kettle with a fat wooden paddle and explained to the fascinated crowd what I was doing.

Part of the appeal of a fudge shop was the childlike wonder of how sugar, cocoa, milk, vanilla, and butter could be boiled down, then poured onto the cooling marble table and worked into thick fudge.

The sights and smells would draw in customers. The theater of it was part of what I loved about a fudge shop. I'd grown up watching my Papa make fudge and thrill tourists with his stories, his deft hand, and the ease with which he cut off scraps and handed out tastes to those who stayed for the entire show.

I lifted the heavy copper kettle and poured the fudge out on the marble cooling table. "The table is made of marble because the stone wicks away the heat at just the proper rate to ensure the fudge sets up without sugaring," I explained to the crowd. "Have you ever made fudge?"

I saw nods from some members of the crowd. Papa used to get more responses to that question, but then he worked in a time when more women made candy at home. Oh, don't get me wrong—Mackinac Island had always been a summer bastion for the ultrawealthy. They would come up from Chicago and Detroit to summer in the giant Victorian mansions that were built in the hilltops to draw in the cool lake breezes and fresh country smells.

Still, in the forties, fifties, and sixties more women were home to try their hand at candy making. Nowadays most women expected to work full-time and foods were increasingly prepackaged for efficiency and the health of busy families.

It was a good thing as far as I was concerned. It meant that more women could be candy makers, chefs, doctors, lawyers, professionals. It also meant the old stories were increasingly exotic to the crowd of observers.

I settled the kettle back into its arms and grabbed a sharp metal scraper with a wooden handle. "The marble is buttered first to keep the fudge from sticking," I said and began the dance around the table, working the fudge by scraping and folding it with the paddle as it cooled. "Chocolate is surprisingly delicate," I said. "It can easily scorch if the kettle temperatures get too high. Once burned, the entire batch needs to be thrown out."

"What can you do if your fudge doesn't set up?" A woman in the middle of the crowd asked. "What did I do wrong? Do I have to throw it away and start over?"

"It's best to make fudge on a cool, dry day," I said as I worked the fudge. "Too much humidity and you have to adjust the temperature you work with. It's also why we use wooden spoons or, in my case, a paddle when we cook the fudge. Metal will absorb the heat and slow down the process."

I worked my way around the table, pushing the scraper under the fudge and folding it toward the center. "You'll notice that I lift the fudge and let it pour through the air. This helps to cool the fudge as I work. As for your very good question, the reason it doesn't set is that it didn't cook long enough. If you can get it back into the double boiler, boil it some more." I stopped and eyed the crowd. "If you want to make candy at home it really helps to purchase a good double boiler. The steam from the water bath is best for keeping chocolate from scorching."

I went back to my work; as the fudge set it became heavier, and I could tell when it was nearly ready simply by how much strain was in my shoulders. "If you can't recook it, then you can melt it down and add powdered sugar to it. Beat in a quarter of a cup at a time until it sets right up."

"Do you like that pat-in-pan fudge?" another woman asked. "Isn't it cheating?"

"I think any type of fudge you make is fine. You don't have to be an expert bakery chef to make a birthday cake. It's the same with candy." I picked up the container of black walnuts, chopped them, and poured them in a generous line down the center of the fudge. Then I took a container of black cherries, chopped them, and poured them on top of the nuts and worked them into the candy.

I ended up with a nice loaf of dark chocolate, black-cherry, and black-walnut fudge. I sliced it up in roughly quarter-pound sections. I carefully cut up bite-size pieces and scooped them on a plate and offered them to the crowd. It was always the best part of the demonstration. It was instant feedback on my work when the audience would have expressions of childlike delight at the fudge tasting.

"A safe fudge," said a male voice to my right.

I turned with my plate and saw that Chef Thomas was in the crowd. Squealing with delight, I handed the plate of fudge to a man shepherding a bunch of Boy Scouts. Then I threw my arms around Chef Thomas's neck and hugged him hard. "Oh my gosh, I'm so happy to see you."

He patted my back and then untangled me from his neck. "Good to see you, too, Allie."

"Frances said you were staying on island for a month

to teach a master class at the Grand Hotel?" I put my arm through his and walked him out of the crowd and over to the pair of overstuffed chairs near the fireplace.

Jennifer came around from the reception desk and took over for me at the candy counter. A great thing about my best friend is that she always knows when to step in and take over. My customers were safe with her.

"Can I get you some coffee or tea?" I asked and waved toward the coffee bar. I hoped to get a barista and a top-of-the-line coffeemaker one day, but for now I had a Keurig machine that offered coffees and teas of every type and flavor in individual cups.

"No, I don't drink that crap," he said. "I only drink coffee-press coffee."

"Oh, right, you hate Starbucks," I remembered. "Even though they grind your beans and make individual espresso."

He leaned back in the chair and studied me. "Life is short. There's no reason to drink anything but the best."

"I have a French press up in my apartment."

He shook his head. Chef Peter Thomas was in his late fifties. He was a short man—only five foot five inches tall. Today he wore a blue button-down shirt and a pair of black slacks. Crossing his legs, he let his top knee fall to the side so that his ankle rested on the opposite knee. He wore no socks and dark brown Top-Siders. A gold wedding ring gleamed on his left ring finger. The rest of him was absent of bling.

His dark blue gaze was attentive. "I'm fine."

"Here." Frances came over with a bottle of Evian water. She handed it to Chef Thomas.

"Thank you," he said and took the water, twisted the top off, and drank.

"You're welcome." Frances turned on her heel and headed back toward the front desk, her midlength, flowered skirt floated around her ankles. She wore a simple pink tee shirt with a scoop neck. On her arms were three inches of bangle bracelets that clattered at her wrists.

"Tell me about your hotel and fudge shop," Peter said. "I thought you said your grandfather would be here to teach you the ropes."

"He was supposed to," I said and leaned back in the seat. "He died unexpectedly a few months ago so I've been learning by trial and error."

"You seem to be doing a decent job," he said and took another sip of his water.

"Thank you." Any kind of compliment was rare from the man. He defined taste and refinement in the restaurant business. "Tell me about the class at the Grand. Have they put you up in a nice room?"

"I've got a nice suite with a view of the lake. Not that I'll have much time to look out the window." He sipped again.

"Frances says you bought about twenty pounds of fudge yesterday."

"Yes, I did," he agreed and then didn't take the bait I laid out to tell me how good it was.

"Who is taking your class? I didn't know there was a culinary school on island."

"Regretfully, I'm not giving lessons to culinary students," he flicked a piece of imaginary lint off his pant leg.

I drew my eyebrows together, confused. "Then who?"

"It's for a reality series," Jenn said as she abandoned the now-empty candy counter. "I heard about it online."

She held out her hand. "Hello, I'm Jennifer. I'm working with Allie for the summer. Helping her get on her feet."

"I didn't know she needed help," he said, stood and shook her offered hand. Then he settled back down and took another sip. For all his protests that he didn't need anything to drink, he'd nearly finished the bottle of water.

"Jennifer is an extraordinary event planner. She's working with me to bring in more events to the McMurphy. And hopefully more events to Mackinac Island. She has it in her head that there should be more movie shoots on island."

"She may be right. Any kind of media event on the island is sure to create more traffic to your shop," he said thoughtfully. "That brings me to the reason I'm here. We had a contestant drop out. It seems she had a fear of water and wouldn't suck it up and take the ferry onto the island."

"Why didn't she fly?" I asked.

"Fear of flying," he sounded put out.

"If she is so afraid, why did she try out for the television show?"

"She thought it would be set in Chicago." He rolled his eyes. "How unimaginative would that have been? Back to the reality series, I told them you would be a perfect addition to the candy-making cast."

"Wow, really?" I said.

"Yes, really." He raised one dark eyebrow. "Why not?"

"I'm not exactly Hollywood material."

"The show is a contest. They're looking for bakers, not actors. Besides, they thrive on quirky creative types like you."

I couldn't tell if that was a compliment or not. I decided

it was. "What kind of time are we discussing? I'm pretty busy with everything happening at the McMurphy."

"Don't worry, it's only a few hours every morning. It should give you plenty of time to entertain your fudgies in the afternoon and evenings."

"Is this one of those reality shows or is this for real?" I gave him the squinty eye.

He laughed heartily. "I did say cast, didn't I? Not competitors."

"Yes, you did."

"Think of it as marketing for your hotel and fudge shop." He waved his hand. "When this airs you will be able to charge whatever you want for your rooms and it will double or triple your fudge sales."

I chewed on my bottom lip. "I'm not altogether certain I want to double or triple my fudge sales. I'm the only candy maker here."

"Trust me, you'll be able to hire as many employees as you need."

"I kind of like small-batch, real homemade fudge."

"Please." He crossed his arms and made a face. "Everyone knows that the fudge shops all make their fudge in a factory in Mackinaw City and ferry it out to the island."

I raised my right eyebrow. "Not mine," I said with my chin high and pride in my voice. "It's what makes the McMurphy recipe so select."

"And that's a message you can get out to your customers." He leaned forward to press his point. "I overheard your lovely receptionist worrying about your customers all leaving for the new hotel built up close to the Grand Hotel."

"They'll come back when they realize it's just another

modular hotel like the ones off island." It was my turn to cross my arms. I realized that I missed these arguments— excuse me, "discussions." Peter Thomas was one of the few people I could do this with, and I found it re- freshing.

He leaned back. His shoulders fell as if in defeat.

My eyes widened. Had I won an argument?

He eyed me sideways, smiled, and went for the kill. "You get twenty grand an episode. I can see that you stay on or leave as soon as you have had enough."

CHAPTER 5

"You should do it," Jennifer said. "Think of the publicity."

"Think of the money," Frances encouraged.

"Don't do it. They'll make a fool of you on television. No amount of money or publicity is worth it." For the first time Mr. Devaney, my cranky handyman, sounded more like the voice of reason than a contrary senior citizen.

It was seven-thirty PM, and we gathered in my apartment after another busy day. The windows were opened wide to let the cool lake breezes blow through. The island didn't offer a lot of nightlife—which was part of the appeal. When the last ferry left with the day-trippers, the entire island seemed to breathe a sigh of relief and life slowed down.

The hourly cannon shots stopped. The shops closed up, and the horses finished their last trips for the day. Even the bike shops closed up, and those who stayed on island enjoyed a slower pace. Bonfires were lit. There was laughter and quiet family times where people made s'mores. Children chased lightning bugs, and the slap of the water against the shore could be heard once more.

It was my favorite time of night. The hotel visitors retreated to their rooms or went out to dinner at one of the restaurants and walked back in the soft air.

I hired two interns to work the night-desk shifts. It was an easy job. All they were there for really was to watch the door and answer questions. The McMurphy didn't offer room service, so for the most part the calls consisted of people locking themselves out of their rooms or not being able to open the sometimes humidity-warped windows.

I brought the large pitcher of sangria I had made into the living-room area of the apartment and set it down on the coffee table in the middle of the arrangement of soft chairs and couches. The apartment on the fourth floor of the McMurphy had belonged to my grandparents— Papa Liam and Grammy Alice McMurphy. It was only recently that I had moved the last of their things out and brought in a few pieces of my own. The big furniture I had kept; mixing my handpicked pieces with their old ones created a comfortable synergy between old and new.

"Mr. Devaney is right." I sat down in my favorite over-stuffed rocker-recliner. It had been Papa's chair, and I always felt comfort when I sat there, as if he were still at the McMurphy, watching over me. "They script those reality shows to have over-the-top drama. The last thing I want to do is have to scavenger hunt the island for bizarre fudge ingredients."

"What in the world could they possibly ask you to put in fudge that can be found in a scavenger hunt?" Frances asked. She looked so pretty this evening. Her skin glowed. That glow was something I'd noticed only on healthy women over fifty-five years old. There was something so lovely about the delicate, refined skin of a woman in the peak of her life. It was my goal to have skin like that when I was older.

Perhaps, though, it wasn't simply the care she had taken with her skin. Perhaps it was the fact that Mr. Devaney sat in the chair beside her. They were so cute and discreet. Someone who didn't know them wouldn't know what was going on. They sat an arm's length apart, but their body language gave them away. Frances leaned on the armrest of the couch nearest to him. Mr. Devaney sat with his legs wide, his left foot, clad in the slip-on leather shoes of a retired teacher, touching Frances's white orthopedic athletic shoes. Her socks were pink to match the scooped-neck tee shirt she had on.

In contrast to Frances's relaxed outfit, Mr. Devaney wore a pair of pressed dark blue Dockers and a blue button-down shirt with the sleeves rolled up. The top button of his shirt was unbuttoned to show the pure white T-shirt underneath. How he managed to stay so pressed and clean when he was my handyman was a mystery to me.

Jennifer picked up the pitcher as I sat down on the stuffed ottoman I used as both footrest and extra seating. "You are silly if you pass up this opportunity. Seriously, you can't buy marketing better than this. If you don't take it I will, I could use the press."

"Oh, please," I said with a wave of my hand. "You already have more business than you can handle. How's the Postma wedding coming?"

"Oh, it's going to be grand." Jenn perked up as she sat back and sipped sangria from one of my bowl-shaped wineglasses. Hers had a pink stem. Mine had a green stem. Frances's had a blue stem, and Mr. Devaney . . . well, he drank a beer from the dark glass bottle. A man had to have his priorities. "I've got the courtyard of the fort reserved. It will be a red, white, and blue affair with cannon fire and fireworks over the lake."

"That is grand," Frances said and sipped her drink. "What ever happened to two people standing before God in a church and saying vows?"

"Oh, those days are long gone." Jenn waved her pink, manicured fingernails. "Ever since the eighties when Princess Diana married her prince, weddings have gotten to be bigger and bigger affairs. It's a show of wealth now."

Mr. Devaney frowned. "The marriage should be more important than the wedding. Save your money to buy a house or put your kids through school."

"Please." Jenn's bell-like laughter filled the air, waking Mal from her nap at the base of the couch. "Buying a house is a fifteen- to thirty-year commitment. No one stays married long enough to see the benefits of money they put in a house."

"You're jaded," I said and savored my sangria. It was a mixture of oranges, strawberries, and blueberries in a crisp white wine. I had changed from my candy maker's uniform to a pair of soft, flowy linen pants in pale blue and a tight, white T-shirt. My feet were bare, and I took note that I should paint my toenails.

"Not jaded," Jenn said with a sigh. "Realistic. So many people lost so much money in the housing crash. Besides, no one keeps the same job long enough to buy a home and live their entire lives in it." She shook her head. There was a bit of sadness in her blue eyes. "Life is not like when our parents got married."

"It wasn't like when our parents got married either," Frances said. "We were glad of that. My parents moved in with my grandparents for the first ten years of their marriage. Thank goodness that tradition went away with my generation. I may have killed my mother-in-law."

Jenn and I were surprised by the vehemence in her voice. "Wow, who knew Frances could be vicious?" Jenn said. I stifled a laugh.

"Now this generation complains that their kids can't afford to leave home. My kids have married kids living in their basement," Mr. Devaney said.

"What goes around comes around." I tried not to snicker. "I haven't said no to Chef Thomas yet. I may not have to say no. I have to go up to the Grand in the morning for an audition. They want to see how I look on video."

"You'll be fine." Frances shifted slightly so that her leg brushed Mr. Devaney's. She tossed down the last of her drink and stood. "Well, girls, it was a fun day but this old woman needs to go home and get her beauty sleep."

On cue, Mr. Devaney stood. "I'll see you home." He made a sweeping gesture, and Frances stepped in front of him as they walked to the door. I noted how his hand touched the small of her back.

"Good night, you two," I said. "See you in the morning."

We waited for them to close the door behind them and listened for the arrival of the elevators.

"Those two aren't fooling anyone." Jenn wiggled back into the couch, her perfectly pedicured bare feet curled up underneath her. Mal jumped up and snuggled beside her.

"I know, aren't they cute?" I sent her a wry smile. "What are we doing wrong that our love lives are not even close to theirs?"

"Speak for yourself." Jenn wiggled her right eyebrow. "I happen to have a date Thursday."

"A date!" I jumped up. "You've been holding out on me." I sat back in Papa's chair, careful not to slosh my beverage. "Spill."

"It's with a certain crime-scene fellow." She smiled that secret feminine smile of a woman interested in a man.

"Shane! Seriously? I don't think I've ever seen you date a science geek."

She shrugged and ran her fingers through Mal's soft, curly fur. "He's cute and I like to listen to him talk."

"You don't have a clue what he's saying," I teased.

"That's the best part," she replied. "I don't have to understand. All I have to do is smile and nod and say things like: right? Wow! I know . . ." She laughed again, causing Mal to lift her head and place it on Jenn's knee.

"You are bad," I said.

"Hey, I wouldn't talk if I were you," she said. "At least I have a date."

"If you haven't noticed, I'm a little too busy to date." I sat back and closed my eyes. "If I agree to be part of the cast of Chef Thomas's show, I won't have any time at all."

"What about that young candy maker who came by this morning looking for a summer internship?"

I opened my eyes and pursed my lips. "I completely forgot about her."

"I thought so. Her resume is on your office desk." Jenn raised her arms in a long catlike stretch. "Look at it in the morning."

"I'm not ready to give up kitchen time to someone else," I admitted. "I waited my entire life to make it mine and now it's here."

"I happen to know your grandfather fostered new talent every year."

"Yes." I nodded and finished my drink. "It's how he took time off to play cards at the senior center. I don't have a hobby or a regular card game to attend to . . ."

"Maybe you should," Jenn said pointedly. "All work and no play makes for a dull life. You're young—you shouldn't be so serious."

"The fate of the McMurphy is in my hands. It's an awesome responsibility and everyone is expecting me to fail."

"If it sinks, it sinks." Jenn shrugged. "It wouldn't be your fault. Your parents aren't exactly here working in the family business." She waved her hand at the apartment. "All I'm saying is relax. You've been waiting your entire life for this—enjoy it while you have it."

I got up to take Mal out for her nightly walk. "Come on, Mal. Let's go out." I took her halter and leash off the hook by the back door.

Jenn followed me to the back door. "Don't be mad at me. Someone had to say it. As your best friend, it's my responsibility to let you know when you get all work and no play."

I helped Mal step through her halter, clipped on the leash, and pulled doggie-poo bags out of the container near the door. Mal jumped up and down, pressing for the door in doggie excitement. "Your concern is duly noted."

"Good." Jenn nodded. "Have fun on your walk. If you find another body, call me. I like to see Shane in his natural environment."

I rolled my eyes. "I think one body is enough for one day."

CHAPTER 6

"I'm Allie McMurphy. I am the owner and fudge maker at the historic McMurphy Hotel and Fudge Shoppe," I said. "Mackinac Island is the fudge capital of the world and I like to argue that my family fudge is the best on island. Our recipe has been around for over one hundred years . . ." I paused in horror. "I'm sorry. I forgot what else you wanted me to say."

"Talk to the camera," came a disembodied voice from behind the bright lights.

I turned back to the tiny red dot and tried to imagine a human face. This television stuff was harder than it looked. "I forgot what I was supposed to say next."

"Talk about the murder you helped solve."

"Oh." I dropped my shoulders. "Why?"

"It adds color to the show," the voice said.

"Come on, Allie, you can do better," Chef Thomas's voice came from my right.

I caught myself looking into the dark at my right and instead addressed the camera in frustration. "I don't see how solving a murder helps me win a fudge competition."

"It's not about winning," the director said. "It's about what you can bring to the show that will make viewers look forward to the viewing every week."

"Peter," I begged. "I'm not the person you want on your cast."

"Look at the camera."

"You are exactly the person we need."

I rolled my eyes. "You owe me for this, Chef Thomas," I muttered and narrowed my eyes. "Paybacks are hell."

"Smile and talk about the dead man you found in your utility closet." Peter's voice held a tone of laughter, and I sent a stink eye in the direction of his voice.

"While remodeling the hotel this spring, I was horrified to find a dead body in the second-floor utility closet . . ." said the voice behind the camera.

Sighing, I turned back to the camera, gave my best fake smile, and repeated what he said, "While remodeling the hotel this spring, I was horrified . . ."

See? I was naturally bad at the television thing. It's not that I didn't want to help Peter out. It was that—well, I was a fudge maker and an hotelier. I wasn't a reality-television person. Now Jenn on the other hand—she had the looks and the personality for television.

I mentioned that to Peter after my screen test. "Seriously, Jenn's smart and pretty and personable. You should sign her up for your show."

"She can't make fudge like you can," he said. We sat outside on the veranda of a small café near the Grand Hotel. A waitress in a gray costume with a white cap and a white apron brought us a plate of tea cakes.

"She doesn't need to make good fudge," I pointed out and helped myself to a petit four. "She just has to look good on television."

"You see, that is why I want you on the show. Not a single person in the cast can cook let alone make decent candy. I was hoping to bring you in so that at the very least I wouldn't have to lie to all of them about who's the best."

"You could bring us in as a team—Jenn can do the talking and the interviewing, etc. I can be the silent partner who makes candy in the kitchen."

"That's not a bad idea," he said and made a face as he bit into a cucumber sandwich. "For crying out loud." He spit out his mouthful. "This place charges more than a five-star hotel. Why can't they get a decent cook?"

"The food's not that bad here." I snagged another cake. "You're being way too fussy."

"Humph," he snorted. "My palate is used to finer food." He flagged the waitress down.

"Yes, sir?"

"Take this back and tell the cook I want today's tea platter, not last week's."

"Is the food not right?" She asked, her brown eyes wide with concern. "Because chef is very good."

"Tell him I want fresh or I'll come back there and show him how to cook." He handed her his business card and turned back to me. I watched as she scurried off with the plate in her hand.

"I wish you hadn't done that. I was enjoying the petit fours."

"You'll like them better when they are fresh." His blue eyes glittered knowingly.

"Okay, so tell me the truth. The director hated me, didn't he?" I held up my hand when he started to speak. "No, don't try to be kind."

"He wants you on the show," Peter said. "And I want you on the show."

"I'm trying to run a business," I whined.

"I hear through the grapevine that you have an applicant for assistant candy maker. Is that right?"

"Who told you that? Jenn?" I sat back and crossed my arms and tried not to pout. "I want to make all the fudge. I want it to be my success or failure."

"Think of her as your assistant. You don't need to chop all the nuts or cut up the fruits or wash the dishes . . . need I go on?"

I relaxed a little and tapped my finger on my cheek. "I see what you mean."

He reached over and took my hand in his. "Do this for me, please. I need to be able to have real fudge. It will be good for you and good for your shop."

I lifted the left side of my mouth in a disbelieving tight-lipped look. "Fine."

"That's my girl." He patted my hand.

Just then the door to the café burst open and a red-cheeked, heavyset man in a chef's coat and hat barreled toward us. He had a platter of tea cakes in his hands, and the waitress followed behind, her eyes wide.

"What is the problem with my tea cakes?" the chef said. "I made these myself not twenty minutes ago."

"If you made them twenty minutes ago, I'll eat my hat." Peter went into full professor mode. "The bread is stale on top and soggy inside. The petit fours are far too sweet and I detect ice crystals in their center, which tells me they were frozen. Take me back into your kitchen. Let me see if you keep them in the freezer."

"No, sir, you cannot go into my kitchen. This is an outrage!"

I watched in part horror and part humor as Peter got up, grabbed the tray, and strode straight back into the kitchen. I could well imagine what would happen next. I remember his "man on a mission for good food" mode. I was thankful it wasn't me he berated this time.

I paid the bill and left a hefty tip on the table. It would be hours before Chef Thomas would emerge from the kitchen vindicated. The poor cook had laid down a gauntlet in front of one of the masters at the cooking school. I almost winced when I heard plates smashing in the kitchen. Almost.

Instead I walked away as quietly as possible. Seriously, did I want to expose myself to those tantrums again? This time they would be far worse—played up for drama and the estimated one million watchers.

But then again, one million watchers who may be using my Web site and calling in orders for me to ship them fudge so that they could taste what Chef Thomas did.

While Papa had left me with a good chunk of money, with the new Grander Hotel opening its doors, it never hurt to do a little publicity. What was that Jenn said? Bad publicity is better than no publicity.

Speaking of publicity, it was high time I went back to the *Town Crier* and got that ad in the paper. I could also use it as an excuse to ask Liz what new gossip was going around about the bones Mal had dug up from under the lilac bush.

Then a thought hit me—would it be too morbid to make neon orange fudge in honor of whoever lost their toes?

Maybe not.

CHAPTER 7

"Rex isn't giving me a lot of details," Liz said. She sat at a desk behind the counter of the *Town Crier*. Dressed in cargo pants, a camp shirt, and fabulous boots, she had her feet up on the desk and her hands behind her curly hair. "I even tried baiting him with my feminine wiles."

That made me laugh. "He seems too no-nonsense to fall for that."

"He's a guy," she said with a shrug, released her hands, and leaned forward on her desk. "I always use the Erin Brockovich trick on a guy."

"Does that work?"

"Often enough." She sent me a fast grin. "Rex has been married twice. The man likes women so I had to try."

"Does he date?" The words came out of my mouth before I could stop them.

"Some, not anyone on island that I know of." Liz shrugged. "Last I heard there was this chick in St. Ignace. Why?"

I paused and looked at her. Sometimes it was best not to say.

"It's like that, is it?" She asked and leaned back, putting her hands behind her head.

"No, not really." I wiggled uncomfortably in my seat. "One—I don't have the time. Two—there was this thing with Trent Jessop that never got resolved. . . ."

"Ah, the legendary coffee-spot incident. Yes, I heard about that."

My cheeks heated up in a blush. "Darn small community." I pressed my hands to my cheeks to try to get them to calm down.

"Hey, I'm a reporter. I hear everything that goes on around here."

"He acted as if it's nothing. So maybe it was nothing."

"Oh, it was something." She studied me. "I happen to know that he doesn't make a habit of doing that in public."

"Oh." It was all I could say. The memory of that incident was enough to throw me off track.

"Is that all you wanted to know? How the investigation is going? Trust me, you could have called."

"No." I pulled my small clutch out of my coat pocket. "I came down here yesterday to put a help-wanted advertisement in the classifieds. Then Mal pulled up those bones and I completely forgot why I came."

She sat up and pulled a paper out of the in-box on the top. "Okay, that's simple enough. What are you looking for?"

"I need a part-timer on the housekeeping staff and someone to relieve Frances at the front-desk reservations."

She handwrote notes on the paper. "Did you try the St. Ignace or Mackinac City employment agencies?"

I made a face. "I prefer someone who knows the

island—maybe spends the summer up here with their family like I did as a kid."

"So a local help-wanted . . ." She scribbled another note.

"Yes." I craned to make out what she wrote, but her handwriting looked more like scratches. "Can you read that?"

Liz laughed. "It's my personal shorthand. I developed it taking interview notes. I didn't want the standard shorthand because people could read it and sometimes a reporter needs to keep information close to the vest so that their byline has some meaning. With so much social media, some things go viral quicker than I can write a decent article."

I winced. "I bet it's tough these days."

"It is." She raised an elbow in a slight shrug. "But the *Town Crier* is a family tradition. I'm not willing to let it go. Besides, we publish online as well as hard copy."

"Then it's a labor of love."

"Yes." She nodded. "There's no money in it."

I drew my eyebrows together in concern. "Do you work elsewhere?"

"Are you wanting to hire me?" She grinned. "I'm expensive."

I laughed. "No, I'm really looking for cheaper help. I was just being nosey."

"I freelance a lot. Newspapers might be going the way of the dinosaur, but everyone still needs competent writers who can put out good copy."

"So my want ad will be written by a pro . . ."

She laughed. "Not sure if it will be read by the person you are looking for. You should put a note out on craigslist or one of the other sites."

"Oh, right. That's a good idea."

"She's good at scaring away business," Angus MacElroy said as he came into the front from the back office. "Take the woman's money." He put his hand on Liz's shoulder. "We could use it to replace the mulch under the lilac bushes."

"Hi, Mr. MacElroy," I said and smiled.

"Don't smile at me," he grumped and pulled the rabbit's foot out of his breast pocket. "I'm still alive and for some crazy reason want to continue to be alive."

"Oh, Grandpa, that line's going to get old fast." Liz wagged her finger at him.

"Remember you said that when this young lady finds my old bones trussed up somewhere."

"Don't worry, Mr. MacElroy, should I find your dead body, I'll call Liz first so that she can take the credit and figure out who did it." I winked at him as I handed over my debit card.

"Have you heard anything else about the bones?" Liz asked her grandfather. "I know you have an ear to the ground when it comes to the locals."

"Everyone is interested in whom it might be, but no one knows of anyone missing, which leads us all to believe it was a fudgie who lost their way." He shrugged. "The only good thing as far as I'm concerned is that toenail polish means those bones most likely belong to a younger female. That's the speculation at the senior center anyway." He put the rabbit's foot in the breast pocket of his dress shirt and patted it. "This may mean your streak of finding old men dead is over. Not that I'm taking any chances." He mumbled the last bit just loud enough for me to hear.

"Angus?" I turned to the old man, who was giving me

the squinty eye. "I'm buying a help-wanted ad. Liz has the particulars. All you have to do is swipe my card."

Angus swiped the card, then pulled a receipt pad out of his drawer and scrawled something on it in ink. He ripped the top off the pad and waved it at me. "Your card and your receipt."

"Thanks!" I stuffed it in my pocket and turned to leave.

"Rumor has it you're going to be part of that reality TV program being filmed at the Grand. Is that true?" he asked.

"I suppose." I shrugged. "I'm only doing it as a favor to my old mentor and hoping it will bring more publicity for the McMurphy."

"Those things are scripted, you know."

"Technically they're not scripted, they're coached. I applied on one condition."

"What's that?"

"That they boot me out early on. I'm too busy to give up a month—especially June—for these shenanigans."

"You know, there's a great story there, Grandpa," Liz said. "We could do a behind-the-scenes look at the making of a reality cooking show." She drew the title across the air with her right hand. "I'll interview Allie. We'll get all the dirt about what really happens at one of those shows."

"I signed a disclosure waiver already." I winced. "All I can tell you is that I did the screen test today. Now if they don't put me on the cast I can tell you about the director and Peter. But until then I'm legally bound not to say anything. And their lawyers are ferocious when it comes to any leaks."

Liz made a face and shrugged. "I kind of figured but a reporter has to try."

"It doesn't mean you can't interview the director and the crew," Angus said.

"I'll introduce you to Peter Thomas. He was my most-hated and then most-loved professor in culinary school."

"I had one of those," Liz said. "It's a good angle." She rubbed her chin. "Not as good a story as a dead body. But then right now that's not going anywhere. For all we know those bones in the mulch were two years old."

"Where's that killer dog of yours?" Angus asked me.

"Mal?" I smiled. "She's with Frances, welcoming the guests."

"Call me if she finds any more bones, okay?" Liz got up and went to her desk to pick up a notepad. "I need to see how close I can get to an insider look at that reality team."

"Don't tell them I sent you, I can't afford to be sued," I said.

"Mum's the word," Angus said and zipped his lips and threw away the key.

I laughed. "I haven't heard that term in years. I think Grammy used to say it when she would sneak me a cookie."

"Just remember," he warned. "Everything you say here is on the record and can and will be used in the paper."

I made the zipping motion with my fingers across my mouth. I was not going to say anything I didn't want in the paper. I took two steps to the door, and one look at the portal reminded me of when we found the bone . . . and Angus saying he might know who the socks and boots belonged to. "Wait." I spun back around. "What about this Karus fella Angus thought might be the dead guy?" I asked, my gaze on Liz as she gathered up her gear. "Has anyone spoken to him? Would he know who else wears argyle socks and steel-toed boots?"

"That's a good question." Liz stepped around her desk. "It's a small community. If two people have footwear in common they would bond over it."

"Maybe it's someone in his family," I mused. "I'd be gentle with how you ask him."

"Oh, I'll be gentle." Liz raised an eyebrow. "I'm always gentle. Aren't I, Grandpa?"

"Gentle as a lamb." He chuckled.

"More like a wolf in sheep's clothing, I suspect." I watched as Liz beat me out the door. I glanced at Angus. "That's two story ideas I've given Liz. The very least you can do is refund the cost of my ad."

"In your dreams, Missy." Angus wandered back to his old computer monitor. He sat down and looked over the top of his glasses at me. "Don't you have fudge to make and a hotel to run?"

"Right." I turned to go. "You'll tell me if she discovers anything about those bones, right?"

"This is journalism, young lady. We make our money selling stories. I'm not stupid enough to give it away free. Buy a paper if you want the latest news. Now, go, be gone." He waved me off. "Don't let the door hit you in the behind on your way out."

Mrs. Goode's Fudge

3 cups of sugar
Dash of salt
⅔ cup of cocoa powder
1½ cups of milk
¼ cup butter
1 teaspoon vanilla
2 cups of chopped peanuts

Prepare an 8" x 8" x 2" inch pan—butter the pan, cover the inside with parchment paper or wax paper. Butter the paper and set the pan aside.

In a large, heavy saucepan mix sugar, salt, cocoa powder, and milk. Stir over medium heat until the ingredients reach a full boil. Let boil unstirred until a candy thermometer reads 125°F or the soft-ball stage is reached. Remove from heat.

Add butter and vanilla—do not mix. Cool until the thermometer reads 110°F, then beat until fudge thickens and just begins to lose its gloss. Add peanuts and pour into prepared pan. Cool completely. Cut into 1-inch pieces. Enjoy!

CHAPTER 8

"Miss McMurphy?"

I walked back to the fudge shop after placing my ad and picking up a few items from the grocery store. I was missing Mal. The sound of crowds of people laughing and talking mixed with the clip-clop sound of the carriage horses. The scent of fudge and caramel corn mixed with sunscreen. I was overwhelmed with memories of summers with Papa Liam and Grammy Alice.

"Excuse me," a young woman put her hand on my arm and stopped me. "Do you work at the McMurphy Hotel and Fudge Shoppe?"

"Yes," I said. "I'm the owner. Is there a problem?"

"Oh, no, no problem." She was shorter than me, the top of her head reaching the same level as my chin, which made her about five foot one inch tall. She had long black hair and brown eyes and the high cheekbones of a native islander. "I'm Sandy Everheart. I stopped by the hotel first, but you weren't in."

"How can I help you?" I asked and tilted my head.

She was slender and wore a white polo shirt and black

slacks and wedge shoes with closed toes. "Were you headed back to the McMurphy?"

I lifted the bags in my hands. "Yes, I was."

"Can we speak in private?"

"Okay, sure, follow me." We were only a few shops down from the McMurphy, and we wove our way through the crowds of tourists and porters and maids and the gardeners who weeded the many beds of flowers.

She opened the door of the McMurphy for me, and the scent of fudge wafted out. I noted how the crowd weaved toward the rich scent of chocolate. I was glad I had a sign that said FREE SMELLS INSIDE. I also had a free Wi-Fi sign, but it wasn't as big a draw as I had thought. It turns out people go on vacation to get away from their computers and cell phones. Unless they were high schoolers—then they had perpetual cricks in their necks from staring at the social media on their phones.

Mal came running up, wagging her stumpy tail and leaping on me for attention. "I can't pick you up until I free my hands," I told her.

"You should teach her not to jump up on people," Frances called after me.

"I know, I know." I put the bags down behind the front desk, then picked Mal up for puppy kisses and hugs. "How do you resist this?" I asked and held her out.

"You can't spoil her if you want her to interact with the residents."

"I know, you're right." I put Mal down.

Frances wore a lilac print dress she had belted around her middle. Even though it was warmer out today, she wore a solid lilac sweater and sat on her perch behind the counter. "Who's this?" she asked and nodded toward Sandy.

"I'm sorry, Frances Wentworth, this is Sandy Ever . . . I'm sorry, what was your last name again?"

"Everheart," she said and stuck out her hand. "Sandy Everheart."

"Nice to meet you, Sandy." Frances shook her hand. "Is there something I can help you with?"

"I'm here to see if there is something I can help Miss McMurphy with."

"Are you looking for a job?" I asked. "Because I just posted an ad in the paper."

"Were you looking for a candy maker? Because that is what I do." She smiled at me, and the expression lit up her face. "I've been through culinary school and I majored in candy making." She reached into the notebook she held and pulled out two sheets of paper. "My resume and references."

"I see." I glanced at the resume. She graduated from a school in New York. "Top of your class, too."

"Yes, I'm very good with chocolate," she said. "For my final project, I created a to-scale miniature of the New York skyline. Here's a picture of the project." She took out her cell phone and pulled up a photograph and showed it to me.

"Impressive," I said. "But I don't need a chocolatier." I handed her back her resume.

"No, please keep it," she said. "I will take any work that you have in the kitchen."

I narrowed my eyes. "Why? It looks like you apprenticed at Li-Lac. In the West Village, New York?"

"I did and I have references." She flipped through her resume to show me the references.

"You should apply at the Grand or the Island House or even that new Grander Hotel. Surely they can do a better job of using your services."

"I tried them." Her shoulders slumped. "They already have their staff hired."

"I see." My heart went out to the emotion in her eyes. "With a resume like this you can work anywhere—Chicago, New York, Atlanta . . . anywhere."

"My home and family are here." She took her resume from me. "I am taking care of my mother. I can't go off to some big city."

"You won't feel bad about washing dishes?"

Her expression lit up. "No, ma'am. I would be grateful for anything you have available in your kitchen."

I studied her and thought, what could it hurt to let someone help with the dishes? Especially if I'm running around for a week or two shooting Peter's reality show. "When can you start?"

"Oh, my goodness, right away. Thank you!" She took my hand and shook it. She then shook Frances's hand and finally bent down and offered her hand to Mal, who gave her her left paw.

"Look at that," Frances marveled. "You've taught Mal how to shake."

Sandy laughed. The sound was clear and sweet as bells. "I think she feels my excitement." She stood. "Seriously, when do you want me to start?"

"Frances will get you the paperwork to fill out," I said. "This is a seasonal position. I'm not sure we will be open in the winter."

"Okay, I understand."

Frances reached into her desk and pulled out employment sheets. "Fill this out and I will need to see your social security card and another form of ID for your personnel files."

"Okay . . ." She reached into her pocket and pulled out a small wallet. "I have them now."

"Wow, you came prepared." I leaned against the receptionist desk.

"I had hoped you would hire me."

"Why don't you come in tomorrow about seven AM. I usually start making fudge for the counter about five AM and I will have dishes that need to be done."

"Perfect," she replied.

"Good." I patted her on the shoulder and left her to Frances. Jenn would be thrilled to have a chocolatier on staff. I bet myself that within a day or so Jenn would put Sandy to work preparing centerpieces for her events.

The next day I got the call from the producers when I was in the middle of a fudge-making demonstration. "The cold marble tabletop cools the hot candy in just the right amount of time to get a smooth and creamy finish."

I did a quickstep around the table, scooping the last of the fudge and forming a long loaf. Frances came over and picked up a spare hand scraper.

"You have a phone call from those TV people." She grabbed a plate and chopped off some of the fudge. Cutting it into bite-size pieces, she nudged me. "I'll take it from here."

"I'm in the fudge business, not the television business," I muttered.

"We can use the publicity," Frances nudged. "You've added another employee and are looking for yet another."

"Right." I sighed and put my scraper in the sink and

went out to the reception desk, where the phone line's light blinked. "This is Allie."

"Hi, Allie, this is Bob Salinger, producer of the Candied Chef series." He paused as if expecting my happy reply.

"Yes, Frances told me," I said.

"We would like you to be a cast member on the show. We need you to come down today to do the opening credits photo shoot and to give some introductory information that we will use throughout the show. Be at the Grand Hotel Ballroom Salon 5 by three PM. Wear your chef coat."

"Today?"

"Yes, today, our shooting schedule is very tight."

"I'm running a business . . ."

". . . that will benefit from your being on our show."

"Right," I said. "I'll be there."

"Good."

I hung up the phone and glanced over to the white and blue puppy bed inside the downstairs crate. Mal was sprawled out on it, her tummy and feet in the air. "It must be nice," I muttered.

I glanced back at the fudge shop to see Frances serving up fudge to a crowd of people. I went over to help. I needed to make at least two more batches of fudge before I left. I'd better get to it.

"—And that's why my boss always made us wear hairnets," an elderly woman told me as I waited at the edge of the counter, holding her boxed fudge. "Be sure everyone wears hairnets. There are so many terrible things in hair."

"I thank you for your advice. My baker's cap works as well as a hairnet," I assured her. "It meets all health codes."

"Yes, I suppose it does," she grumbled and snatched the bag out of my hand. "The gal at the reception desk wasn't wearing a hairnet. I know she works behind the counter on occasion. I saw her there this afternoon."

"Right, so in future, I will be sure that Frances and anyone here at the McMurphy Hotel and Fudge Shoppe wears a hairnet prior to handling the fudge. You see we have a clear demarcation between the fudge shop and the lobby." I pointed out the black-and-white tile floor that butted up against the wooden floor of the lobby. "We also have glass walls on these two sides that meet the inspector's code. I can assure you that my fudge is made in-house and is served fresh by the cleanest standards this side of a clean room."

"Yes, well I certainly hope you have a clean kitchen," she said as I gently walked her out of the front door of the McMurphy.

"You have a nice day, now." I opened the door for her, and she stepped out, gathering her sweater around her shoulders as a fresh breeze blew in off the lake. Seeing that she was properly distracted, I slipped back into the shop and closed the door behind me. "Free at last," I said to Frances, who sent me a wry smile.

"You're going to be late for your photo shoot." She pointed at the clock on the desk showing that it was five minutes past the time I'd been slated to show up.

"Darn it." I pulled off my dirty chef coat and hat and grabbed a fresh chef coat out of the linen closet tucked into the back of the elevators. "Do we have hairnets?" I asked Frances as I grabbed the rest of the required objects and walked to the door.

"I'll get right on those," Frances called after me.

I went out the back door with a full head of steam. Why didn't Papa Liam ever use a hairnet?

"Because your Papa Liam had been bald since he was twenty-two years old," came the reply.

Startled, I glanced up and saw Mr. Beecher making his way toward me down the alleyway between the McMurphy and the Oakton B and B behind it. The old man always reminded me of the snowman from that classic Christmas cartoon. He had a white mustache, laughing dark eyes, and a wide, bald head. He preferred to wear fedoras no matter what the weather. In the heat they were straw; in the cooler weather they were felt. He usually wore a dress shirt, a waistcoat, and a jacket over black slacks with shiny dark shoes. He was as old as Papa or maybe older. I wasn't sure and thought it rude to ask.

"Hello, Mr. Beecher," I said. "You startled me. I didn't realize I had asked that question out loud."

"Where are you going in such a distracted hurry?" he asked as I reached him.

"I was asked to be part of the reality fudge-off being filmed at the Grand. I was supposed to have been there five minutes ago, but got shanghaied by one of my clients who was concerned that none of us were wearing hairnets."

Mr. Beecher nodded. "No need for them really. You young people wash your hair much more often than we did back in our day. As long as the hair is clean and pulled back, you're good."

"That's what I told her, but she kept complaining. Some people like the attention they get when you are trying to sell them something. You are a captive audience and they are reluctant to let you go." I raised my eyebrows. "On that note I've got to get going. See you later, Mr. Beecher," I called over my shoulder.

"Knock 'em dead, my dear." His words floated back after me.

"I'll certainly try," I called over my shoulder. "That is, if they don't fire me for being tardy."

CHAPTER 9

"Good, you're here," called a young man in cigarette-shaped black pants and a white T-shirt with the sleeves rolled up. He was as thin as a rail, with brown hair that was cut very short in back, but the bangs were left long so that they could be side swept and reached his cheekbones. "I'm Austin and I'm the stylist for the show." He grabbed me by the arm and pulled me into a partitioned portion of one of the ballrooms at the Grand. Inside were racks of clothing and shoes, shelves with accessories, and ten chef's hats—one with each person's name on it. They read from left to right, Bruce, Cathy, Tony, Jabar, Emily, Amber, Erin, Mark, Tim and on the very end was a hat with my name on it—Allie.

There was loud pop music playing and a makeup artist worked on one middle-aged woman's makeup while a hairstylist tsked over a young man's faux hawk.

"What are you?" the stylist looked me up and down. "A size eight?"

"Usually a size six," I answered, feeling that his question was rude considering we just met. "Sometimes an eight. It really depends on the cut." I tilted my head. "I'm Allie McMurphy, by the way."

"Yes, yes, I know who you are—I have your picture and your personal file. They've got you cast as the girl-next-door. So you really need to be a size four." He chewed on his bottom lip and gave me that look again. "I can make do for now. But I suggest you drink only water and eat only fresh veggies and broiled chicken or fish. Your hair is good as long as Mike can straighten that wave out. Your cheekbones are good, but you're a little too pear-shaped for the television." He brought his left hand up to his cheek and put his right hand on the left elbow and cocked his hip. "I suppose it's okay if you are overweight. This is supposed to feel as real as possible and the reality is that nowadays girls your age are a little more . . . how do you say it? Fluffy? Is that right?" He looked at me as if expecting an answer.

"I'm not overweight by any means," I protested.

"Don't take it personal." He patted me on the shoulder. "Every single one of us is starving ourselves to look decent on television. Maybe if you spend a couple hours in the gym each day you can tone up and that will help your look."

"I'm a fill-in replacement," I told him. "I don't expect to last much past the first cut."

"Well, that's not up to you or me," he said. "The writers are upstairs as we speak hashing out the story arc. You know—mean girl, crazy man, hunky chef, girl-next-door—which, by the way, is a better part than the original. She was to play the stupid blonde. Since you are not blond and I don't have the time to make you blond—"

"I don't want to be blond."

"That's beside the point. We already have two blond girls." He walked me toward a rack of clothing that was marked "girl-next-door."

"That's a lot of clothes," I muttered. "What're they for?"

"Wardrobe already picked out what you'll wear for the season. We have to have twenty-two outfits in case the writers decide to keep you in for the full twenty-two episodes."

"But I thought I was supposed to wear my McMurphy uniform." I waved my hand over my pink polo and black pant ensemble. "They asked me to bring my own chef's coat." I lifted the coat in my hand to show him that I did as I was asked.

"Oh, dear me, no." He shook his head and studied me again. "No, no, no. We can't have that dreadful pink polo on television. You'll clash with everything. Black slacks are so passé, with your figure you should be wearing skirts. How good are your legs?"

"What kind of question is that?" I began to get perturbed by his personal breakdown of my body and my uniform.

"Austin's just doing his job, Allie," Peter Thomas came up behind me and brushed a kiss on my cheek. "You can't take these things personal. Remember that tough skin I gave you in CIA—this program is a good place to use it."

"Hello, Chef," Austin gushed with stars in his eyes. "I see you're wearing the tailored shirt and pant that I suggested. Nice belt . . . no socks, yes. You look fabulous."

He clapped his hands. "You'll be drawing in the female viewers like crazy this year."

"Bruce Jones, you're up for filming," said a young woman in black slacks and a black T-shirt; she had brown hair tied up in a ponytail, dark slashing eyebrows, and red painted lips. She looked from her clipboard to the room and spotted the young man with the purple-tipped faux hawk. "Oh, no, Tim. They said no way to that hair." She glanced at the watch on her left wrist. "You have five minutes to make it better. Go!"

Then she looked back at her clipboard. "Cathy Unger you're up."

The middle-aged woman stood up and walked toward the young woman, who made a twirl sign with her finger. Cathy did as she was asked.

"You look great," the woman said. "You're shooting in Salon D." Then she glanced my way. "Are you the girl-next-door?"

"She is," Peter said, patting my back.

"She needs to get dressed and in and out of hair and makeup. She's up in ten." The woman's blue eyes were as serious as the black eyeliner she used. "Let's go people. No one here is paid to just stand around."

The room got very busy for the short while she was in it. As soon as the door closed behind her, the tension in the air lessened by quite a bit.

"Wow, she is large and in charge," I said to Peter.

He let out a roaring laugh. "That's Caroline Haute. She's the brains behind the show. She's the one who ensures everything comes together." Peter leaned toward me. "She loved your test shots. Especially the story about the old man who died in your attic."

"You mean my utility closet . . ."

"Whatever, it's a great story. Now I'm leaving you in Austin's capable hands. Knock 'em dead." He winked at me and strode off. It was the second time I had heard that in less than an hour. I hoped to goodness it wasn't an omen of things to come.

CHAPTER 10

"You look bright-eyed and bushy-tailed," Frances said to me as I poured my second cup of coffee and put a plastic lid on it so that I could carry it with me. It was seven in the morning, and I had finished four batches of fudge and two pots of coffee—yes, pots.

"Peter didn't tell me that shooting this show would take hours. I didn't get home until two AM, then the alarm went off at five so that I had time to make fudge for the shop before opening." I sipped the hot coffee and burned my tongue on the thick brew. It didn't matter—I had that tired brain that made you want to gulp hot coffee in a sad attempt to get the caffeine to your brain. Seriously, they should provide IV caffeine for this type of morning. "I'm hoping a brisk walk with Mal will shake some of the fog out of my brain. I made the first cut. They have us in stereotypical roles."

"What does that mean?" Frances asked as she sat down at her reservation desk.

"There are eight of us cast members. Let me see if I remember this right. There is Bruce. He's from Kansas so they have him playing the country boy even though he told me he was from the Kansas City metro area and didn't know a cow from a bull. Then there's Cathy. She's the middle-aged mom. Tony is from New Jersey and gives off the Jersey Shore vibe."

"What's that?" Frances asked, her expression perplexed.

"Apparently there is a reality show set on the Jersey Shore. Anyway, then there is Jabar. He is the token African American. Emily is the smart one—she got cut last night."

"Oh, that's too bad, I like smart girls," Frances said and put her elbow on the desk and her chin in her palm and studied me.

"Right?" I agreed. "Apparently smart girls don't make for good television. So then there is Amber and Erin; both are blond and mean-girl types." I ticked them off on my fingers. "Jon is a tattooed kid from Seattle and then Tim is heavy set with a purple tipped faux hawk. Jon is supposed to be a free spirit type and Tim is supposed to be crazy and mean, but in truth he is a big teddy bear."

"Wow, this show is scripted?" Frances seemed confused.

"I can't talk about it," I said.

"Then what part are you playing?"

"I'm playing a type not a part."

"Fine," Frances waved her hand and straightened. "What type are you playing?"

"The girl-next-door," I replied. "Kind of boring and easy to cut from the show early. I figure that means tonight unless they decide to get rid of a guy first to keep the numbers of men and women even. That happens sometimes. Anyway, I'm supposed to shoot a cooking segment tonight. They have some crazy ingredients for us to use."

"What kind of crazy ingredients?" Frances asked as she typed away on her computer, scheduling the reservations that had come in through the Web site during the night.

"I have no idea but it's supposed to be outrageous—you know, to cause the 'ugh' factor, and we are supposed to give the judges something gourmet out of it." I put Mal's halter around her little body and then hooked the leash to it. She grabbed the leash from me and ran toward the back door, holding the leash in her mouth. "Mal, no!" I ran after her. She stopped and sat with her leash still folded up in her mouth. Her black button eyes blinked at me to ask why I was taking so long.

She had gotten up with me in the morning but had gone back to her crate to sleep while I made fudge. She knew she was not allowed in the tiled area of the lobby. My greatest fear was that she would get underfoot while I was transferring hot sugar from the copper kettle to the marble tabletop. So while she liked to be up when I got up, there wasn't anything she could do but sit at the tile entrance and watch me cook. After a while she went back to her bed until Frances came in at seven AM.

Frances always welcomed Mal with a treat shortly after I took her for her morning walk. It was a comfortable routine. I'm certain Mal thought she could walk herself, but I refused to be the kind of doggie parent who let her dog out the door and trusted she would come back. Mal was only six months old. She still needed guidance and a firm hand.

I reached down and snatched the leash out of her mouth. "All right, here we go." I opened the back door and ensured that I stepped out first. The reading I had done on dog training said that according to dog social manners, the leader, or alpha, went outside or inside first. The best way to get your dog to listen to you is to ensure that you are always the leader. This meant being diligent about entering and exiting a building.

"Good morning," Mr. Beecher said as he walked down the alley, leaning on his cane. "Nice day for a walk. The lilacs are really blooming now."

"Hi, Mr. Beecher, have you been to the Beanery for coffee already this morning?" I walked Mal to her green spot near the fence by the back of the Oakton B and B.

"Ever since I turned seventy years old, I've gotten up early. Not much to do, so I putter around the house until the Beanery opens at six AM. I've got a standing order of Earl Grey tea, with room for cream, and cinnamon-raisin toast. They make a homemade loaf fresh every morning."

"Sounds wonderful," I said as Mal finished up her squat and bounced up to say hi to Mr. Beecher.

She did a pirouette to catch his attention, and he laughed at her antics. "That's one cute doggie you've got there," he said.

"She's pretty smart, too," I said. "If you ever bring a treat make sure she does all her tricks for you."

"Will do that." He chuckled. "Have a good morning." He patted Mal on the head and walked on.

I took the chance to guzzle more coffee, and soon enough Mal was tugging on the leash to get walking. We cut through the alley and up to Market Street. Today we started toward the elementary school along the bike trail that went around the island. I loved that trail. It was a simple eight-mile ride that got you out into the woods and hills that were in the less-developed parts of the island. Of course, Mal and I would not go all the way around. I didn't have the time. So we wandered near the cottages that faced the lake.

Suddenly Mal followed her nose off the path, through the grass, to a freshly manicured flower bed.

"No, Mal." I tugged her leash. She was light enough I could pull her back to me if I needed to, but this morning I was tired and more interested in my coffee than Mal's snooping. My wandering thoughts had me thinking how much we would know about the neighborhood gossip if we humans could sniff it out like the doggies did.

Then I realized I really didn't want to know everyone's business. Some secrets were best left alone.

"Get the dog out of the garden." A harsh voice drew my attention. Mrs. Cunningham, a member of the historical society on the island, came around one of the large maple trees that edged the property.

"Oh, right, sorry." I pulled on the harness. Mal was having none of it, causing me even more embarrassment. "Come on, Mal, out!" She did pop out then, but this time she had another bone in her mouth. She bounded up and dropped the bone on my shoe.

I blinked at it. She sat and looked at me with a proud expression and a tilted head. "Please be a chicken bone, please be a chicken bone."

Mal grew impatient and nudged me with her nose.

"I see it," I said and bent down and picked it up.

"What did your dog take from my garden? I just put that mulch down yesterday. I paid over a thousand dollars for the flowers and mulch and work. If she pulled up one of my new plants you are entirely to blame." The old woman came running up wagging her finger at me. In her left hand was an iron rake, which she used to push at Mal.

"Stop it!" I ordered and picked up my puppy. "Don't you dare hit her with that rake or I'll rake you. She's just a puppy."

"That pup ruined my garden. You can't deny it. I saw her dig up whatever you are holding. It belongs to me."

"I'm afraid it doesn't belong to you." I studied the bone in my hand. "You need to call Officer Manning. This looks like a human bone."

"A what?" she screeched at me. Mal took the moment to reach out and lick the old woman's cheek. "Hey!"

"Sorry." I pulled Mal back. "Don't get too close—she likes to kiss everyone."

The old woman wiped her cheek with her hand, and I saw her gaze soften. "I had a pup that was like that once," she said, her tone just a little softer. "Old mutt would try to French-kiss you every chance she got." She reached out and petted Mal's head. "Now what was that nonsense about Officer Manning?"

I put Mal down and handed the woman the bone. It was about an inch long and looked as if it had been cut by a very sharp knife at a very strange angle. "That's a bone."

"So it is," she said. "Probably chicken bone." She eyed it.

"It's not hollow enough to be a chicken bone," I pointed out. "Do you see that odd cut?"

"Yeah, what about it?"

"Those same strange cuts were on the foot bones Mal found a few days ago under the lilac bush near the *Town Crier*." I pursed my lips. "We really should call Officer Manning—he's working on the case."

"I have no idea how a bone got into my landscaping." She took a pair of bright blue reading glasses with glitter on the cat-eyed edges and placed them on her nose to get a better look. "Lots of critters living and dying out here. I never thought I needed to bother the cops over a few bones."

Mal pulled on the leash, drawing my attention. Then she put another bone on my shoe. "Where are you getting these?" I asked her as I picked up another small bone with sharp-angled blade cuts.

"She better not be digging up my garden," Mrs. Cunningham warned. Her gray eyebrows crumpled and her brown eyes flashed. She forgot that she had been charmed by Mal only a moment ago, stormed the few feet to the garden, and shouted, "Shoo!"

Mal danced around her and did a fast semicircle with another bone in her mouth. Mrs. Cunningham chased after her, which was silly since I had ahold of Mal's leash. They played hide-and-seek around me. At least Mrs. C had put the rake down.

"Stop it!" I put my hands on my hips and tugged on the leash.

Mal sat down beside me and looked up at the old woman, who wagged her finger at Mal. "Stay away from my flowers."

"There's another bone." I held out my hand, and Mal dropped her treasure in my palm. This one had a flake of bright red polish on it. "That tears it. I'm calling Officer Manning. Animal bones do not have polish on them."

"Good, call him. I want to lodge a complaint about that animal of yours." She pointed at Mal. Mal did a pirouette on her back legs, then sat back down and tilted her head.

Mrs. C could no longer stay mad. "Well, heck." She straightened. "Aren't you just the cutest thing ever?"

Mal held out her paw to shake.

"What's she doing?" Mrs. C asked.

"She's making friends," I said as my phone speed-dialed Rex's direct line. The phone rang in my ear. "Shake," I said and reached down and shook Mal's paw. "See?"

Mal held her paw out to Mrs. C. The old lady chuckled and shook Mal's paw, and suddenly they were fast friends.

"This is Officer Rex Manning. Leave a message at the beep."

"This is Allie McMurphy. I may have a second crime scene." I hung up and dialed the police station.

"Island Police, this is Charlene, how can I help you?"

"Hi, Charlene, this is Allie McMurphy. Mal has dug up more bones that may be of interest to Officer Manning's investigation."

"That's one busy dog," Charlene said. "Are you sure it's a bone?"

"There are at least three, and yes, they are bones. Can you tell Officer Manning to come to 442 Mockingbird Lane?"

"That's the Cunningham cottage, right?"

"Yes." I sent a smile to Mrs. C, who was on her knees petting Mal. The puppy had that effect on people. One moment they were expecting the worst, and the next Mal was licking their face and dancing for their attention. It seemed Frances knew what she was doing when she picked Mal out for me.

"Hang on for a moment while I contact Rex." Charlene put me on hold. "Sunshine Day" played in the background.

I looked at the bits of bone I held in my hand. They

were larger than the toe bones, but still smaller than an arm or leg. The cuts on the bone looked more like knife cuts than teeth marks. Mal found both sets of bone bits in fresh mulch. Maybe the body was cut with the mulch.

"Allie?" Charlene's voice came back on the line.

"Yes, I'm still here."

"He's on his way. He said don't touch anything."

I studied the bit of polish on the edge of the last bone. "Too late."

CHAPTER 11

"Charlene tells me you found more bones?" Rex zipped up on his bike. He hopped off, hit the kickstand, and came over to where I stood.

"Not me, Mal." I nodded toward the lawn where Mal entertained Mrs. Cunningham by playing fetch with a pinecone. "Mrs. C said she just had her gardens done." I held out the bones. "Mal dug these up under the pansies."

At the sound of her name, the dog came running up to Rex. She jumped on her hind legs and danced, not touching the officer. I had taught her not to jump on people. So she figured as long as she didn't touch them she wouldn't be in trouble.

"Mal!" I scolded her. She sat down and raised her paw.

"Hello, pup." Rex took off his bike helmet and leaned down to shake Mal's paw. "I heard you found more evidence for me. Is that true?"

"She is quite a clever little minx," Mrs. C said as she came up to us. "She found three pieces of bone and brought them to Allie."

"I told her they were most likely animal bone, but she insisted on calling you."

"This last one has a bit of red nail polish." I held up the bone with the flake of polish stuck to it. "These bones have the same sharp edges as the *Town Crier* bones."

Rex pulled latex gloves out of his pocket, put them on his hands, and then carefully took the bones from me. "They could be phalanges," he muttered. "Hard to tell when they are cut up like this."

"Do you think the skeleton could have gone through the mulcher?" I asked. "Both sets of bones have these sharp edges and both were found in the fresh mulch."

"It could be," he muttered and carefully put the pieces in a baggie and sealed it. "It looks like she dug for these." He walked over and squatted down to see where Mal had pushed the mulch aside. "But she didn't dig past the bottom of the mulch."

"So they could be buried in the mulch alone, right?" My heartbeat picked up, and I felt a rush of excitement at the thought that I may have stumbled upon a possible solution to finding only the toes and boot last time.

He hit his walkie-talkie button. "This is Manning," he said. "Responding to possible body dump at the Cunningham cottage. Send in the CSU and backup to help keep the crime scene clean."

"Roger," Charlene's voice echoed through the speaker.

Rex took a pen out of his pocket and poked around in the mulch. The sunlight glinted off another white piece of bone. He put the pen beside it and snapped a picture of the placement.

Mal strained on her leash as if to say, "Let me help, let me help." Her stubby tail wagged.

I pulled her back, disappointed that I couldn't squat down beside Rex and watch him fish up more parts. Mrs. C stood over him pointing out possible bits of bone, all thought of Mal disrupting her newly groomed gardens gone.

"So much for our morning walk," I said to my playful puppy. I hit Jenn's number on my cell phone.

"Hi, Allie, what's up?" Jenn's voice sang out of my phone.

"Mal found more bones."

"Cool! Where are you?"

"I'm off Market on the west coast of the island. It's the white, blue, and green painted lady."

"Oh, you mean the Cunningham house?"

"Yes." I shook my head and made a face. "How do you know?"

"I was scouting places for a tea party. Mrs. C is so pleasant to talk with. She said she would consider a Victorian tea party as long as the party was kept to the lawn and her first floor."

I eyed the woman. She was thin and suntanned. Her skin had that fine texture of a woman past menopause. Her gray hair was tucked up under a straw hat. She wore a long-sleeved shirt over a T-shirt and brown denim pants. Garden gloves stuck out of her back pocket. She looked like pictures of Katharine Hepburn. It was hard to imagine that tough woman would go for a tea party for tourists in her home. But then Jenn could talk an Eskimo into buying ice.

"Need me to come get Mal?" Jenn asked, shaking me from my odd thoughts.

"Yes, please. I need to stay until I've given my statement and she's getting restless."

"No worries, hey, your new help just walked in. What do you want me to have her do while you're out?"

"Ask her to do the dishes and clean up the kitchen.

Hopefully, I'll be back to do a show of fudge. I can walk her through helping me to make the fudge and entertain the tourists."

"Sounds good. I'll be right there. After all, there is a certain crime scene tech I'm interested in . . ."

I laughed. "Of course. Officer Manning just put in a request to have him come out."

"Wait—do you think this is a different body or more of the same person?"

I bit my bottom lip and watched Rex carefully place each bit of bone in its own baggie. "It's hard to tell at this point," I said. "But if it's the same person, then they liked red nail polish on their fingers and neon orange on their toes."

"So whoever the bones belong to, they were proper on the outside and fun on the inside."

"Yes, I suppose that could be true." I walked Mal away from the crime scene. "Or two separate people— one who liked bright polish and one more conservative with the red."

"Can they take DNA from bone and see if they match?" Jenn asked. I heard a door close behind her, and the rush of wind on the phone told me she had stepped outside and was headed this way.

"That's a good question for your boyfriend."

"It is, isn't it?" She giggled. "Not exactly dinner conversation, though. I'm going to have to bone up on my science to keep Shane's interest. No pun intended . . ."

"Oh, I bet you can do that without trying." I remembered how Shane Carpenter's hazel gaze couldn't stay away from Jennifer's cute figure. He might wear heavy black-framed glasses, but they couldn't hide his interest in my best friend.

Mal jumped up and down. "I see you," Jennifer said and hung up.

I let Mal drag me toward Jenn. "That was fast," I said.

"What can I say, I'm motivated by eye candy." Jenn took Mal's leash and angled her head so she could see around me. "Who's here?"

"Officer Manning," I said. "You're too early for anyone else."

"Then I'll drag my feet." Jenn laughed. "How did you find these bones? Mal again?"

"Yes, she has a super sniffer." I bent down and patted Mal on the head. "Mrs. Cunningham thought Mal was digging up her pansies and chased her with a rake."

"That's terrible," Jenn said and gathered Mal up into her arms. Mal rewarded her with a kiss on the cheek. "Poor baby, chased by that mean old woman."

"That mean old woman owns the Cunningham house and is a senior member of the island historical society," I pointed out. "Plus, she forgave Mal when she realized that Mal was digging up bone bits, not flowers. They're fast friend now, right, Mal?" I patted Mal's head, and she reached for me. "No, you go with Jennifer. Your work is done here."

Mal reacted by resting her head under Jenn's chin. Jenn giggled and patted her. "She's a little drama queen."

"Right?" I noticed that Shane Carpenter walked over from the administration building with his tool bag in hand. He was a tall man at six feet and thin without being skinny. His CSU uniform was made up of a white button-down shirt with the county logo over the pocket and a pair of black cargo pants with pockets that held things he might need. His light brown hair was cut short on the sides and hung longer in the front, meaning he had to keep pushing it out of his eyes and away from his glasses.

"More bones?" he asked.

"Yes, Mal found these as well." I patted Mal's head. She ignored me for the attention of the newcomer. Mal sat up and tried to get Shane to take her so that she could kiss him as well. Shane wasn't having any of her antics, and she fell back on Jenn in disappointment.

"What about these bones made you call us?" Shane asked as he went over to where Rex kept the evidence bags of the three bones Mal dug up.

"They look like the bones we found at the *Town Crier*," I said as he picked up the bone bits. "See how the cuts are similar? Then this piece looks like it has a flake of red polish. I wondered if they were finger bones."

"Yes, they look like phalanges." He tipped his head and studied them from all angles.

"Do you think they belong to the same body?" Jenn asked as she cuddled Mal. "Or is there more than one body in the mulch?"

"I highly doubt there are bodies in the mulch," he said, and I noticed that his gaze hit Jenn's in a sizzle moment. The look was so intense that I took a step back to get out of the way.

"So, it's safe to walk the streets of Mackinac Island alone?" Jenn batted her eyes at him. "Or should I get an escort?"

"You have an escort anytime you feel uncomfortable." He nodded his assurance. "But I doubt you have anything to worry about here."

"Well, that's good to know." She sent him a small smile, and he turned away and walked over to Rex.

"Okay, wow, what was that?" I said as quietly as possible.

"Nice, right?" Jenn said, and she squeezed Mal so hard the puppy squeaked. "Sorry, Mal."

We both took a deep breath and watched the men discuss the work in front of them. After a few minutes of quiet contemplation, I turned to Jenn. "Okay, well, I'll give my statement. Can you take Mal home? Frances can watch her. I won't be too long."

"Sure," Jenn said and sent one last look toward her date. "Oh, I put Sandy on KP duty. I've inspected the guest rooms that were vacated and have a list of small repairs that I gave Mr. Devaney."

"Oh, I bet he liked that," I said sarcastically.

"Yep." Jenn giggled. "The only time that man is happy is when Frances is around. Too bad I can't send Frances to do room inspection."

"Well, you could," I pointed out, "but you'd be stuck doing the financials."

"Yeah, no." Jenn laughed. "I might be decent with numbers but accounting makes me want to stab myself in the eye with an ice pick."

"Yikes, okay, no accounting for you. What's on your agenda this week?"

"I've got a wedding and an engagement party. Why?" She tilted her head. I didn't usually ask her what she was doing in her business because she always anticipated the McMurphy's needs and was there with a solution before I even knew there was a problem.

"The new girl," I said.

"Sandy?"

"Yeah, she's a chocolatier. Have her show you her

portfolio. I was thinking you might be able to use her in your party planning."

"Hmm, what's a chocolatier doing washing your dishes?"

"She has family on island and by the time she graduated, all the fudge shops and hotels had already hired their kitchen staff."

"Really?"

"I think she needs someone to give her her first break." I shrugged. "Not everyone with a dream has a family business to help make it come true."

"Now that's the truth," Jenn said and put Mal down. "No worries. I'll look at her portfolio. It would be nice to have access to a chocolatier. I could design centerpieces and desserts."

"That's what I was thinking." I smiled.

Mal tugged on the leash, and Jenn took off in the direction of the McMurphy. "See ya!"

I waved and turned in time to see Shane Carpenter eyeing Jenn like I eye a spectacular piece of fudge. Man, that guy had it bad for my friend. I hope my friend knew what she was getting into. Jenn didn't have any plans to stay on island permanently, and Shane looked like he was here to stay.

Mom's Dark Chocolate Coconut Fudge

4 cups dark chocolate chips (2 bags)
1 can sweetened condensed milk
2 tablespoons butter
1 teaspoon vanilla
2 cups flaked coconut

Butter an 8" x 8" x 2" pan, then line with wax paper or parchment.

In a double boiler*, melt chocolate, sweetened condensed milk, and butter until smooth and thick.

Remove from heat. Add vanilla and stir until combined. Pour half of the fudge into the prepared pan and spread evenly. Press coconut in a thick layer into the bottom layer of fudge. Cover the coconut layer with the remainder of fudge. Cool. Refrigerate overnight. Remove from pan. Cut into pieces. Store in a covered container.

*Invest in a double boiler for making fudge. Using a water bath (fudge pan inside a larger one and with steam/ boiling water) to heat the fudge keeps the chocolate from scroching and or sugaring.

Also, a good candy thermometer is necessary if you choose to make the kind without sweetened condensed milk.

CHAPTER 12

"If I had to guess, I'd say that those bones belong to one person who died and somehow got mixed in the mulch." I looked into Rex's pretty blue eyes. "It's the only thing that explains why the bones were in two separate neighborhoods on island."

"That's the working theory," Rex said as he eyed the growing pile of bones that were being separated from Mrs. Cunningham's precious flower garden.

"I've sent scrapings from both bone samples to the county lab for analysis. We'll know in about six weeks if the bones belong to the same person," Shane said.

I winced at the delay. "Six weeks?"

"That's fast. Most counties are swamped with work and can be anywhere from six months to two years behind on such analysis."

"That's terrible." I said. "How can we fix that?"

"Pay more taxes," Rex said. "Not exactly on anyone's list."

"A chipper-shredder would explain the cut marks on both of these sets of bones," Shane mused. "But if the body is one person who went through the chipper, their remains could be scattered throughout town. There's really no telling where all the bits are without sifting through every garden on island."

"Is there only one mulch company?" I asked and hugged myself at the thought of someone being scattered about town.

"There are two on island," Rex said. "The Island Compost and Mulch Center is where people can recycle food scraps and downed branches."

"Oh, right, I remember Papa Liam took me out there one time as a kid. The smell was enough to discourage me from going back."

"Ed Gooseworthy is the supervisor out there," Shane said. "Find out if he'll let me swab his shredders and go through the mulch."

"Good idea," Rex said.

"Wait." I put my hand on Rex's bicep. The man was strong as an ox. "What's the second place for mulch on island?"

"The horse stables," Rex replied. His gaze studied my expression.

I drew my brows together and pursed my lips. "So, like Jessop Stables?"

"Yes," Rex said. "There has to be someplace for the straw and manure to go when the horse stalls are cleaned out."

"Not to mention a place for the street sweepers to deposit the stuff they clean up," Shane said.

"And the Jessops run a composting yard?" It kind of made sense, but it was tough to wrap my mind around. The Jessops were extremely wealthy and well bred. The idea that they made part of their money on horse manure was odd.

"Exactly," Rex said.

"Who would buy that?" From their reactions, I must have looked completely confused.

"It's a very good mixture for gardening," Shane said.

"They age it for a year or two so that it isn't so strong it burns the plants. After that it's great for a wide variety of gardens."

"Oh." I suddenly understood. "That's why the mulch smells so funny when they first put it out."

"Between the manure and the rotting vegetation, the mulch not only prevents weeds from growing but it actually feeds the plants it's put around."

"So, wait." I made a face. "Are you saying that someone might have gotten trapped in the compost and then run through the chipper-shredder?" I shuddered. "Sounds like a terrible way to die."

"If it's true it would make a heck of a story," Liz said as she walked up behind me with her notepad and pen in hand. "I bet I could write an entire *True Crime* story on something like that."

"I'm certain both the Island Compost and the Jessop Compost and Mulch Service have safety procedures in place to keep that from happening," Rex insisted.

"If the body did come through the garden center it might not be as old as we think." Shane raised one eyebrow in thought. "Depending on the temperature of the compost pile, the body would decay a lot faster than if it were buried or simply left to rot."

"So it could be someone who was here in the last thirty days?" Liz asked.

"Precisely." Shane nodded. "I need to get into both places and take temperatures and do some decay experiments."

"How much can bones tell you about someone?

Enough to help point us in the way of determining who they belong to?" I asked. I mean, I would hate for some-one's family to never know what happened to their loved one.

"If we get enough bones, we can determine quite a few things about a person."

"Great!" I felt my eyes light up.

"Hold on." Rex held up his hand as if to stop my ex-cited thoughts. "That kind of determining can take months to put together."

I felt my shoulders slump in disappointment. "So it's still more important to do the old-fashioned detective work."

"It's what they pay me for," Rex said.

"I heard through the grapevine that you were actually picked for the reality-show cast," Liz said. "Congrats! I tried to get in with Bob Salinger for an interview but I'm not having any luck. You would think they'd want the publicity. Could you make some introductions?"

"You're doing a reality show?" Rex and Shane both looked surprised.

"Sort of." The heat of embarrassment moved into my cheeks. "I don't think I'm the one you want to ask, Liz. I told Chef Thomas I'd do it only if I was the first one to go."

"How come you want to be tossed?" Liz asked. "I happen to know your fudge can compete with the best. It seems to me you'd want to win."

"Oh, sure, it would be nice to win the hundred-thousand-dollar grand prize and be able to put the award in the fudge-shop window, but I don't want to take away my time and efforts from my real job, the McMurphy."

"Okay." Liz nodded. "I can understand that. Tell me, how long does it take to tape one of those shows?"

I winced. "I'm not supposed to say anything about the filming. They make you sign a nondisclosure that is ironclad."

"How ironclad?" Rex asked, drawing his eyebrows together.

"For-as-long-as-you-live ironclad," I said. "They don't want their filming practices to get out."

"So what can you tell us?" Liz asked, her notebook out and pen ready.

"Nothing." I laughed. "Off the record, we were shooting until the wee hours in the morning. A lot more goes into a show like this than you see on television."

"I imagine that's true," Shane said. "Like a real-world investigation versus a sixty-minute television show."

"I still think what you do is cool," I said. "If I hadn't been so determined to make the McMurphy go another generation I might have been a chemist or biologist. There are a lot of similarities between science and candy making. It's all about melting points and air mixtures and proportions."

"Precisely," Shane said and grinned at me.

"While you two are geeking out, I'm going to call in a couple more teams to scour the island gardens with mulch and see how many pieces we can find," Rex said.

"Oh, boy." I felt my eyes grow wide.

"What?" Rex asked with a lift of his chin.

"I think I found another bone," I said and pointed behind him. Daisy, the Saint Bernard, was at it again. This time she had a long bone that was maybe six or eight inches long. Thing is, it didn't look like an animal bone. Plus it had the same strange cuts on the ends.

"Are you sure that's a human bone?" Shane asked. "Hard to tell from this distance."

"Is that a chance you're willing to take?" I asked.

"Well, crap." Rex went after Daisy for the second time this week.

"I'm not chasing her today," Liz said and shook her head. "That dog is a lot faster than she looks."

"Where do you think she got that bone?" I asked.

"What direction did she come from?" Shane asked.

"From the post office."

"I'll send a team that way first. If we can get some of the bigger bones we might have a better chance of identifying the body."

"Do you think it's murder?" I asked.

"Hard to tell at this point," Shane said. "I'll take all the pieces we can uncover and take them back to the coroner's office. Maybe looking at a bigger picture will help." He shrugged. "That said, if it was heart disease we'll never know."

Daisy doubled back to run past us. Rex was closing in on her, muttering dark things under his breath.

"A little help?" he asked as he ran by.

"You look like you're doing a fine job without us," Liz said, and we all laughed.

CHAPTER 13

"You got a phone call from the film crew," Frances said when I came through the back door. "Filming starts an hour early today. They want to see what different light looks like."

"Oh for crying out loud," I muttered. "When am I supposed to get my work done?"

Mal came running to greet me. She slid the last foot or so on the polished wood floor with a wild doggie grin.

"Well, hello there," I said and reached down to give her pats. She immediately fell to the floor and rolled over to get her tummy rubbed. "Yes, you are cute," I whispered as I rubbed her belly.

"Hi, Miss McMurphy." Sandy walked out from a spotless fudge shop. "I've got all the supplies restocked and the dishes done."

"Wow, this looks great." I noted how she straightened the shelves and put everything back exactly where I preferred it to be.

"I know how important it is for a chef to keep their equipment and supplies stocked and in order. I remember where you kept things from the last time I was here and put them back in their place. I hope that's okay." Her brown eyes shone with the joy I felt whenever I was in the kitchen.

"Perfect, thanks," I said. "Let me wash my hands and put on my chef coat and hat. I've posted my list of fudges and you can catch the orders as I start the show."

"Great," she replied. She wore a white polo and black slacks. I had ordered pink-and-white-striped bib aprons for whoever helped me at the counter. Her feet were clad in black athletic shoes that mirrored mine.

Her shoes were how I knew she was a serious chocolatier. Anyone who enjoyed being in the kitchen knew two truths: First, it was easy to get lost in creation and have time fly by unnoticed. Second, you needed good shoes to keep your legs from growing heavy from standing for untold hours.

I washed my hands, dressed for the kitchen, and went straight to work. Dark chocolate black cherry was the flavor of the day and had been nearly sold out. A quick peek told me that the cocktail fudges were still popular for the 21-and-over group. They were such a draw that I made sure I had at least one flavor always on the shelf.

"Cocktail fudges were a clever addition," a male voice said behind me. I turned to find Chef Thomas in the lobby heading my way.

"Thanks." I greeted him with a kiss on the cheek. "How did you get away from the film crew?"

"The writers are working on script changes based on last night's shoot." He turned to Sandy. "Hello, I'm Peter Thomas."

"I know," Sandy gushed and shook his hand. "They spoke of you as a legend in my school in New York."

"Really?" His eyes sparkled.

"This is Sandy Everheart,"—I introduced her—"my summer intern. Actually, she has an impressive resume herself as a chocolatier."

"And you're working in a fudge shop because?" He tilted his head and studied her.

She smiled. "My grandmother lives on Mackinac. I was born and raised here. It's my home."

"What made you decide to become a chocolatier? Isn't that a bit unusual for a local?"

"Chef!" I was aghast at the rude question.

"No, it's a good question," she replied. "Many people thought I was crazy to leave and go all the way to New York to pursue my dream. But I grew up watching the fudgies' delight at candy and vowed early I wanted to be able to put that joy on people's faces. I specialized in cocoa because it is also a native American plant. What I learned is that sculpting in chocolate is as important a medium as sculpting in pottery. With the addition of joy at its consumption." She clasped her hands in front of her. "There is something so incredible about art that is not meant to last. It makes it even more precious."

"Good answer," Peter said. "I'll be here all summer. Perhaps I'll commission a centerpiece for the close of the television shoot."

"I think the staff will like that," I said. Sandy was a small woman but my admiration for her grew with every word she said.

"I heard your pup found more bones this morning." Peter turned to me. "Is that true?"

"Yes." I offered him one of four stainless-steel barstools that were meant to give watchers a seat at the show. "She must know what the body smells like. As soon as we got close she knew right where to dig."

"So what's the story? Is there more than one body buried in the flowers?"

I gathered sugar and water and cocoa with a touch of salt. The base to the fudges was pretty much the same. It was how you put them together that made the difference. "They think it might be one body that ended up in the mulch and got spread about the island."

"They should use your dog to find all the bones," Peter said.

"That's an idea," Jenn said as she came around the fudge shop from the stairway where I assumed she had been working in the office. "We could charge a finder's fee."

"Har, har," I said. "Then Mrs. Finch could hire out her Saint Bernard. So far Daisy has found as many bones as Mal. The only difference is Mal brings the bones to me. Daisy on the other hand has to be run down and the bones forcefully extracted from her jaws. In fact, the last time I saw Officer Manning he was chasing after Daisy."

"Me, too." Jenn's blue gaze twinkled. "He and Daisy would make a great dog and pony show."

The door to the McMurphy opened with a jangle of bells. I glanced up to see a woman in her thirties with brown hair and brown eyes walk into the lobby. Her entrance wouldn't have been remarkable except she looked vaguely familiar, and I wanted to see what she said to Frances.

"It's Tammy Gooseworthy," Sandy said and blew out a long breath. "She's the new pastry chef at the new Grander Hotel."

"Really? I wonder why she's here?" I watched her through the glass wall that separated the fudge shop from the rest of the lobby. I noted that Tammy wore a pair of dark-wash jeans, nude stilettos, and a crisp, white blouse. Not exactly the standard outfit of a pastry chef.

Frances pointed toward us, and Tammy turned. It was then I noticed she carried a basket. I looked from the basket to her face and noted that she was not looking at me. She was looking at Peter.

"I think you have a fan," I said as she headed our way. I noted that her lipstick and fingernails matched with a bright red color. Again, most pastry chefs didn't have their nails polished. It was best to keep them cut short and without polish. Clean hands were the epitome of good housekeeping in keeping a kitchen and all of its patrons healthy.

"Chef Thomas?" Tammy asked as she made her way toward Peter.

"How can I help you?" Peter asked. I noted that he didn't get up off his stool. I saw a flash of emotion cross Tammy's face. She hid it in a blink of an eye and pasted a smile on her face.

"Hi, Tammy Gooseworthy." She held out her free hand. "I'm the new pastry chef at the Grander Hotel."

"A pleasure," he said as he let go of her hand after a few short shakes.

There was a moment of awkward silence before Tammy spoke again. "I heard you needed another chef for your reality show. I was hoping you would consider me for the part." She held out the basket for him to take. "I've put a variety of fudges I've developed for the Grander inside. I hoped maybe you'd try them." She shook her head so that her hair floated off her shoulders. There was a brief moment of disarray, and then her hair floated right back into place.

I tried not to think about my wavy hair and how if I

didn't tuck it up in my chef hat it would be a wild mop. In fact, I doubted if my hair had ever rippled like that when I shook my head.

Mixing ingredients for the next batch of fudge, I tried to ignore the conversation, but it was hard in such a small place.

"I'm afraid that space has already been filled," Peter said as he pushed the basket back toward her. "I'm sure your fudges are fine, Ms. Gooseworthy—was it?"

"Yes," she said with a sharp nod of her head. "If you don't mind my asking, who did you get to fill the spot?"

"My ex-student." He waved one hand in my direction. "Allie McMurphy. Have you met?"

"No." She turned to me. I saw her slow perusal go from the top of my head to the tip of my toes. "Wait, aren't you the one who killed Joe Jessop?"

"No." I shook my head. "I found him already dead."

Mal took that moment to come running out from behind the reception desk then tried to stop as she hit the tile of the kitchen floor. Instead of stopping she slid into Tammy with a solid thump. Mal didn't weigh more than ten pounds, but she could trip you up if you didn't know she was there.

I watched as everything seemed to go into slow motion. Mal hit the back of Tammy's calf. Tammy wobbled on her precariously high heels, then lost the fight for balance and went down, hands thrown out, basket tumbling to the floor. She landed on all fours with a *woof* sound coming out of her chest.

Apologetic, Mal licked Tammy's face. Wouldn't you know Tammy's hair swung out and then fell in a perfect bob as the woman tried to get her bearings.

"Mal!" I scolded the puppy, who looked up at me,

then carefully backed up to the wooden floor of the lobby, plopped her bum down on the floor, and tilted her head as if to say, what? Do I get a cookie?

I handed the wooden stir spoon to Sandy and went to help Tammy up. "I'm so sorry. She's just a puppy and has to learn better manners. Are you okay?"

I wrapped my hands around Tammy's right elbow and helped her to her feet. Tammy yanked her arm out of my hand and brushed back her perfect hair. "She should not be allowed out if she isn't trained. Really." Tammy narrowed her eyes. "You could get sued for allowing that menace in a public lobby."

"Mal isn't a menace," I said calmly and held up my hands to take a step back. "She's a puppy and like most kids is still learning her boundaries. See—" I waved my hand toward Mal. "She knows she isn't supposed to be in the kitchen area."

"Look at my fudges," Tammy cried out at the ruined basket and the lumps of fudge on the floor. She picked up the broken basket and put the floored fudge back inside.

"It's a good thing you wrapped the fudge. No harm, no foul," Jenn said as we all stood around and watched Tammy try to regain her dignity.

"I believe I'm done here," Tammy said with a perfect clip. The only thing that gave away her anger was the stiffness in her shoulders. "Thank you for your time, Chef Thomas. If you decide that you want a camera-ready cast member, I hope you think of me and the Grander. We are new to the island and would like you to consider using us in your television shoot."

"I appreciate the invitation." Peter crossed his arms.

"It's not up to me to choose the location. I will, however, let the director and producer know of your offer. I'm sure they would be happy to consider it."

"Thank you." She reached her free hand into her pocket and withdrew a business card. "Here's my card. Call me anytime. I do have some experience in front of the camera."

"Right, will do," he said and took her card.

She stared at him a moment as if debating whether to ask more of him, and then she must have decided not to do anything. "Okay," she said. "Well, thank you for your time and consideration." She gave a short nod and turned, making a wide berth around Mal.

The bells jangled on the door as she walked through it. We all watched as she seemed to gather herself together and head down the street toward the Grander Hotel.

"You should give Mal a treat," Jenn said and drank coffee from the mug in her hand. "Your puppy has a way of making friends with all the appropriate people."

I was back at the kettle stirring the cocoa and sugar mixture as it boiled to a soft-ball stage. "She looked upset," I said as the candy reached the proper stage and I pulled it from the heat to add butter and vanilla and rum flavoring. "I couldn't tell if it was because Mal slid into her or if it was the fact that I had already filled your open cast slot."

"You're on television now," Peter said. "You should get used to people not liking you. It comes with the territory."

"Wait." I put my hands on my hips. "I thought I was

doing the television thing to get more customers, not make enemies."

"Honey, you can't make an omelet without breaking a few eggs," Jenn said.

"Yes, well, let's hope I didn't just dump my eggs on the floor."

Easy Dark Chocolate Paddy's Peppermint Fudge

4 cups dark chocolate chips (2 bags)
1 can sweetened condensed milk
2 tablespoons butter
1 teaspoon vanilla
2 cups of mint chips

Butter an 8" x 8" x 2" pan, then line with wax paper or parchment.

In a double boiler melt chocolate, sweetened condensed milk, and butter until smooth and thick.

Remove from heat. Add vanilla and stir until combined. Pour half of the fudge into the prepared pan and spread evenly. Press mint chips into the bottom layer of fudge. Cover the mint chip layer with the remainder of fudge. Cool. Refrigerate overnight. Remove from pan. Cut into pieces. Store in a covered container.

CHAPTER 14

"I appreciate you loaning Mal to us," Rex said as he brought my puppy out from the back of the police station. "I would have never thought to use her as a cadaver dog."

"It was Jenn's idea." I said and took Mal's leash from him. I stooped and picked her up. She licked my cheek and settled comfortably against my chest. "So she helped?"

"Yeah." Rex put his hands in his back pockets. "I've got three teams out now digging through the first three spots she hit on. There were five more but I don't have the manpower to safely extract bones so I've had Officer Wright rope them off with crime-scene tape. We needed to let everyone know that they were off-limits."

"What about Daisy?" I asked with a grin, remembering him chasing after the surprisingly agile Saint Bernard.

"I put her in a cell in the back. I think she swallowed one of the bones. This way we can check if she passes it. Besides, it's better to keep her locked up until we find all the bones. Since Mrs. Finch won't lock her up, I did."

"Good thinking," I said. Then I thought of a cold, dark jail cell and had to ask, "Is Daisy comfortable?"

"She's good. Officer Lasko brought in a big dog bed and water and food bowls." He paused and then added, "She has a soft spot for dogs."

I scratched Mal between the ears. "I can understand why. Our fur babies are important to us."

"Yeah, I get that."

The door to the police station opened behind me, and an older woman walked through. She had white hair curled closely around her rectangle-shaped face. Her back was hunched by osteoporosis as older women's sometimes are. She wore a red maxi skirt with tiny white dots on it and a white T-shirt under a red, long-sleeved corduroy shirt. Over that was a jacket made of black polyester. On her feet were bright white athletic shoes.

I watched with fascination as she ignored both me and Rex and walked straight to the back.

"Hold on—" Rex told me, and then he followed her through the office to the back. I stepped over to the open door. This was going to be interesting. "Mrs. Finch, you can't go back there."

"I can darn right go wherever I want. I'm a taxpayer. This building and your salary are all paid for by me. I think that entitles me to come back here. Besides, you have my Daisy in here. I see her locked up like a common criminal."

"Locking her up is for her own good," Rex countered and stepped between Daisy's jail cell and Mrs. Finch.

The old woman put her hands on her hips. "Don't make me call your mother, young man, because I will if I have to."

"You don't scare me, Mrs. Finch," Rex said and

crossed his arms over his chest. "There is an ongoing crime-scene investigation. Daisy has removed two bones from two separate scenes. She is to remain in the jail cell until it has been determined that all the human bones that could be found were found."

"Let her out and she'll track down your bones for you." The old woman waved her hands as if to shoo Rex out of her way.

"No," he said clearly. "You need to turn around and go home, Mrs. Finch, or I will have to arrest you for impeding a police investigation."

At that point Mrs. Finch gave him the stink eye and sat down on the jail-room floor. "I'm not leaving until Daisy gets to." She crossed her arms and legs and stared straight ahead.

Daisy sniffed at her from behind bars and licked her ear.

"Mrs. Finch, please get up. I need you to leave, now."

"This is a sit-in." The old woman stared straight ahead.

"Mrs. Finch, please, don't make me arrest you."

"Do what you must," she said with dramatic flair. "I won't leave until Daisy can leave."

"Fine." Rex blew out a long breath. He reached for a key on his belt and unlocked the jail cell next to Daisy's. "Then I have no choice but to incarcerate you."

He bent down and picked up the stubborn old woman. She stiffened so that when he picked her up he could only lift her under her folded arms. She popped up, legs still crossed as if she were on a flying carpet. Rex unceremoniously took her into the cell and deposited her on the cot. Then he left her there, locking the jail cell behind him.

"I'm going to call the newspaper," she threatened him. "They need to know about police brutality."

"Have at it." Rex waved her phone in the air. "I have your phone. You get one phone call. I suggest you call your lawyer."

He turned on his heel and headed back to me. I hurried back to the space where he left me. "Crazy old woman," he muttered as he came through the hall door.

"So that was Mrs. Finch? How old is she?"

"She must be in her nineties."

"That's a lot of gumption for a woman that old," I said and bit my bottom lip. "What are you going to do if people rally around her? If Liz or Angus got wind of her protest it would be plastered all across the front page."

"Then I'm sure I will be patted on the back for job well done. That woman and her dogs have been terrorizing the island for at least the last thirty years."

I laughed. "If she's in her nineties, I'd suspect she has been terrorizing for a lot longer than thirty years. What are you going to do if people really protest?"

"I'll open the jail cell. Either she'll go on her own or she'll stay on her own. At least for now I know my crime scenes are safe."

Mal wagged her tail in my arms and put her paw on Rex's arm as if to agree with him.

"Thanks again for the use of Mal," Rex said and glanced at the clock. "Wait, I thought you were supposed to be at the Grand by seven PM for that reality show."

"I am," I said. "How did you know?"

"It's a small island," he answered. "News travels and you are going to be late."

I followed his gaze to the wall clock that read 6:50 PM. "Oh, look at the time. You're right. I'm going to be late.

Best of luck with Mrs. Finch and let me know if you want Mal to help out any more."

"I will—be careful out there," Rex called after me. "Remember to lock your doors."

"Okay, bye." I waved behind me and scooted out the door. There was no time to let Mal walk and do her business. At this rate I'd be lucky to be only five minutes late. If I let Mal down, I'd either have to drag her after me or miss my curtain call altogether while she continued to sniff the local gardens.

Decision made. I scurried back to the McMurphy and put Mal in her crate. "You'll get your walk when I get home, okay?"

Mal wagged her tail and circled her blanket-filled crate three times before she settled into a peaceful ball of fluffy curls. I raced upstairs and grabbed my duffel bag full of supplies. We'd been told we would need to bring clean underwear, a toothbrush, and toothpaste, along with a brush and face wipes.

The director couldn't guarantee we'd get home until morning, and he wanted us to have an overnight bag just in case.

Duffel in hand, I slipped out the back of the McMurphy. The late-night light was soft as the moon had slipped over the horizon. Mackinac Island was far enough north that summer twilight lasted a long time as it fought with the sun and the darkness that followed it.

It occurred to me that I forgot to ask what kind of bones they had dug up. Did we know if the victim was a man or a woman? Or if they had been murdered or merely died of natural causes.

I guessed I'd find out more in the morning. But for now I was late, and I knew that wouldn't sit well with

Peter. If the great chef had one pet peeve, it was tardiness. I had learned that long ago when I was in school.

This would be my first time ever being tardy for Peter. I winced at the thought of how angry he'd be with me. Shaking off the haunting feeling of dread, I hurried faster to the Grand Hotel. I guessed I'd find out what my consequences for being late would be. Like it or not, I had signed a contract that listed the times I was supposed to report in. Would this be the last time I was allowed on set?

CHAPTER 15

"You're late," Austin said as I rushed through the door of the Salon D. He pushed his long bangs out of his eyes. Today he wore round black-rimmed glasses. His slim body was covered with a white T-shirt and blue jeans.

"I know." I made a face and grabbed the outfit he held in his hand on my way to the curtained dressing area. It should have been uncomfortable changing behind a curtain in such a public place, but at this point, I was beyond embarrassment.

"Let me guess, your dog dug up more body parts." He stood outside the curtain as I ripped off my clothes and quickly dressed in the styled outfit.

"No, the police had Mal sniffing gardens to look for more evidence. I was at police headquarters picking her up." I stepped out in a denim skirt and checkered blouse. "Really?" I asked as I waved my hand over the outfit.

He held his hands as if they were a camera lens. "Perfect girl-next-door. On to hair and makeup." He pushed me to the director-chair seats.

"Just don't braid it, okay?" I sat in the chair. "And avoid the *Gilligan's Island* Mary Ann look."

"Ha, Mary Ann is exactly the character you're cast as."
He grabbed up a brush and brushed out my shoulder-
length brown hair. "You're going to be team cooking
tonight," he said. "It will be very anxiety provoking.
Things will go horribly wrong but your team will pull it
out in the end. Of course, not before you get bullied by
the mean girl and step in to encourage the African American boy."

"Do you mean Jabar?" I asked as he scraped my hair
to the side, put it in a low ponytail, and sprayed all the
wispy hairs into place. "I've tasted his candy. He's
very good."

"Not tonight," Austin said as he placed a chef's hat on
my hair, pinned it into place, and then sprayed so much
hairspray I coughed until my eyes watered.

"Justine, get over here." Austin snapped his fingers at
the young blond makeup artist. He checked his watch.
"She's five minutes late. I don't know if they will want to
write that into the script or not. After all, you are supposed to be staying at the mansion on the hill with the
others."

"I live on island, people are going to figure out I
wasn't staying with the others," I pointed out as Justine
dutifully finger tapped foundation on my face.

"Oh, there you are." Patrick, the redheaded, freckled
producer's assistant, came rushing into the salon. "Cameras are rolling. So what we're going to do is rush you
into the kitchen while Chef Thomas is giving instruc-
tions. There's a red X on the floor in front of the two
fudge cooling tables. Take your place on the X and Chef
will rip you a new one. Can you squeeze out any tears?"

I grabbed the script story he had in his hand to quickly
figure out what all was going to happen in tonight's

shoot. "I think I can," I said with a nod of my head. "I know he certainly made me cry while I was in school. I'll try to relive those moments."

"Good." He rushed me out of the salon and down the hall into the kitchen set. "Look apologetic" were his last words as he shoved me into the lights and cameras.

The director rolled his fingers for me to enter. I swallowed when I heard Peter giving instruction. No one was ever late for his class. Lack of punctuality was an insult and the first time he ripped you a new heart. The second time you were thrown out of the class to cool your heels for an entire semester. Trust me, no one wanted that.

It seems my tardiness played well with the writer's vision for the show. I stood on my spot and waited, wishing I were able to join the rest of the cast behind their respective tables. But no, I was left to cool my heels while a twinge of embarrassment colored my cheeks.

Finally, dramatically, Peter turned to me. He was no longer my friend. The man was once again the soul-searing demigod chef who held your dreams in his hand. "You're late!"

I squirmed. "I'm sorry, I had an emergen—"

"No excuses!" he shouted. "Do you have any idea what kind of opportunity you are given here? Do you know how many others were rejected so that you had this opportunity?"

"No . . ."

"And you waste my time and the time of your fellow contestants by being late."

"I apologize."

"Not good enough! You must be taught there are consequences for blowing an opportunity like the one you have here today."

I looked at the eight remaining cast members. "Sorry."

The director held up his hand, which was a cue for "hold your places." The cameras turned their lenses on the other cast members. The self-taught candy maker looked empathetic while the rest of the cast held various expressions from horror to disgust to glee at the prospect of my consequences.

Then the director made a whirling motion with his finger and the cameras once again turned their cold eyes on me and Chef Thomas.

"This is an elimination round," Chef Thomas announced. "The challenge is to come up with a fresh savory fudge recipe. Each team will be given two minutes to take two ingredients from the challenge table and the rest of their ingredients from the pantry. Work together or go it alone at your own peril. You have thirty minutes and each team must present one plated savory fudge for judgment."

The camera panned to the group. The teams were split into guys versus girls, who looked alternately eager and horrified by the variety of cheeses and savory meats on the table.

Then Chef Thomas turned to me. "For your consequence, you are your own team. You will have a five-minute wait period and then you will get one minute to gather what you need from what's left at the savory table and the pantry."

The director pointed the lenses on me, and I looked rightfully horrified. Then he pointed to a spot in the corner with a stool and small workspace. I went to the spot as directed.

"Your time begins . . . now!" Chef Thomas said, and

the two teams ran to the savory table, grabbing the best ingredients, then rushed to the pantry.

After the appropriate amount of time, the cameras once again pointed at Chef Thomas, who made a big deal out of timing my "one" minute to gather what I needed.

I didn't waste time thinking about the savory. I was left with Slim Jim sausages and sharp cheddar cheese. Grabbing a bag of potato chips off the shelf, I raided the pantry for the staples in fudge making—sugar, cocoa, and cream.

"Time!"

I went back to work. The idea was to create the basic fudge, then chop the savory into chip-size bits, and garnish with crumbled potato chips for a taste of an American picnic.

The cameras rolled while we worked. The other teams had a person to create the fudge and a person to set up the plates and the rest to prepare the ingredients. Since Slim Jims were already cooked, I didn't have to waste time cooking bacon or sausage like the other two groups did.

More importantly, I was used to working alone and so my inner timekeeper moved quickly and efficiently. Another part of my consequences was the lack of a candy thermometer and an electric food processor to chop. It was not a problem for me. Papa Liam had believed in the original McMurphy recipe—that meant learning what a true soft-ball looks like in a bowl of ice water.

"Five minutes—" Chef Thomas sounded the alarm. The other teams scrambled. The team of guys was embroiled in a personal dispute over whose recipe was best and how best to crumble bacon and plate the fudge. The female team had their fudge done, cooled, and plated with three minutes to spare. All of the members gave each other a high five.

I ignored the butterflies in my stomach. It was hard not to get caught up in the competition part of cooking. I remembered to breathe through the process and trust the flow.

"One minute," came the call, and the cameramen closed in on me. I cut my fudge, sprinkled the garnish, and plated as they counted down: "five . . . four . . . three . . . two . . . one! Time's up!"

Everyone's hands went up to prove they were done, and the team members clapped in relief.

Next, I stood at the table in front of the judge. On my plate was a simple piece of red, white, and blue checkered fabric. Three pieces of garnished fudge rested in a pyramid. I glanced at the others' work.

The female team had chocolate and caramel garnish on the plate. Their fudge was extra creamy vanilla with a brie base and bacon garnish. The quarreling men's team had two presenters vying for Chef Thomas's attention. They explained their Swiss cheese garnish and bacon-infused dark chocolate fudge.

The camera moved to me and my simple plate. "It's an American Picnic theme," I said. "There are bits of Slim Jim and cheddar throughout. The garnish of salty potato chips helps contrast the savory with the sweet of a simple cocoa fudge recipe."

The judges were Mrs. Birdwell, head of the historical society, Karla Heys, the owner of the Heys Candy Shoppe on the island since 1875, and Chef Thomas.

The judges gave their impression of each type of fudge. Each judge was directed to give a good or a bad critique. They were instructed to question the quarreling team as to why there were two spokespersons, and they made a big deal about how the Swiss cheese garnish, while yummy, did not qualify as use of a savory ingredient in the fudge. They praised the creamy quality and smoky bacon flavor of the chocolate.

Finally, they came to me.

"Why are you not a part of a team?" Karla Hays asked.

"I arrived late," I said and stood with my chin up and my hands clasped behind my back.

"Why were you late?" Mrs. Hansen asked me.

"I have no excuse," I said as I thought of how Chef Thomas worked at school. No reason was a good enough reason to be late. "I worked alone on my project and it shows in the simplicity of my plate."

"You are excused while the judges debate the merits of your work. Remember this is an elimination round. One or more of you will be going home," Chef Thomas said.

We all filed into a small room with a waiting room set. Here one camera was placed in the middle of two couches. We were directed where to sit and to act relieved to be done, but nervous about the results.

"You did a good job on a last-minute project," Cathy, the leader of girls' team said.

"Thanks," I replied and slumped into my assigned seat. "I hope the design and flavors weren't too simple."

Meanwhile the camera focused on the still-fighting leaders of the guys' team. The director had worked up Tony, the loudmouthed New Jersey fudge-shop owner, and Jabar, the African American culinary-school graduate.

I glanced at the watch on my wrist. It was two AM. I

had my fingers crossed that I would be eliminated this time. These late night shoots were killing me.

Thirty minutes later, we were called in for the judgment section. I stood with my fingers crossed behind my back that this silliness would finally be done.

The judges already taped their sections. In fact, Mrs. Birdwell and Karla Hay were no longer in the room. I envied their early release. The director left Peter to give the news of winners and losers. He was directed to read from the script while the cameras focused on the contestants. The two sections would be spliced together in editing and look as seamless as if they were all in the room with us.

Peter started with the vanilla fudge team, expressing his delight at the flavor, texture, and presentation.

"Team A," Chef Thomas said. "You are the winners of this round. You are free to leave."

The girls hugged each other in relief and gave high fives as they left the room.

"Team B and Chef McMurphy, one or more of you are going home."

"And cut," the director said. "Contestants, move to the closer red Xs. Set up for close-ups on the contestants."

We were herded together, and our plated fudges were replaced with copies, made by the prop crew, that would not melt under the lights.

"And five, four, three, two, one . . ." The director pointed to Chef Thomas.

"Team B, your lack of ability to work together on a team assignment is appalling. In the fudge business your egos must be checked at the door. Couple that with your lack of two savory ingredients in your fudge and you are clearly not up to par on this challenge."

He turned to me. Winked. Then read. "Chef McMurphy, your tardiness is appalling and unacceptable in this competition. The simplicity of your plate was rudimentary. That said, you took your loss of time well and used what was left over to create a surprisingly tasty fudge. Chef McMurphy . . ."

He paused while the director counted down with his fingers.

"You are still in the competition. You may leave."

CHAPTER 16

I was all set to be eliminated. I must have looked as stunned as I felt. It took me a moment to realize that I was to leave, and I nodded and walked out. We were told to rally in the waiting room, where the single camera caught our reactions to our placements.

Team A gushed over my making it through this section. They hugged me and patted me on my back. I smiled at the praise and expressed my surprise.

Fifteen minutes later the remaining contestants came in. The writers had indeed let go both of the leaders of Team B, leaving only Tim the faux hawked teddy bear of a guy from Indiana and Jon, the younger tattooed kid from Seattle.

After our reactions were shot, we were told we could go home. I changed out of my wardrobe in the ladies' room, exhausted.

"Chef Thomas really likes you," the self-taught woman said as I came out of the stall dressed in my yoga pants and T-shirt with the McMurphy logo, the wardrobe on a hanger. She ran a brush through her light brown hair.

"He was my advisor in culinary school," I said.

"I've bet they've scripted you to win. I'm Cathy, by the way." She offered her hand.

"I know, it's on your hat on set," I said and shook her hand.

Cathy giggled. "It certainly is. You're Allie, right?"

"Yes," I said and smiled back. "I hope they don't have me scripted to win. I've got a business to run and these early morning shoots are killing me."

"It's worse if you're a loser. They take you out to the mansion they supposedly have us housed at and shoot some 'off-kitchen footage' to put in between the contests. Jabar and Tony were handed a huge script to flesh out the conflict between them. They'll be shooting until noon tomorrow."

"Good Lord," I muttered and splashed water on my face. "I guess then I should be happy to be let go at only . . ." I checked my watch. "Three-thirty AM."

Cathy laughed. "Don't worry, you'll get used to the odd hours if you do any more of these reality shows."

"Have you done others?" I asked, drawing my eyebrows together.

"Sure." She patted my shoulder. "Everyone on the circuit knows each other. Jabar and Tony have played best friends and worst enemies. It depends on the direction of the show. In reality they're life partners saving up to buy a house in San Diego. Jabar wants to own a candle shop. Tony wants to counsel boys in trouble."

"Then why do reality shows?" I asked as I took out a facial wipe and carefully took the television makeup off.

"Reality shows pay well, silly. Why else would we all be doing this?"

"Publicity?" My voice rose up an octave. "That's why

I agreed. Well, that and Peter asked me to fill in for a cast member who didn't show."

"Oh, yes, Aimee. She got a callback as a Broadway stand-in. Lucky girl is off the reality circuit."

"So you're an actress?"

She laughed. "Sure. Of course. If you get a big enough fan following in reality shows you can move on to talk-show hosting or being a reporter on the entertainment channels. My agent is angling for me to have my own Web series. *Getting Chatty with Cathy.*" She splashed the words across the air, then shrugged. "Web series are the next big thing."

"So what you're telling me is that nothing is what it appears?"

"Pretty much." She applied mascara.

"Wait, if you are all actors, then who makes the fudge?"

"Oh, ha, we memorize the recipes the night before. That was a really great trick by the way . . ."

"What trick?" I asked as I splashed water on my face and patted it dry.

"Coming in late. It gave your character an edge."

"I don't understand."

"Having been singled out more people will be aware of who you are and will begin to either root for or against you depending on their desire. Did they script you as late?"

"No," I said with a shake of my head. "I was stuck at the police station."

"Wow." She lowered her arm and looked me in the eye. "Why? Are you okay?"

"No, I'm fine." I sent her a half smile. "My dog dug

up more bones today. I loaned her to the police to check out other yards and see if she sniffed out any more."

"Crazy, I thought you finding that dead guy was part of the script."

"No." I shook my head and zipped up my duffel bag. "I actually found him."

"Was it horrifying?"

"It wasn't pretty. Anyway, I was late because I went in to pick up my dog and get her back home. It took them longer than I thought it would. So no, being late wasn't planned."

"Wow, the director acted very fast then. Good show."

"Yeah," I said. "Good show."

"So wait, if the dead guy story is real then you really make candy for a living?"

"Yes," I said. "I'm Allie McMurphy. I run the family business—the historic McMurphy Hotel and Fudge Shoppe."

"Wow, cool. Tony spent two weeks studying how to make that cheese-flavored garnish. The rest of the cast will think it's awesome that you made the fudge yourself. A real candy maker . . . that's so cool."

"Have a good night," I said and opened the bathroom door.

"See you tomorrow," Cathy said and went back to her grooming.

I had to wonder what would happen if word got out that the show was rigged. Would people even care?

The next morning I stumbled around the fudge-shop kitchen, exhausted but triumphant. I managed to cook up the fudge of the day—a plain chocolate, a dark chocolate, and a caramel. I was placing the last tray in the candy display case when Jenn came downstairs.

"You look like you need this." She handed me a mug of thick, bold coffee with a splash of half-and-half from the coffee bar that Frances had set out when she came in at seven AM.

"Oh my gosh, thank you!" I sipped the coffee and closed my eyes as the warm, creamy beverage slid down my throat. I felt like an addict getting their first hit of the day. Shamefully, my coffee addiction was just that—an addiction. Thankfully it didn't cause me trouble like it did my mom. She had to limit herself to one caffeinated beverage a day or she got the shakes.

"You came stumbling in very early this morning," Jenn said and sipped her mug. "Who is he?"

"I wish." I sat on one of the stainless-steel stools. "Unfortunately it was all work."

"The reality show?" Jenn sat down beside me, her hair perfectly in place, her makeup at a minimum because unlike me she didn't have huge bags under her eyes. That was due to a solid eight hours of sleep. "How's that going? Have they eliminated you yet?"

"It's going." I made a face and wrapped my hands around the mug and drew it to my chest. "And no." I sighed. "It seems I'm creating a 'fan base.'" I said the last with one-handed air quotes.

Jenn laughed. The sound of it was bell-like and sweet. "How are you creating fans? Well, besides being your wonderful self."

"That's just it, I'm not myself. I'm playing the girl-next-door."

"I can see that."

"They try to cast to type," I repeated the words the

producer had told me. "Anyway, I was late to the shoot last night."

"Oh, boy . . ."

"I got waylaid picking Mal up from the police station."

"Oh, remind me to ask you how that's going," Jenn said. "But first continue with this . . . you were late . . ."

"And they made a giant deal over it." I winced again at the thought. "I'm going to be so humiliated when this episode airs."

"Really, what happened?"

"I got the 'no excuses' talk from Peter in full professor mode."

"Ouch." Jenn had heard of Peter in full professor mode countless times from me and my classmates who she was friends with.

"Right? Then the director had me singled out to accomplish a team task on my own with six minutes less time."

"And you exceeded all expectations."

"I can't help myself." I shrugged. "I get in competition mode and it's all over." I frowned. "Come to think of it, I should have failed miserably and let them eliminate me." I hit my forehead with my right palm. "Darn it."

"It's okay," Jenn said. "I think they might have a twelve-step program for people with your competition problem."

"I think you're right. What's the first step?"

"Admitting you have a problem," we both said at the same time.

I shook my head and drank more coffee.

The front doorbells jangled as Chef Thomas walked in. "Good morning, ladies," he said, far too chipper for my liking.

I gave him the stink eye. "I need to have a word with you," I grumped. "You promised I only had to do one or two shoots. Why didn't you remind me last night that I was supposed to fail?"

"I told them you would get wound up and actually win the thing. They didn't believe me." Peter went to the coffee bar and poured himself a cup of bold, black coffee.

"Hey," I said. "I thought you didn't drink non-gourmet coffee?"

He chuckled on his way over to where we sat. "This morning I'll drink anything with caffeine. This late night taping is going to be the death of me yet." He sat down next to me. "How's it feel to win?"

"But I didn't win," I said.

"Yes, you did." He took a slug of coffee. His blue eyes twinkled at me. "No one else could have done what you did in that short of time with those ingredients. It seems I taught you well."

"What did you have to put in the fudge?" Jenn asked.

"Can't say." Peter and I spoke at the same time.

"Not until the episode airs," I said and touched her arm. "But I don't want to watch."

"Interesting," Jenn said. "When does the first episode air?"

"It's a late-summer fill-in show. The first date it airs is July third," Peter said.

"I can't believe I let you talk me into this show." I sighed. "Right now all I want to do is go to bed and sleep for twenty-four hours."

"What's the deal, anyway?" Jenn asked Peter. "Why shoot so late into the night?"

"The hotel is quieter at night. That means less background noise for the mics to pick up."

"Huh, never thought of that," I said. "So the other members of the team sleep during the day?"

"Yes," Peter said. "It's the perfect job for a night owl. I've never been able to work all night and sleep all day."

"I have my day job." I waved at the full candy counter. "I don't have time to sleep."

"Just don't be late again," Peter said pointedly. "You'll be in breach of contract if you do."

Frances walked into the lobby from the back door. She took Mal's leash and harness off and let the puppy go. Mal hit the floor running and did her stop-and-slide routine to Peter. He was ready and had braced himself. Only his coffee splashed when she hit his legs with her entire weight.

"Well, hello, Mal." He reached down and patted her on the head.

When he straightened, Mal went to Jenn and begged for pets from her. Finally she came to me. I picked her up and squeezed her until she squeaked.

"Hey, puppy. Did you have a good walk?" I glanced over to Frances. She left her walking shoes on the mat in the hall and had slipped into more comfortable house shoes.

"She did fine," Frances said as she went for more coffee. "I heard from the gossip trail today that they are close to identifying the bones Mal dug up yesterday."

"They are?"

"Mal dug up bones?" Peter asked.

"Yes, it's why I was late last night. She found a second area of mulch with bone deposits in it. So I loaned her out to the police to see if she could find any more sites."

"Did she?" Peter asked.

"Yes, she found six sites in all," I said. "There may be more but last I heard those sites were keeping the police busy."

"Word is they found a partial jawbone," Frances said. "There was some distinctive dental work done."

"Ah, so the mysterious person will soon be announced?" Jenn said.

"According to Mr. Beecher, the authorities think they can find out the 'who' in this mystery but are still tracking down the 'where' and the 'why.'"

"I bet it all falls into place when they identify the body . . . well, in this case the bones," I said.

"Allie, what was going on with Mrs. Finch and Daisy? I heard they were both arrested and detained against their will."

"Oh, right." I put my coffee down and stood so that Frances could have my stool. "It was the oddest thing. Rex detained Daisy—the dog." I added the last bit to clue Peter in on the topic. "She keeps taking the bones that Mal digs up and has to be chased down. Then the last time, she swallowed the evidence so Rex took her in and put her in a cell until she passes the evidence."

"That's one way to do it," Jenn said.

"It was smart," I said. "There aren't enough police on one shift to protect the crime scenes. With Daisy locked up they're certain to stop at least one plunder of their sites."

"And Mrs. Finch—why did she get arrested?"

"She wasn't actually arrested. She staged a sit-in in protest of Daisy's freedom being curtailed. Rex told her she could sit-in as long as she wanted but she had to do it in the locked cell next to Daisy. The last I saw

Mrs. Finch was sitting cross-legged on the cot while Daisy sat beside her on the other side of the bars."

"A sit-in? Now that is a story for the paper," Jenn said. "Where is Liz?"

"Angus is on it," Frances said. "I passed him on Mal's morning walk. He had a camera in hand and was quite happy to create a mountain out of a molehill."

"I think Liz is still investigating the reality team." I turned to Peter. "No worries. I told her I was under contract to keep the details quiet. But the last I saw her, she was headed to the Grand to find out what she could figure out on her own."

"That sounds dangerous," Peter said. "I understand that the crew is surrounded by security. Which is another reason to shoot at night—no curious tourists wanting to see us film."

My cell phone rang. I pulled it out of my pocket. "Hello?"

"Allie, it's Liz."

"Hey, Liz, we were just talking about you."

"Well, you're going to be talking more. I walked in on a crime scene."

"What? Where?" My voice grew loud. Everyone with me turned to stare. I raised my hand to let them know I needed to hear more before I would repeat any information.

"Do you know the ladies' room in the ballroom area where the show is being taped?"

"Yes, I was just there last night. It's where the girls in the group change into our street clothes. Why?"

"There is a dead woman on the floor. Her purse is emptied out beside her."

"Oh, no, do you know who it is?" My group of friends

stepped in close to figure out what I was talking about. I held out my hand to indicate they needed to wait.

"I only caught a glimpse but I think she had caramel brown hair."

"Cathy," I muttered and slumped against the wall. "I was just talking to her there."

"There's one more thing, Allie."

"What's that?"

"She had a half-eaten piece of fudge wrapped in red, white, and blue checkered cloth beside her."

"Oh, no . . ."

"Shane says it looks like poisoning. He's already bagged the fudge. So quick question . . . was your fudge from last night plated on that material?"

CHAPTER 17

I hugged my waist. "I can't say."

"So that's a yes?" Liz pressed through the phone.

"No, it's an 'I can neither confirm nor deny anything about the show.'"

"What's going on?" Peter asked behind me.

I put my hand over the phone. "Cathy's been found dead."

"What? When? Where?"

"Who's that with you?" Liz asked.

"It's Chef Thomas."

"Oh, I want to talk to him."

I held out the phone. "It's Liz MacElroy, reporter for the *Town Crier*—our local paper. She wants to talk to you."

Peter stared at my phone as if it might bite him. "Can't," he said and crossed his arms.

I put the phone back to my ear. "He can't."

"What do you mean he can't? He doesn't know how to or he won't?"

I looked at Peter's closed-off face. "He won't."

"Darn it," Liz muttered. "Okay, look, I'm hearing your

name getting thrown around. If you give me an exclusive, I'll give you a heads-up on what's going on."

I chewed on my bottom lip. It was a tough decision. I had a signed contract saying I would forfeit all payment for the show plus have to pay them $20,000 in fines for each time they could follow a source back to me. That said, I needed to know why my name had come up. Had I been the last person to see Cathy alive?

"I can't say anything about the show."

"Fine," Liz said. "So tell me, did you see Cathy in the bathroom this morning?"

"Yes," I said.

"What is going on?" Jenn asked.

I held up my finger, asking her to wait.

"She was alive when I left her," I stated. "That's a fact."

"Okay," Liz said. "If you learn anything else you'll give me the exclusive?"

"Yes, of course, we're friends, right?"

"Yes. Okay, so it turns out that the hotel installed cameras in the hallways where the show is being shot to keep anyone from trying to steal a prop."

"Okay," I said.

"Word is that the video shows Cathy going into the bathroom last night and five minutes later you go in. Twenty minutes later you come out. Cathy never does. No one thought anything about it. They figured she left earlier than you when the camera monitor was looking at other footage."

"No," I said in horror. "No, she was alive when I left."

"Let's hope you don't have to prove that."

I hung up the phone, grabbed an empty stainless-steel stool, and sat down hard.

Frances and Jenn surrounded me. "Are you okay?"

"You look white as a sheet. Are you in shock?"

"What? No," I said.

Frances put the back of her hand on my forehead. "You're clammy. Put your head between your knees."

I allowed them to guide me into a folded position.

"Breathe," Jenn said. "In and out—whoosh."

"Cathy died?" Peter asked.

I turned my head to look him in the eye. "Yes. Apparently two of us went into the ladies' room and only one came out."

"Oh, that's terrible," Frances said.

Mal barked at her tone.

"It's okay, puppy," I said from my folded position. I tried to sit up. "I think I'm okay."

"Do they know how she died? Was it a heart attack or something more sinister?" Frances asked.

"They wouldn't know for sure yet," Jenn said. "Shane tells me it takes a full autopsy before they determine cause of death—even if they find a person hanging. They are to presume nothing and make their evaluation based on the evidence. If the body is inconclusive, then they go to the evidence around the body."

"That makes sense," Peter said. "Obvious assumptions are sometimes obvious and sometimes misleading."

"What is Cathy's death going to do for tonight's shoot?" Jenn asked.

"I have no idea," Peter said. "But I'll find out." He turned to leave, went to the front door, and paused. "They found her at the Grand?"

"Yes, in the bathroom in the hallway where the sets are," I replied.

He pushed through the door and put on his sunglasses, then melted into the swelling crowds of Main Street. In the coming week the crowds would get even larger as Mackinac Island celebrated the Lilac Festival.

"Are you okay?" Jenn asked me again.

"Yes," I said and stood. "I think all I need is a good four or five hours of solid sleep."

"Good morning, gang." Sandy came in from the back, cheery. "How's everything?"

"Oh, thank goodness," Jenn said. "Sandy, can you handle the fudge shop? I'm going to take Allie upstairs. She needs some sleep."

"Sure, not a problem." Sandy grabbed a striped apron and wrapped it around her waist. "Looks like all the fudges are already made. Go on, boss. Get some sleep. You know the first rule of the kitchen . . ."

"Don't be late?" Jenn said.

I laughed. "No, it's don't work sleep or health impaired. It's simply too easy to get burned or maimed or any number of awful things."

"I can do this," Sandy reassured. "Go on, get some rest. Things will look better with proper rest."

"I certainly hope so . . ."

CHAPTER 18

I woke up to pounding on the door to the apartment. It matched the pounding of my head. I hate how much it hurts to wake up from a nap. Especially when you haven't gotten enough sleep.

"I'm coming," I held my head as the pounding started again. I wore an oversized T-shirt and a pair of silky boxers. My hair was mashed up on one side of my head. I suspected I had dried drool running down the right side of my mouth. Too bad. Whoever woke me deserved to be frightened by my appearance.

"Allie, open up."

That was a familiar voice. Darn it. I opened the door to see Trent Jessop standing at my door. The man was a gorgeous sight for the eyes. Well over six feet tall, he had broad shoulders, dark eyes, and dark hair that was so expertly cut it didn't matter who touched it, it fell right back into place. Next to him I felt even more roughed up. "I'm up," I turned my back on him so he was saved from the full effect of me after a three-hour nap. I was up, but I was not awake.

"Are we alone?"

I stopped in my tracks. "Excuse me?"

"Okay, I'll take that as a yes."

"I'm sorry, why are you here, Trent?" I made my way to the kitchen and put water in the teakettle and put it on the stove. I went through the steps for making French press coffee. The French press took more effort than a drip machine, but the coffee was worth it. I'd been making it so long that I could and often did make it in my sleep.

He followed me to the kitchen. "Rex sent me over."

"Okay . . . why? I was sleeping—something I'd rather do at night but the television show tapes all blessed night long."

Trent chuckled and crossed his arms as he leaned against the doorjamb. "You're not a morning person, are you?"

"What gave me away?" I sat down on the stool and realized that I was in pajamas with bed-head hair in front of the hottest guy on island, and in several states, if you asked me. I jumped up. "Can you watch the water? I need to get dressed."

"You don't have to dress on my account."

I turned to see him smiling, his eyes on my bare legs. "Yes, I do." I scurried off to my bedroom, ripped off the T-shirt, and put on proper undergarments and a fresh McMurphy pink polo and a pair of black jeans. Then I went to the bathroom, washed my face, and brushed my hair. A look in the mirror reminded me that I was who I was and that was all that mattered.

I walked back into the kitchen to find that he had made the coffee in the press and set it in a cozy to steep.

"Where do you keep your mugs?" he asked as he opened then closed cupboard doors.

"Here," I said and walked over to the sink. "I keep them to the right of the sink with the glasses." I put down the mugs. "Actually, Grammy Alice kept them there, Papa Liam left them there, and now I leave them there." I shrugged. "I guess they're there no matter who owns the kitchen."

"That's deep for a woman who just woke up and has yet to have a cup of coffee." His eyes twinkled at me as he picked up the French press and poured us both a cup.

"Half-and-half?" I asked and pulled out the pint from inside the refrigerator.

"No, I like mine straight-up black."

"I like cream." I splashed more than enough to turn my coffee a lovely creamy brown. I put the pint back in the refrigerator and took a sip. My eyes rolled back and the pounding in my head lessened. "Now, let's try this again. Why are you here?"

I opened my eyes to see that he was once again leaning on the breakfast bar. This time he had a deep-red mug in his hands.

"Did you know that the cops got a warrant to search Jessop Compost and Mulch?"

"I heard them talking about that being a possibility," I said. "Mal found more bones with those unusual cuts. Since the bones were found in the mulch in two different yards, the natural conclusion was—"

"—they came with the mulch," he finished.

"Exactly, and Rex told me that there are only two companies who sell mulch on island, you and Gooseworthy—"

"—so they got a warrant for both."

"You have to quit doing that," I said.

"What?"

"Finishing my sentences. It's unnerving."

"Unnerving?"

"Yes." I contemplated him over the edge of the mug. "It's something old married couples do."

He broke out in a deep, rich laugh. "And we're—"

"—not even dating," I finished.

He laughed even harder. "Someday we're going to have to remedy the situation."

Okay, I had been lifting my cup to my mouth. His words made me bobble the mug and splash coffee all over the floor. "Darn." I put the cup on the counter and grabbed a paper towel to wipe it up.

"Didn't mean to make you spill your coffee." He raised one eyebrow. "Does the thought of us dating make you nervous?"

"I am not awake enough for this conversation," I muttered and threw the paper towel in the trash. "Why are you here, Trent?"

"Apparently I'm here to terrorize you." He sipped his coffee.

"That is not an answer." I hugged myself and leaned against the counter.

"Okay, that's fair. I guess I needed to know what was going on with this investigation of yours."

"My investigation? Oh, you mean the bones Mal found?"

"There's another investigation?"

My head had cleared from my nap. "Yeah, one of the cast members of the reality show died last night." I picked up my coffee and took it to the small dining table on the other side of the breakfast bar that separated the kitchen from the living space. "At least that's what Liz told me. I had an hour's sleep before I had to get up to make today's fudge. It's why the nap."

He sat down across from me. "What made you agree to do the reality show? I mean, aren't those shows about people humiliating themselves for money? You don't seem that type to me."

"Huh, thanks," I said. "I didn't think I was the type either, but my old mentor, Chef Thomas, is hosting the thing. They had a cast member bow out and he was looking for a quick fill-in." I shrugged. "I thought I'd only be shooting one or two and it seemed like a quick favor."

He tilted his head and studied me. "You are loyal to your friends, aren't you?"

"Isn't everyone?"

"No." He shook his head. "In my experience your loyalty is a rare gift."

"Huh."

"Okay, so I don't need to worry about you investigating me, right?"

"Right." I sent him a wry smile. "If anything, I need to worry about them investigating me."

He drew his eyebrows together. "Why?"

"It seems that I was the last person to see Cathy alive."

Almond Butter Fudge

For the First Layer
1 cup dark chocolate chunks
1 cup smooth almond butter
2 T. corn syrup
½ t. sea salt

For the Second Layer
1 cup full-fat coconut milk
2-¾ cups semi-sweet chocolate chips

Prepare the first layer. Line a 1-½ quart square baking dish with wax paper so that, when pressed, just an inch or so hangs off around the edges. Set aside. In a double boiler melt the chocolate chunks completely. Stir in the almond butter, corn syrup, and salt, mixing until smooth and until all ingredients are incorporated. Spread into the bottom of the lined dish and set aside.

Prepare the second layer. In a small saucepan over low heat, combine the coconut milk and chocolate chips. Stirring frequently, cook until the mixture is well combined and the chocolate has a glossy finish. Pour this mixture over the first almond butter-chocolate layer, smoothing slightly with a spatula. Score with a sharp knife into 1-inch squares.

Chill in the refrigerator for 6 hours or overnight. When ready to cut and serve, remove the fudge from the pan by lifting out the paper. Place on a cutting board, and then use a sharp knife and cut into 1-inch pieces following the score marks. Serve.

CHAPTER 19

"The Lilac Festival starts in tomorrow," Jenn reminded me after I walked Trent out of the apartment and went into the office. The business office for the McMurphy was located on the fourth floor next to the owner's apartments.

When Jenn, my best friend from the hotel management degree program, offered to come out and spend the summer on island and help me run my first season with the McMurphy, I had moved a couple of bookshelves and tucked a second desk in the small twelve-foot-by-twelve-foot room.

Our desks faced each other, computer monitors on opposite sides so that we could see each other. Unfortunately, the rest of the office was a mess of stacked files, books, and on Jenn's side, a giant box of samples for linens, print materials, and all the things an event planner might want to order for an event.

Behind me the entire wall was filled with bookshelves—one dedicated to fudge recipe books old and new, one filled with Papa's books and paraphernalia, and the final one held cloth boxes that served as my filing system.

"Oh, man," I sat down. "Lilac Festival . . . I still feel as if it's May."

"The parade floats are looking awesome," Jenn said. "Frances went over to the exchange building and snapped some pictures on the work in progress. I understand it's a flurry of activity. You really should consider entering a float in next year's parade."

I turned on my computer, then put my left elbow on the top of Papa's big mahogany desk that now served as my desk. "I hoped to have a float this year, but there is simply no time."

"No worries, it's best to scope out the floats this year. I'll snap some pictures of the ones we like best and we can brainstorm at the end of season for what our float will look like. I understand the planning starts in January."

"Yes." My computer booted up, and I typed in my password. "Frances is cutting lilacs to festoon the hotel lobby. I have lilac fudge and candied lilacs on my planning sheet."

"I love the smell of lilacs in bloom, don't you?"

"Yes," I said with a smile. "Grammy Alice used to love Lilac Festival. She was on one of the first planning committees. It was thought that we should have a horse-drawn float parade. Then the best time for it would be when the whole island smells of lilacs and all the flowers are in bloom so that the soft scent of flowers would fill the air. Quite a difference from the busy, smoggy summer days in Chicago or Detroit."

"I'm excited to see it up close." Jenn scrolled through the pictures she had in her e-mail. "We should offer a lilac tea on Sunday. What do you think? We could set up the front half of the lobby with three or four round tables and use fine china and offer a variety of delicate teas, plus lilac petit fours, cucumber sandwiches, and lady-fingers adorned with sugared lilacs."

"Sounds fabulous," I said. "We could see if Sandy wants to make white chocolate centerpieces—perhaps a small replica horse-drawn carriage? If there are only only three or four tables that need centerpieces, she might be able to sculpt multiples if she keeps it simple."

"Oh, great idea," Jenn said. "I'll go down and see what Frances and Sandy think. If we're going to do this, we need to act quickly. We should leave an invitation in the mailbox of every guest room. I can make some simple posters to go up around town. Is it a go?"

"Yes, maybe we can take donations for the Mackinac Island Children's Clinic," I said. "Let's see if we can have a presence in the festival without a float."

"Great idea." Jenn left filled with excitement.

I was deep into bill paying when the phone rang. "McMurphy Hotel and Fudge Shoppe, Allie speaking."

"Allie, Peter Thomas," his voice boomed through the phone line. "We're having a cast meeting for the show in an hour. Can you be at the Grand? Salon A."

"As long as I don't have to be ready to shoot, I'll be there," I promised.

"Great, thanks."

I finished my bills, made a long list of other things I needed to attend to, and headed downstairs. Mal greeted me with a running slide into my legs. I picked her up and patted her on the head. "Are you being a good pup?"

Mal licked my cheek as her answer.

"Hey, Allie," Jenn said from behind the reservation desk. "Frances and Sandy are on board with the tea. We were thinking of offering it on both Sunday afternoons."

"That way, it takes advantage of all ten days of festival time," Frances added from her perch behind the reception desk.

"It will give me time to craft something for the last tea's centerpieces," Sandy chimed in. She wore a pink bandana over her black braided hair, a pink McMurphy polo, black slacks, and the pink-and-white apron of our uniform. "The first tea is four days from now. I can craft something simple for that tea."

"I like it," I said to my smiling team and put Mal down. She wandered off to snag a dog toy and shake it.

Mr. Devaney came up from the basement. Mal dropped her toy and ran over to get her pets from the new person in the room. "There's a plumbing issue in 221 and stuck windows in 333." He reached down and patted Mal.

"Mr. Devaney, have you ever worked on a Lilac Festival float?" I asked.

He straightened and narrowed his eyes suspiciously. "Why?"

"We're thinking we should enter a float next year," I said.

"That's a year away. I could be dead by then," he groused.

I put my hands on my hips. "Well, if you're alive next spring can you help with the float? Frances will be in charge of overseeing the project."

He looked at Frances and then the hopeful faces of everyone else. "I suppose."

"Good." I looked at my team. "Let's get on the festival tea. I have to go to the Grand—they're having an emergency meeting of the show cast."

"When will you be back?" Jenn asked.

"I'm hoping to be back in time for the evening fudge demonstration."

"Good," Frances said. "Let those reality folks know that you're running a business. Put your foot down, young lady. You need to sleep."

"Are the bags under my eyes that noticeable?"

"Yes," all three women said at the same time.

I made a face. The front doorbells jangled, and a couple came in. "Hello folks, how can we help you?"

My team scrambled to their various work pursuits.

"We're planning a wedding on island in September and are looking for a place to house the family," the young man said. His green eyes sparkled in delight as his right hand brushed the woman's left arm.

"We offer a special if you rent the entire hotel for a weekend," I said. "We also offer an event planner's services as part of the weekend fee." I waved toward the reservation desk, where Frances and Jenn were. "Please come in. I'm Allie McMurphy. My family has owned the hotel for over one hundred years."

Mal raced up to greet the newcomers. Thankfully, she didn't slide into them but did a pretty pirouette and then sat and held her paw out to shake.

The woman laughed. "Hello, are you the entertainment here?" She reached down, patted Mal on the head, then straightened. "What we love about the island," the woman said, "is all the tradition in this lovely, peaceful setting."

"I'm Thad. This is my fiancée, Rose. We are looking for a place where we could rent either an entire floor or an entire building," he said.

"Depending on the dates we can certainly help you." I glanced at my watch. It was time for me to go. "Frances, this is Thad and Rose. See if we can meet their dates. If so, please give them a tour."

"Will do." Frances waved the couple over. "Let's see what we can do to accommodate you."

"I have to get going before I'm late again," I told Jenn. "You can reach me by text or cell."

The air outside was soft and fragrant. My thoughts were not on the walk down the alley that split the block between Main Street and Market Street. I felt bad for Cathy. She would never again know the sights and smells of early summer.

"You just think you're so much better than us."

"What?" I turned to see Tammy Gooseworthy hovering by the side door to the part of the Grand Hotel where the cast and crew entered for shooting. Her brown hair was hair sprayed to create a helmet-like bob. She wore a white short-sleeved button-down shirt with the Grander Hotel logo embroidered on the top pocket, black slacks, and athletic shoes.

"You have something going with Chef Thomas, don't you? It's got to be the only reason he picked you to be in his show." Her expression was one of cold disdain, her nose in the air as she looked down at me.

"Chef Thomas was my mentor," I said. "I didn't hide that. Why are you so upset anyway? I understand you're the chief pastry chef at the Grander Hotel. Congrats, by the way." I took hold of the door handle. "I've got to go in, they're waiting for me."

"He should have had auditions." Tammy followed me inside. "I have more years' experience than any other member of this so-called cast. I've done some digging and most of these people aren't even qualified to be here." She followed me as I kept walking.

"Seriously, Tammy? A woman has died. Just put in your application for next year's show." I stopped her in the hall. "Besides, it's not like the Grander Hotel needs the publicity."

"This isn't about the Grander." She waved her hand. "This is about honor. Mackinac is the fudge capital of the world. We need a true local in this contest to show people why we're the best."

"Fine," I said to get her to quit following me. "There's Bob Salinger. He's the producer. You really should be talking to him about this."

"I will!" She stormed off toward poor Bob.

The woman was trouble on wheels. I was so swamped I didn't have time to argue over why I was in the show. Right now I was very close to saying, "Fine, have at it. I quit."

CHAPTER 20

"Cathy's passing has been a great loss for us," Brian Bere, the associate producer said. He had a ball cap across his heart and his head bent. "A moment of silence, please, for our girl, Cathy."

The cast and crew were all herded into the dressing room. There were about thirty of us all told. I noticed that Jabar and Tony were holding on to each other with tears running down their cheeks. Emily, the first cast member to be let go, was also here. It was a solemn gathering.

"Thank you," Brian said. He wore a tan T-shirt and a pair of cargo shorts in camouflage green. His calves were bare and his sockless feet were encased in classic boat shoes. "Now, I know you are all wondering where do we go from here?" He gave a dramatic pause. "The producers and directors feel that as long as no one is in direct harm, Cathy would want us to go on."

There was a round of applause from everyone whose summer paychecks depended on the show going to air.

"With Cathy gone, there is no need for an elimination

episode. It's been decided that each of you will go home for twenty-four hours and a small camera crew will go with you. You are to show off your hometown and the people who support you."

"Awesome," I said. I could use twenty-four hours of respite from taping.

"I'm sorry but that's not going to happen for a while," Rex said as he came into the room.

The sound of all thirty of us protesting was close to deafening. Rex put his hands in the air with a signal to stop. When that didn't work, he put his fingers in his mouth and whistled one short, incredibly loud burst.

The room went quiet in an amazing amount of time.

"The preliminary report is that Cathy Unger was poisoned," Rex said. "We need everyone who was here the night she was murdered to come to the station and be interviewed."

"The show will provide a lawyer," Brian said. "Don't say anything until the lawyer gets here. I don't think I need to remind you that you are all under contract. Our contract has withstood one lawsuit. Don't think for a moment it won't withstand another."

I looked from Brian to Rex and back. Brian looked thin and young in comparison. Rex's gorgeous blue eyes studied the cast and crew as if he could ferret out a killer simply by looking at them. Brian, on the other hand, turned away from us and dialed a number on his cell phone.

Whoever Brian spoke to was not happy. The associate producer spent a long time explaining and reexplaining what was going on. Finally he turned around.

"Go to hair and makeup," he said. "We're going to

shoot. Peter, when you're done see me. We need to figure out what we're going to shoot for this episode."

"Wait," I said. "I thought this was only a team meet. I didn't know we would be shooting in the daylight."

"That phone call was to the guys footing the bill for this show. If you want to get paid, you will stop asking questions and go to hair and make-up as I said." Brian gave me the evil eye.

I held up both hands in surrender. "Okay, I just need to let people know where I am."

"Don't take too long," Brian said. "Time is money."

"Keep in mind, I will be asking you individually to come down to the police station to be interviewed," Rex said. Officer Lasko entered the room looking very official and as intimidating as a woman with a gun could look. "In the meantime, do not talk about what happened that night. I don't want my reports to be a group memory." He looked us over one more time. "Officer Lasko will remain with you while you tape the show." He waved his hand toward her. "Keep yourselves busy and always in view and hopefully we can get the interviews done as quickly and quietly as possible. First up is Tony Sergeant. Come with me, please." Rex nodded toward the big chef.

Brian put a hand on Tony's bicep. "Remember, don't say a word until our lawyer gets there."

"How long will that be?" Rex asked, his hand on his hip belt.

"He's flying in from Chicago," Brian said. "So no more than an hour."

"Fine," Rex said. "I'll send someone over to get him in one hour." Rex turned back to the room. "Remember, do not talk to anyone about Cathy. I need independent stories."

"They won't," Officer Lasko said, her gaze intent. "I'll make sure."

Wardrobe and makeup were slow, quiet affairs. I had spoken to Jenn. She promised to keep things running at the MacMurphy in my absence. A half an hour from our initial meeting, Brian came in with script pages for everyone.

"Here's the storyline for tonight. When we shoot the at-home visit, we'll air it with a dedication to Cathy. This taping will air the following week."

I looked at my part. "Wait, we break into teams of two except for me?"

Brian nodded. "We need to see if you can pull off crazy fudge or if last night's fudge was just a fluke." He raised an eyebrow and looked me straight in the eye. "The choice is up to you."

"I thought there wasn't an elimination this week."

His eyes were serious. "We're shooting for next week."

"Oh." I looked at my part. "Okay."

They came and took Tony to the police station while we were blocking and staging the next competition.

Once again we were all standing behind two marble-topped fudge tables.

"Welcome chefs," Peter said when the cameras rolled. I noted that the other two judges were missing. "Today's challenge will be judged on how you work through a difficult order. I will be the only judge tonight. You must impress me with your negotiation skills and your ability to substitute when an ingredient goes missing from your work area.

"As an extra challenge, the pantry has been stocked with minimal ingredients. Everything is first come, first served. It will be up to you whether you want to work together or apart."

The cameras took in our looks of horror and fear. There were certain key ingredients needed in every fudge base. "On your mark, get set, go!"

We rushed to the pantry. Tim was the first guy inside and swept as much as possible into his arms. That left precious little for the remaining staff. Jon went through and snatched up a giant grouping of extras. The two mean girls, Amber and Erin, worked in tandem as well, grabbing the ingredients they needed from opposite ends of the pantry table. Everyone rushed back and negotiated their exchange. I was left with a jar of peanut butter, some powdered sugar, a box of cocoa, a stick of butter, and a pint of milk.

I grabbed it all up and went straight to work. There were two candy thermometers that were passed around by the others. I quickly melted the butter and peanut butter together, then stirred in the powdered sugar for a peanut butter fudge base. I scored it and put it in the refrigerator. All that was left to do was to create a fudgy ganache. Once I made that I added a top layer and then ran a hot butter knife through it to swirl the two fudges together.

"Five minutes!" was announced. The two girls had squabbled over the candy thermometer. Neither one had it long enough to ensure their fudge was at the right temperature. The two guys worked together and had their fudges done and plated. I melted a bit of the ganache and drizzled it on the plate and then put a pyramid stack of three fudge pieces on the plate.

"Five, four, three, two, one—Stop!"

I raised my hands to show that I had indeed gotten my fudge to the judge's table.

Chef Thomas looked them all over for a scoring of presentation. He quizzed us on our choices. Finally came the taste test. Peter held up the first piece of my fudge, when the associate producer came running onto the set.

"Don't eat anything!" He smacked the piece of fudge out of Peter's hand.

"What? Why?"

I thought Peter was going to deck Brian for smacking the candy out of his hand.

"It's been confirmed. Cathy was killed by poisoned fudge."

Rose's Chocolate Peanut Butter Fudge

5 cups milk chocolate chips
2 tablespoons butter
1 can sweetened condensed milk
1 teaspoon vanilla
1 bag of peanut butter chips (2 cups)

Butter an 8" x 8" x 2" pan. Line with wax paper or parchment paper.

In a double boiler, melt milk chocolate chips, butter, and sweetened condensed milk until smooth. Be careful not to burn.

Remove from heat. Add vanilla and stir until incorporated. Pour half of the fudge into the prepared pan. Layer peanut butter chips. Cover chips with the remainder of the fudge. Cool. Refrigerate overnight. Remove from pan. Cut into pieces. Store in a covered container.

CHAPTER 21

"We need to take apart the pantry and check all the ingredients to ensure the poison didn't come from something we had on set," Brian said. He held his hands out and down to make his point. "Deep breath, everyone. Officer Rex Manning requested that they take samples from all the pantry stock and check out the pots and pans."

"It's going to ruin our shoot," the director argued. "We only have thirteen days left to make this series. We can't stop shooting just because a woman was poisoned."

"We can shoot without the taste test," Peter suggested as he wiped the candy residue from his fingers. "Then edit it so it looks as if we tasted it."

"Good, good, go with that," the director said and moved the cameras into close-up position.

Peter continued with his critique as if he had really tried the fudges. When he got to me, his eyes narrowed and his voice got low. "Pat-in-pan fudge is not real fudge, is it, Miss McMurphy?"

"As long as it's labeled pat-in-pan it can be presented as fudge," I argued. "Besides, the fun thing about making fudge at home is to know how to make it quick and easy."

I crossed my arms and waited to hear what he had to say about that.

"Pat-in-pan is a sucker trick when a chef doesn't have the time to create real fudge. It is disqualified."

"Okay," I nodded. "I accept your opinion as a judge."

"That said, the chocolate ganache fudge is the perfect blend of cocoa and cream. The combination is superb."

Okay, so did he like it or hate it?

"You are all dismissed to the waiting room while I mull over my decisions."

We left the room, filing over to the waiting set.

"I didn't know you could make fudge with powdered sugar," the first of the pair of blond women left in the competition said. "I'm Amber. Your fudge looked really easy."

"It is easy," I said and shrugged. "My Grammy taught me how to make it when I was in kindergarten. It's a very good simple fudge to make when you don't have time to make the real thing."

"Well, it will be interesting to see what Chef Thomas decides," said the other blonde. "I'm Erin and I'm hoping my contract is done. It creeps me out to think that Cathy's dead." She rubbed her forearms as if to ward off a chill.

"It has to be my time to go," I said and yawned big. "Working two jobs is killing me."

"Let's hope not literally," Amber said.

The director and camera crew shot footage of us awaiting our fate in the waiting room set. Thirty minutes later we were ushered back into the cook set and took our places on the appropriate Xs.

"Welcome back, candy makers," Peter said. "It has been a tough time for everyone since the loss of Cathy. It has been decided that everyone will get a pass this week.

Go home and come back fresh tomorrow and we will continue to find out which of you deserves the cut."

"And done," the director said. "Thanks everybody. Terrible day. I'm so glad you all are up to the challenge of continuing to shoot the show."

"Do we have a choice?" I whispered to Erin.

She shrugged. I suppose my question was a moot point.

After dressing in my own clothing and washing the makeup off my face, I grabbed up my duffel and looked at the other two ladies. "Okay, I'm going to be a little superstitious. Last night I walked out alone and left Cathy. I refuse to leave anyone in the bathroom tonight."

"Well, aren't you sweet," Amber said and gathered up her stuff. "Come on, then, we'll leave together."

"Hey, wait one minute and I'll come too," Erin chimed in. "Trust me, I don't want to be the one left for dead." She threw her makeup in her duffel, and we all walked out together.

"That's one less thing to be superstitious about," I said.

Rex and Peter were waiting in the hallway.

"Hey guys, what's up?" I adjusted the strap of my duffel bag.

"Allie, Rex has some questions for you," Peter said, his face solemn.

I drew my eyebrows together. "Okay. What's up?"

"I'd rather we talked in private," Rex said in full-on police mode.

"Oh, that can't be good," I said and walked to where he pointed.

"There's a small conference room to the left. I'll be in in a moment."

"Sure, what about Amber and Erin?"

"They're free to go." He waved them down the hall.

"This is not looking good for me," I muttered as he ushered me into the conference room.

"Have a seat. Can I get you some water?"

"Sure," I said. "Wait—is this an interview? Do I need a lawyer?" A pain started to throb in my left temple. It was most likely caused by too much coffee and too little sleep. "I'm sure Frances can get her cousin over here in about a half an hour."

"No." Rex shook his head. "There's just some things I need to clear up."

"Sure," I said as he left. "Great." I sat down and put my duffel on the floor beside me. A glance at my watch told me it was only one AM. If this didn't take long, I might be able to get back to the McMurphy in time to get five solid hours of sleep.

I closed my eyes for a minute to fight the pain. Then I put my head down on the conference table and was out.

I had this weird dream where a giant Saint Bernard was chasing me with a chipper-shredder machine. "No!" I woke up with surprise to realize I was still in the hotel conference room. I wiped the drool off my face and used the sleeve of my sweatshirt to clean up the small puddle of drool on the table.

I stretched and got up. "Hello, Rex, did you forget about me?" Sticking my head out into the hallway, I saw that no one was around. The hall lights were dimmed for nighttime, and the cast and crew had all gone home. "Hello?" No answer.

This was crazy. I grabbed my duffel and walked out. Being nice and answering questions was one thing, hanging around to be interrogated was another. "You can call my lawyer," I muttered and moved down the hallway.

There was a commotion outside the main lobby. I imagine the guests above that area weren't too happy. After all, you paid a lot of money to stay on the island. In exchange you expected fresh air and a quiet, good night's sleep.

I walked around the crowd and headed home. I'd learn soon enough what Rex wanted to tell me. I yawned as I walked down the street to Main and then walked up it to the McMurphy. Right now I needed my bed more than I needed another disaster.

Frances met me at the back door to the McMurphy. "Oh, good, there you are," she said and opened the door. "Come in. Did anyone see you leave?"

"What? No, I don't think so. Rex brought me into a conference room and promised to be right back. I fell asleep, and since he didn't keep his promise, I left."

"Good. Don't talk to anyone. My cousin William is on his way over."

"What are you talking about?"

"They found the skull of the person in the mulch." Frances walked with me up to the apartment. "That's probably what Rex originally wanted to talk to you about."

"Originally?"

"Yeah, unfortunately, they just found Chef Thomas lying in a heap on the ground next to the Grand Hotel. The EMTs are working on him."

"Oh, my God, not Peter." I dropped my duffel on the landing. "Is he okay? I need to see him."

"He's unconscious but alive." Frances held me by the arms. "They're flying him to the hospital in Mackinac City."

"I want to go with him," I protested.

"You can't," Frances said and took me by the hand and led me upstairs. "You have to stay here and get some sleep. Things will look better in the morning."

"How can I sleep when Peter is hurt and unconscious?" Panic surrounded me. "What if he doesn't make it through the night?"

"That's why I'm here," Frances said and took my keys from me and unlocked the apartment. "You need an alibi."

"What? Why?"

"The evidence against you is stacking up." Frances put my duffel down and then walked me to the bathroom. "Get ready for bed. We'll talk in the morning."

"I don't want to get ready for bed. I want to find out who hurt Peter."

Mal stepped out of her crate and took one long leisurely stretch before bounding over for her welcome-home pats. I absently picked her up. She licked my face, and I sent her a tired smile.

"Peter is in good hands. You need sleep and an alibi. I'm providing both. Now go." Frances shooed me toward the master bedroom. "Do you need me to fix you any warm milk?"

"I'd rather you brewed some coffee. What about the other members of the cast and crew?"

"What about them?" Frances put her hands on her hips and tilted her head.

"Are they under lock and key as well?"

"They'd better be," Frances said. "The way people are getting hurt, it's not safe for any member of the show to be alone. Especially you."

"Why me?"

"Because you make it a bad habit of being a suspect."

CHAPTER 22

"Chef Peter Thomas is in critical but stable condition at Bradford Health Systems intensive care," the radio announced. "All work on the reality show, *Fudge Not, Lest Thee Be Fudged* has been suspended. Cast and crew members have been asked by the local authorities to stay in their rooms until further notice."

"Well, I guess that means they won't let me off the island to see Peter." I said as I came out of the bathroom showered and wearing clean clothes. I had to admit after a few hours of good sleep I wasn't so grumpy.

Frances looked concerned. "The test results on the reality woman's death came back. It seems that she did indeed eat poisoned fudge."

"Oh." I made a face. "That had to be bad."

"It's not so good for you either," Frances said.

There was a pounding at the apartment door before I could ask why. "I'll get it."

I opened it to find two police officers outside. One was Office Lasko. I was not a favorite of hers. "Good morning," I said as cheerily as possible. "Can I offer you two some coffee?"

"No, thank you," Officer Polaski said.

"We need you to come down to the station immediately," Officer Lasko stated with a good amount of glee.

"Okay, why?" I asked.

"I've already called my cousin," Frances said. She stood beside me with her hands on her hips. "Allie, don't say anything until he gets here."

"Should we read her her rights?" The younger office asked.

Lasko's right eye twitched. "Not yet. We're only asking questions at this time. Allie McMurphy is a person of interest in the ongoing investigation of the poisoning death of Cathy Unger. Miss McMurphy, please come with us."

"Okay," I said as Lasko took me by the arm and forcefully showed me the way out. I glanced over my shoulder. "Tell your cousin William to meet me at the station."

Frances picked up Mal and held her. "Remember, don't say anything until your lawyer comes. You have rights, don't let them trample them."

"Will do," I said and noticed how the lobby, usually dead this time of day, was suddenly filled with people milling about. One such person was Liz. "Hey, Liz," I said and waved as the police officers escorted me from the building.

"Allie, wait, what do you know about the attack on Chef Thomas?"

"Can't talk now." I pointed out the police. "I'm kind of busy. But I'll give you an exclusive when I get back."

Sandy was coming in as I was escorted out. "Cancel today's fudge demonstrations," I instructed her. "Today's specials are posted on the wall."

"Don't worry," Sandy shouted after me. "I'll make sure you keep running."

"Don't forget to work on your centerpieces."

"Will do," Sandy said and disappeared into the McMurphy. The streets were far less crowded this time of day as the ferries started running at eight AM and the first boats of tourists hadn't come in yet. Thankfully only those who stayed on the island would watch as Lasko escorted me down the street to the white administration building. I went in happy that my hands weren't cuffed and that I had put shoes on when I got up this morning.

"I hope you have coffee," I said and stifled a yawn. "I'm going to need it."

"You won't be so nonchalant when we arrest you," Officer Lasko said with her you-are-the-bad-guy voice.

"What are you arresting me for?"

"We are not arresting you," Rex said as Lasko escorted me to a tiny conference room. "I need to ask you some important questions about the reality show."

"She lawyered up," Lasko said as she put me into a room and closed and locked the door.

Rex came in twenty minutes later with a Styrofoam cup full of black coffee. "Hi, Allie, please have a seat."

"I need to stand if that's okay with you. Where'd you go yesterday? And why all the drama?" I waved my hand toward the door.

"Sorry about that." Rex sat down and pushed the coffee over to my side of the table. "Lasko wants to be in a crime drama."

I blew out a breath and picked up the coffee. It was black and thick, which was pretty much what I needed right now. "What's going on, Rex?"

"You know your friend Peter Thomas was attacked last night."

"Yes, I heard. First you put me in a small conference room at the Grand, and then I fell asleep, and when you didn't show, I left."

"Again, my apologies." Rex ran a hand over his face. "We don't usually have so much excitement on island. I'll have another talk with Lasko about communication. When I got delayed she was supposed to let you know you could go home."

"I don't think leaving me there was an accident."

"What?"

"Never mind." I wrapped my left arm around my waist and clung to the coffee cup. "It's not important. What is important is that I wanted to be with Peter, but Frances said it would be best if I didn't go. Why is that, Rex? I consider Peter a good friend. Has anyone contacted his family? His daughter should know. Someone should be there."

"Calls have been made. I have an officer with him. He won't be alone when he wakes up."

"Good."

"You spoke to Jessop the other day."

"Yes, I did." I sipped my coffee. "He wanted to know if I still held a grudge. I told him no. I explained why you all got a warrant to check out Jessop Compost and Mulch."

"Who else have you spoken to about the bone bits?"

"No one." I wrinkled my forehead. "Wait—Liz knows, but not because I told her. She was there when we found the first pieces. Remember?"

"I do," Rex said. "As was Daisy."

That memory brought a smile to my face. "Do you

still have Daisy and Mrs. Finch in lockup? Or did Daisy pass the bone?" I made a face. "I would not want to be the one on duty to check."

Rex grumbled. "Daisy is in lockup. Mrs. Finch is still protesting."

"Is all of this connected?" I tilted my head thoughtfully.

"That's what I was hoping you'd tell me. You seem to be up to your eyeballs in all three investigations." His pretty blue gaze studied me.

"I don't know how that happened." I sat down, nervous for the first time. "Mal found the mulched bones. Then Peter asked me to do this favor for him, and now here I am, exhausted and worried because a woman died and a man I admire is unconscious in the hospital."

He waited for my thoughts to catch up with me.

"Then there's my first solo Lilac Festival. Thankfully Jenn, Sandy, and Frances have a handle on the fest." I grew quiet. "You have questions for me?"

"Did you know Heather Karus?"

"Who?" I scrunched my forehead and shook my head.

"Heather Karus. She's a local. Her family's been on the island for almost fifty years. Her dad was a smithy at Jessop Stables. Her mom was a housekeeper. Heather let everyone know she was above her family. She left the island to get her MBA but didn't like it. Last I heard she went to culinary school and returned when her mom took sick."

"Oh, no, I never met her. I mostly knew my grandparents' friends. What does Heather have to do with any of this?"

"What about Cathy Unger? It's been reported that she,

Amber and Erin bested you on tape the night Cathy died. Is that true?"

"Well, yeah," I said. "But that was my fault. I showed up late. They couldn't let me win."

"That's not how it looks on film."

I blew out a breath and dropped my shoulders. "They edit that stuff for conflict. Forget I said that. I can't legally tell you anything about the show."

"That's pretty much the reaction I got when I interviewed the other cast members." Rex sat back. "Their lawyer is slick. He thinks he's dealing with a backwoods police force."

"He doesn't know about your time in Detroit?"

Rex shook his head. "Let's not disabuse him of his opinion," Rex said. "It works to my advantage to be considered a bumpkin."

There was a knock on the door. Rex took a deep breath and blew it out. "Speak of the devil."

The door opened. "Sorry to interrupt," Officer Lasko said when she opened the door. "I've got two lawyers here who claim to be representing Allie McMurphy."

"Two?" I asked.

"Two." Lasko opened the door wider, and Frances's cousin William and a second more well-dressed man tried to beat each other through the door.

The two popped through roughly at the same time. Rex stood. "I'll let you work this out."

"Thanks," I said.

Rex left and closed the door behind him. William was slower and the slicker, well-dressed man grabbed Rex's chair. "Allie? I'm Mark Abrahms. I'm the attorney the show has on staff. It's my job to ensure you are fairly represented in any inquiries."

"Hi, Allie, Frances called me. Since we have a history together I'm certain you want me to be your lawyer in this case." He shuffled his portly body from one leg to the other and placed his briefcase on the table.

"Gentlemen." I sat back and studied them both. "Mr. Abrahms, Mr. Wentworth has represented me in the past. I have a history with him and he understands my personal requirements."

William puffed his chest up. "Get out of the chair, my man. It's me she wants."

"That said"—I gave William the staredown—"Mr. Abrahms understands the contract that I signed for the show backward and forward, don't you, Mr. Abrahms?"

"I wrote it."

"Then it's clear I need both of you." I got up and pushed my chair over to the other side of the table. "Sit down, William. We need to find out what's going on."

"I don't want to take your chair," he protested.

"It's fine," I said and picked up my nearly empty coffee cup. "I don't want to sit."

"Let's begin, shall we?" Mr. Abrahms asked and pulled a notepad out of his briefcase. "What have you told the officer?"

"Even more important, in my opinion," I said, "What did the officer tell you?"

CHAPTER 23

"The parade starts in ten minutes," Frances announced as I stepped back into the McMurphy for the first time since my ignominious escort out.

"The crowd is huge this year," I said and hung up my jacket. The June mornings started out chilly but quickly warmed up.

A glance out the front windows showed that people were five or six deep from the front door to the road. In the back people had kids on their shoulders and stood on step stools. So many backs were pressed to the glass that no one could see inside to the racks of fudge offered.

"It's very rare to have an entire parade of horse-drawn vehicles," I said. "I remember as a kid being so excited when the festival started. I dreamed of being the Lilac Festival queen or maybe the princess and getting to ride in the white carriage and carry flowers while I waved at the crowd."

Sandy giggled as she came from behind the counter. "The festival queen is picked by the students in the island's public schools. Did you go to school here?"

"No, and let me say when I found out you had to be a

full-time islander I begged and pleaded with my parents to let me move in with Grammy and Papa. But they said no. As an adult I can understand why. I was only eight years old, after all."

"I love parades." Jenn came downstairs. "We have a great view. Shall I take pictures?"

"That's a great idea," I said. "We can put them on the McMurphy Web site. That way people can see if they stay with us they can watch the parade from their room windows."

"Brilliant." Jenn grinned. "I'm running upstairs for my camera."

"How are we on fudge?" I asked Sandy. "Sorry I was busy this morning. That was not planned."

"I kind of got that," Sandy said. "I think the police officers on either side of you were the biggest tip-off. Are you okay?"

"I'm okay," I said. "Rex wanted to question me."

"Did he?"

"The lawyers wouldn't let him."

"Lawyers, as in more than one?" Sandy tilted her head and studied me as if I were a new and interesting bug.

"Lawyers—as in two," I replied and took a clean chef jacket out of the drawer where I stored jackets and dishtowels. "Frances's cousin William is my current lawyer and then the show provided a fancy one from Chicago."

"Wow, you one-two'ed him." She made fists with her hands and made a knockout punch.

I laughed. "I didn't need all that. Rex was simply trying to figure out what all is going on. Between the bones and then the chef show incidents, he is running ragged."

"That female officer looked like she would cuff you in a heartbeat."

"Right?" My eyes widened. "She doesn't like me much."

"Huh, that wasn't the least bit evident . . ." She shook her head at her own sarcasm.

"I'm going to sugar lilac flowers for this week's festivities. I meant to do it last night but got carried away."

"I've got some fresh blooms," Frances said and went out the back and brought in armfuls of the fragrant blossoms.

I mixed up the dried egg white as Sandy put out the blotting paper and the fine berry sugar.

"That's a lot of blooms," Sandy said.

Frances smiled. "I just love them."

The sounds of the parade outside filled the air and mixed with the scent of lilacs. We worked quickly and carefully, picking each petal, dipping it, and then rolling it gently in sugar. Tweezers helped us handle them without crushing.

Finally we finished as the parade ended with the parade marshal, Mrs. Hutchins, in Victorian dress, waving and tossing out individually wrapped pieces of fudge.

As the crowds broke up, we cleared the sugared petals to dry on drying racks and I started up the lilac fudge base. A demonstration now held a fascinated audience. Frances opened the door wide to let the fresh air in and the scent of lilac fudge out.

It was days like this that reminded me why I had worked my whole life to this one end—entertaining fudge making on a brilliant lake island.

CHAPTER 24

"What do you know about Heather Karus?" I asked Frances. It was Saturday morning and I worked on my laptop in the lobby of the McMurphy while Mal slept at my feet. That way I was readily available to help her with the burgeoning Lilac Festival crowds.

"Heather? She's a pretty girl. I believe she was the Lilac Festival queen her senior year. Why?" Frances asked from her perch behind the reception desk, working on her reservations.

"Something Rex said this morning. Do you know what she did for a living?"

"What do you mean did?"

"I have a feeling Heather may be our bone donor."

"Oh," Frances gasped. "Really? Why?"

"Rex asked me if I knew her and since she isn't a member of the cast or crew of the reality show, I'm guessing she's our body."

"Oh, poor thing," Frances frowned and went back to her computer. "She recently came back to us. I believe she was interviewing for the head pastry chef at the Grander Hotel."

"Huh, Tammy Gooseworthy has that position," I said and pursed my lips. "What is with her anyway?"

"What do you mean?" Frances turned to me, took off her reading glasses, and gave me her full attention.

"She was following Peter around, trying to audition for the cast of the show."

"Ah, well, she has always been supercompetitive," Frances said. "I remember when the school was having a fund-raiser and a bake sale the year she was a sixth grader. That girl went door-to-door drumming up business and was proud of her trophy for raising the most money."

"She was like that when she was twelve?"

"And later, she won all the awards in school. The girl was a fiend about beating everyone." Frances shook her head. "It was an island-wide relief when she went away to college. There's something not right about her intensity and need to win."

"You know, she followed me into the casting salon, telling me that she should be on the show and not me or any of the other cast members."

"Really? What did you say?"

"I sent her to the producer. Let her terrorize him for a while. Besides, that's not how these shows work."

"It's not?" Frances said.

"No, it's not," I said, "and that's all I have to say about it." I typed Heather's name into my search engine. Up popped pictures of the Lilac Festival and a lovely girl with light brown hair and blond streaks. She waved her hand at the people watching the parade.

Her bio online included an impressive number of achievements in high school and college. Then another interesting fact came to life. "Huh."

"What?"

"Did you know that Tammy's brother Fred was dating Heather?" I asked. "Here's a picture of them in high school and according to her Facebook page, they were still a couple."

"Oh, that's right. I remember asking Steven when those two were going to get married. It was hinted that it would be this time next year."

"If Heather is missing, why wouldn't Fred mention that?"

"I think Fred is overseas right now."

"What? Why?"

"He's at Le Cordon Bleu doing a year of French cooking." Frances took off her reading glasses. "Come to think of it, Heather might have gone over there to visit. I can find out if you want."

"Sure," I said. "It still doesn't tell me why Officer Manning was asking me about Heather. I figured he really came to question me because Tammy raised a ruckus about my being in the reality show." I shrugged. "Maybe there's a connection there somewhere."

"Speaking of the show, aren't you supposed to be shooting tonight?"

"They released everyone to go off island to shoot footage of their home and family. Since I live here, they can film me anytime," I said absently.

"Better let Mr. Devaney know in advance. He doesn't like surprises."

"Oh, right," I said. "Let him know that they'll be popping in unannounced. They want to catch us off guard to get the 'real'"—I made air quotes—"us. So that should anyone come to see us or stay at the McMurphy they can see the piece and say, yes it's really like that."

Frances laughed. "Oh, dear."

"Have you heard anything from Peter or his daughter?" I asked.

"No, there are no further updates."

"I still feel as if I should go visit."

"They wouldn't let you past the visitors' waiting room," Frances reminded me. "Besides, we need you here for the festival."

"I can't make centerpieces and fudge," Sandy said from the other side of the glass wall. Sandy used the fudge kitchen to do her chocolate sculpture. It was the perfect solution as we closed the fudge shop down by seven PM. The lights in the kitchen were bright enough that people could gather at the window and watch her work. "Besides, you know the McMurphy fudge recipe and I don't."

"It's a good thing or you'd beat me at my own talent," I tossed back.

Sandy shook her head at my silliness. My thoughts went to our competition and then Tammy Gooseworthy's competition. "Wait, is Tammy the same Gooseworthy family that owns the Island Mulch and Compost Center?"

"Yes," said Frances as she looked at her screen through the bottoms of her lenses. "Ed Gooseworthy is her father."

I didn't like where my thoughts went next. "You don't think Tammy would be capable of putting a body in the chipper-shredder. Do you?"

Frances paused and looked at me. "No, I don't. Do you know how messy that would be? Tammy hated her father's business because it was smelly. That girl gives neat and OCD the same name. Have you ever seen her with a spot on her?"

"Well, I've only seen her twice, but now that you mention it both times she was wrinkle free and sparkling white."

"It's an obsession," Frances said. "There's no way she would do anything as messy as disposing of a body."

"Ok," I said. "Then is there anyone she knows who might do that for her?"

"Now that is a different question," Frances said and tapped her chin. "Ed employs mainland workers for the season. Then there is his foreman Vincent Gross. Those guys are used to dealing with rotting vegetation on a daily basis. I doubt one body would bother them one way or the other."

"Well that is certainly suspicious." I closed up my laptop. "But there is no real motive for them to kill anyone and an act so terrible must be motivated by terrible emotions."

"Unless it was an accident," Frances said.

"How do you accidently kill someone and throw their body in a chipper-shredder?"

"That's a good point," Frances said. "This is all speculation. For all you know Heather is in Paris with Fred."

"True." I pouted. "Come on, Mal, let's go out for your night walk."

Mal popped up and stretched, then wagged her little tail. When I pulled her leash off the hall tree, she started to do twirls.

"You like to go out, don't you?" I said as I put her halter on and then attached the leash. A quick look at the time told me it was nine PM. I had to be honest—I didn't like it when Officer Lasko escorted me through the streets like a common criminal. I needed to do something about that.

I opened the back door and let Mal pull me across the alley to the small patch of grass. The night was cool and clear. The stars were particularly clear.

"Will you call in your lawyers if I say hello?"

"Oh, hi, Rex," I said. "Are you lurking here to talk to me?"

"Not lurking, taking a shortcut to my place." He stepped up to me. "It's a shame you had your lawyers stop our discussion. That's all it was, you know, a discussion."

"I know that, but they don't and they are being paid to be suspicious." Mal finished her squat and came over to bounce up for Rex to pat her on the head.

"Hello there, girl," he said and stroked her under the chin. "Did you check out Heather?"

"Excuse me?"

"I asked you about Heather to see what you could discover about her."

"Ah, sneaky." I turned down the alley away from the McMurphy and the police station to the quieter side of the island. "In fact, I did. You're not thinking she's our bony victim, are you?"

"We got a partial jawbone with some identifying dental work. We should know the person's ID soon."

"And are you sure it's only one person?"

"We're ruling out multiple bodies at this time." Rex shook his head. "It's not likely more than one body went through the mulcher. Hiding more than one body is extremely difficult."

"That makes sense." I took a deep breath of soft summer air. "Heather is dating Tammy Gooseworthy's brother Fred. Right? Frances thinks she might have gone to Paris to visit him."

"When I get the ID on the jawbone I'll check out that connection."

"So you are pretty sure it's Heather. Why?"

"The rumors don't add up."

"You don't believe she ran off to Paris to see Fred?" I asked.

"It's not what I believe," he said, his expression grim. "I called Paris. Fred hasn't seen her. As much as I don't want it to be Heather, she appears to be a missing person, which makes her my number one suspected victim."

"Let's hope she calls home soon," I said.

CHAPTER 25

"Have you heard the news?" Jenn's voice came through my cell phone early Sunday morning.

"What news?" I had hit speaker when it rang so that I could continue experimenting with my second lilac fudge—this one dark chocolate cream. The base boiled in my copper pot.

"They identified the bones from the mulch."

"It's Heather Karus—" we said at the same time.

"When did you hear the news?" Jenn pouted. "I thought I had an exclusive because I was in the police station when the call came from the lab."

"Oh, right, you and Shane—How is that going?" I asked. In my mind it was a bit of a mismatched pair.

"Oh, it's going well," Jenn said. "We may be passing the 'just dating' stage and into the 'sort of a thing' stage."

I laughed. "Soon to be 'a thing.'"

"If I have anything to say about it."

"I didn't hear the announcement about Heather. Rex had his suspicions and asked me if I knew her. Thankfully nothing ties her to me. So at least on that issue I'm not a suspect. Although if Officer Lasko had her way she'd figure out how it was my fault."

"How's your friend Peter?"

"I haven't heard," I said and took a small glass bowl with ice water in it and spooned out the boiling base to see if it created a soft ball in the water. "His daughter, Constance, promised she'd call me the minute he wakes up."

"I'm so sorry."

"I know. Unfortunately I am linked to Cathy and Peter. The producers are very close to giving up on the show altogether. If Peter doesn't wake up in the next two days they'll either get a substitute or pack it in."

"My guess is they'll bring in a substitute host. Will Peter be angry to wake up to being replaced?"

"I don't know," I said and dumped the water. The base had to boil a little longer before it would set up properly. "Maybe," I said. "Frankly, I was surprised to see him linked to this kind of show. It doesn't seem his thing."

"Maybe the school put him up to it. It's terrific publicity."

"Yes, that's what they keep telling me," I said and put new ice water in the glass bowl. "How's the first tea planning coming? It's this afternoon, right? If this fudge comes out I'll debut it."

"Yes, everything is ready," Jenn said. "We will have five tables of six. I've got lilac-colored linens for the tables and delicate white chairs on rent. Did you see the so-called simple chocolate centerpieces that Sandy did?"

"I did," I said. "She's an artist."

The first set of centerpieces was made of delicate boughs of chocolate lilacs surrounded with white chocolate leaves.

Sandy had built molds of the tiny trumpets with delicate petaled tops as well as molds of the branches. She'd made the chocolate, poured it in the molds, carefully separated each petal, and placed it on the branch connecting them with tiny drops of liquid chocolate.

The centerpieces rested inside clear plastic boxes in the large candy freezer downstairs.

"I've created place cards and got the 'All Things Print' shop off Market Street to donate the printing. These are hand-printed with an old press on handmade paper. The name tags match the place cards and the invitations. It's enough to make a Victorian lady of the finest breeding sigh in satisfaction," Jenn said.

"It's times like this that I'm sad that the McMurphy doesn't have a stretch of lawn like the Grand or the Island House. We could totally create an outdoor afternoon tea."

"Ooh, I like that," Jenn said. "I'll work on that for next year. Ok, I've got to go—my sexy scientist is ready to go."

"See you in a couple hours," I said and hung up. I tested the fudge base again and was happy with the soft ball in the ice water. It was an old-fashioned way of doing things. Now they had digital thermometers that read out the stage the boiling fudge was in. Somehow there was something more satisfying in trusting my own skill.

When I finished the fudge, I let it cool, then folded in bits of white chocolate infused with lilac. In the end I was satisfied with the recipe. So I cut it into single pieces, placed them in delicate paper cups, garnished them with sugared lilac, and took them downstairs.

The tea went off without a hitch. We had a three-piece orchestra in the back corner where the coffee bar usually stood. Jenn finished the afternoon by asking guests to write their get-well thoughts for the children on hand-made paper using a quill and inkwell. We were careful to use ink blotters and offered Lava soap to scrub away any ink residue.

As I thanked the ladies for coming and reminded them that the proceeds were going to the children's clinic, Liz walked into the hotel.

"You might want to keep some of those proceeds for your lawyer."

"Why?" I asked. "I never met Heather."

"The poison that killed Cathy was found in the fudge you made."

I froze. "What? How can they say that? If my fudge was filled with poison then all of the judges would be dead. I watched them all taste the fudge. We have footage."

"The contents of her stomach don't lie. The last thing she ate was your fudge. There is corroborating evidence in the residue of the gingham fabric it was carried in." Liz pulled out a pocket recorder. "What are your thoughts on this new discovery?"

"My thoughts?" I swallowed hard, my brain searching for reason. "One: I didn't poison the fudge. Two: I didn't have a reason to kill Cathy. And three: Don't you think you ought to be looking for whoever put Peter Thomas in a coma?"

"Is it true you don't have an alibi for the night Peter Thomas was bludgeoned?"

"Oh, for crying out loud." I shook my head. "I was put in a conference room by Police Officer Rex Manning."

"But you didn't stay there. You went home at some unknown time."

"I didn't stay there because Officer Manning never

came back. I have a witness for what time I returned."
I waved my hand to Frances. "Frances was here when I
returned."

"According to an eyewitness, Chef Thomas humiliated you on camera."

"I was late and Chef Thomas doesn't excuse lateness.
It doesn't mean I hurt him."

"Cathy and Erin's team beat you out of first place that
night. How competitive are you?"

"Not that competitive," I said. "Come on, Liz this is
nuts."

"If so then why have the police issued a warrant for
your arrest?"

"What? No—They have no proof. They couldn't have.
Because I didn't do it."

"Better call your lawyers," Liz said and turned off her
recorder. "Because Officer Lasko is going to be here in
a few minutes with her handcuffs."

"What's going on?" Jenn said as she stopped by us.
"Liz, you missed a great afternoon tea. I'm thinking the
second tea set up for next week is going to draw an even
bigger crowd. Should I tell them to come dressed in
Victorian garb? That might be a fun twist."

"Jenn, call my lawyer," I said as I moved to the back
door.

"Why?"

"Liz, tell her why," I said and stuffed my arms through
my Windbreaker. It was overcast and the wind off the
lake was cool. Mal followed me out, poking me on the
leg the entire time. "No, Mal," I said frustrated. "Stay!"

"Where are you going?" Jenn asked.

"To see Rex before Lasko gets here with her handcuffs."

"Oh, that doesn't sound good," Jenn said. She picked

up Mal, and they both watched me trudge out into the alley and down to the administration building.

If they did have a warrant for my arrest, I wanted to turn myself in. The last thing I needed was to be dragged through the street in handcuffs. No matter how much Lasko wanted to do it. What did I ever do to that girl? I didn't have a clue.

I walked straight to Rex's office. "What is this ridiculous rumor that there's a warrant out for my arrest?"

"Where did you hear that?"

"I have my sources," I said and sat down in the left chair of two that faced his desk. His office was cramped by the big desk he worked at. Funny how he could look like an action figure even when doing paperwork behind a desk in a tiny office.

"Darn it, I told Lasko to let me bring you in." Rex slapped down the pen he had in his hand. "Did she make a scene?"

I held up my wrists. "I got here before she could. Now please tell me what is going on? Because I know I didn't poison Cathy Unger or put Peter into a coma."

Rex got up and closed his office door. "What about your lawyers?"

"I'm not paying them. So let's figure this out so that we can both go home happy."

"You were the last one to see Cathy," Rex said. "We have a time-stamped piece of video showing that you both went in to the bathroom but only you came out."

"Nice try but that is not motive or means of murder." I crossed my arms.

"Cathy Unger was poisoned by a piece of your fudge. Fudge that we have film evidence of you making."

"If I had poisoned the fudge then every one of those

judges would be dead. They tasted the fudge I cooked. I have no idea what fudge Cathy tasted or even why she tasted it. When I left her she was talking about my character on the show possibly going into the finals—"

"Your fingerprints were lifted off the gingham square the fudge was wrapped in."

"I touched all those squares when I tried to figure out how best to plate my fudge."

"No one else had reason to kill Cathy. You, on the other hand, stand to win a one-hundred-thousand-dollar competition. It is a competition, right?"

"The winner gets a check, yes. They are also expected to do two tours of promotion to ensure the series gets plenty of press." I raised my chin and narrowed my eyes. "I don't have time for promotion tours and I never planned to win. And I certainly don't need to kill off the competition to win."

"You didn't mean to kill Cathy—only make her sick enough to miss the competition."

"Is that the reasoning you're going with? Because it's still wrong. Rex, seriously, I have no need or desire to kill anyone."I blew out a breath. "I'm going to say this only one more time. I agreed to be part of the cast when my friend and mentor, Chef Thomas, begged me. He told me that one of the cast members bowed out at the last minute. He promised me there would only be a couple nights shooting as I would most likely be voted off early. I agreed to do it as a publicity bit for the fudge shop. I'm thinking about offering fudge for sale online year-round."

I ran a hand over my face and rubbed my temples. "I don't care that much about the competition."

"That's not what it looks like when we run the footage. They say you can't hide the truth from the camera."

"They also say the camera adds ten pounds," I quipped. "Neither one is anything I want to think about." I crossed my arms and leaned back. "Really, Rex—I come in as a friend and get questioned like the main suspect. What's up with that?"

"I have to ask the tough questions." His blue eyes were clear as day and flat like a cop's should be. "Now, did Cathy tell you anything that might suggest she was in danger?"

"No." I shook my head and tried to think about what we had said to each other in the ladies' room. "We talked about how my being late created a good incident for the writers."

"And that's it?"

"We talked about reality shows and how the cast is chosen. I guess the cast members know each other. There's some kind of circuit where they try out for multiple shows. Cathy said that after a while everyone knows everyone else."

"So there's a casting call."

"Yes, there is," I said. "I can't legally tell you any more than that."

"Do you know if anyone was rejected by the cast or crew? Someone desperate enough to open a spot on the show by literally killing the competition."

"I wasn't around for the original casting so I have no clue."

"Okay, have you seen anything or anyone hanging around? Or doing anything inappropriate?"

"Tammy is the only one hanging around bothering people, but you know that. Everyone else has been great from my stylist to the hair and makeup guys to the handler, director, and producers. Seriously, I have no idea who wanted Cathy dead or why they used my fudge to do it."

"Maybe someone doesn't like what was going on with the show and decided to take Cathy—and you—out of the competition."

"I don't see why. Seriously, everyone loves each other."

"Really? Because that is not what I see when I look at the footage."

"It's television magic, Rex. The squabbles and such are encouraged when the cameras are rolling to bring drama to the show."

"I see," he said. "I'm going to be very specific here, Allie."

"Okay."

"All the evidence points to you." I opened my mouth to protest, and he held up his palm to stop me. "Let me finish."

I snapped my mouth shut.

"What evidence I have is purely circumstantial and—for the most part—won't stand up in court. Not if you have a good lawyer, anyway."

"I have two lawyers."

"Yes, you do."

"Then why the big deal about arresting me?"

"I want to ask you for your help."

"Okay."

"I believe that whoever killed Cathy is connected with the show. I'm not allowed to learn the 'trade secrets' that may or may not have gotten her into trouble. That said, I believe that whoever killed her is trying to frame you. Imagine, if you will, two members of the cast down in one blow. I know if I wanted in on the competition, I'd be the first one in line, hoping that your friend Thomas would bring me in much the same way he brought you in—as a last-minute substitute."

"That sounds like Tammy," I said. She's been the only one making a stink because she isn't in the competition. As far as official stand-ins, I have no idea if there are any. I'm certain you can ask the director or the producers, they should know what the emergency procedure is for changing the cast."

"I did."

"And?"

"Their answer was not helpful. That's why I've brought you in to the station. I want to try to draw the killer out. Get him to flash his motive a little bit. If he believes you were arrested and are the only suspect, he might drop his defenses and show up to audition for the open position."

"Wait." I sat up. "You're arresting me to draw out the killer?"

"Yes."

"So I'm supposed to what—wait in jail like Mrs. Finch and Daisy? While you run around chasing killers?"

"Yes—er—no."

"That's helpful." I slouched back in my seat like a grumpy teen.

He made a face. "I don't plan on keeping you in jail. You'll be free to go."

"Great!"

"But I'm going to keep you under house arrest. I need to make your arrest as real as possible to generate the audition process."

"So you want me to stop going to tapings and stay at the McMurphy? Cool, I can do that." I rubbed my face a second time. "I'm exhausted from all these tapings. It will be nice to concentrate on my fudge shop—especially during Lilac Festival time."

"This arrest has to look and feel absolutely authentic. I want you to call in your lawyers. I want you to put up a fuss. Can you do that?"

I shook my head. "I let them talk me into this whole thing to get some publicity. I'd been promised good publicity, Rex. I've had nothing but hassels and humiliation."

He leaned back and studied me with his poker face. "Help me catch this killer and you'll get good publicity."

"In the meantime, I get to be hassled and humiliated by Officer Lasko."

"Leave Lasko to me," he said. "Will you do it?"

"Do I have a choice?"

"What was it your friend Jenn said?"

"Any publicity is good publicity." I ran my hands over my face. "Fine. I'll do it. I just hope I don't regret it."

Joy's Almond Fudge

3 cups of sugar
Dash of salt
⅔ cup of cocoa powder
1½ cups of almond milk
¼ cup butter
1 teaspoon vanilla
1 cup shredded coconut
1 cup roasted almonds

Prepare an 8" x 8" x 2" pan—butter the pan, cover the inside with parchment paper or wax paper. Butter the paper and set the pan aside.

In a large, heavy saucepan—note: during the boiling process the fudge can boil up and overflow if you don't use a large enough pan—mix sugar, salt, cocoa powder, and almond milk. Stir over medium heat until the ingredients reach a full boil. Let boil unstirred until a candy thermometer reads 125°F or the soft-ball stage is reached. Remove from heat.

Add butter and vanilla—do not mix. Cool until the thermometer reads 110°F, then beat until fudge thickens and just begins to lose its gloss. Quickly pour half the fudge in the pan and spread to cover the bottom. Layer coconut over the top and pour the remainder of the fudge over the coconut layer. Place almonds in an 8" x 8" grid—one almond per inch. Cool completely. Cut into 1" pieces. Enjoy!

CHAPTER 26

Being arrested is just as scary when it's fake as it would be when it's real. I lawyered up, and Rex handed me over to Lasko to process. Meanwhile, the associate producer, Brian Bere, came over with my lawyer and the show's lawyer.

"No, no, no," Brian said and rushed toward me.

Officer Wright stepped between us to keep Brian from grabbing me. Officer Lasko had one hand on the butt of her gun, and the other clutched my arm.

"You're going to have to keep back," Lasko said. "The arrestee is in the middle of processing."

She dragged me away to the fingerprinting room. I glanced back. "How's Chef Thomas?"

"He's the same," Brian said to me and then turned to the lawyers. "Let's fix this mess and get my cast back on track, okay?"

Four hours later, I was in an ankle monitor device and marched over to the McMurphy under house arrest. The fingerprinting was done by computer scan now, so I didn't have any ink residue to worry about. The mug shots were terrible, along with the endless amount of paperwork.

By the time I was fully processed, the lawyers had a court order to relinquish me to house arrest until the grand jury met to see if the police had a case that would pass the most rigorous scrutiny in court.

"House arrest is better than jail time," my lawyer William said to me.

"I was told I needed to wear this ankle bracelet even in the shower." I cringed. "Really? Why?"

"You've been deemed a flight risk. They have to know where you are at all times," Mark said. "It was a condition of your bail hearing."

"Fabulous," I muttered. A crowd had formed in front of the McMurphy.

"Hey, Allie, is it true you were arrested in the murder of Cathy Unger?" Liz led the pack of reporters—both print and television.

"My client is innocent until proven guilty," William said.

"Miss McMurphy's house arrest is in lieu of jail time and bail. The arraignment hearing has been set for a week from today," Mark added. "My client will take no further questions. Please send all inquiries to my office."

Photo flashes went off like lightning, and I covered my eyes against the flash as they walked me into the McMurphy. I turned my back on the front glass windows and the crowd of reporters.

I rubbed my wrists. "At least they took the cuffs off," I said. "It's almost claustrophobic to be tied up like that."

"Are you okay?" Jenn raced down the stairs from the

office. "It's all over the radio that you were arrested in the murder of that fudge contestant."

"I'm fine, just a little roughed up."

Brian came through the door next. The sounds of questions thrown at him and the flash of lightbulbs followed him into the lobby. He stopped and tugged on the tail of his shirt to straighten it. "What a mess. How long will she be out of commission?"

"At least a week," I said.

"Not long," Mark said.

"Could be a month to six weeks," William said.

"Crud! Crud," Brian said and pulled on his hair as he paced the length of the McMurphy. "I've got money guys on my tail. I've got one contestant being buried and another under arrest. My host and lead judge is in a coma. My insurance company better cover these delays. If it doesn't, I'm screwed."

"Wait," I said. "Don't you have an emergency plan in place for replacing contestants?"

"Right, the emergency plan." Brian took out his phone without missing a step in his pacing. He pressed a button. "Yeah, hey, get me your head of casting. This is Brian Bere. I've got a mess going on up here in the wilderness. Yes, I know, it is an emergency. I need a new host and I need at least one if not two new contestants and I need them yesterday if that's possible." He paced back and forth. "Good, make it so." He turned off his phone and put it in his pants pocket.

"We're good," Brian said. "I'm going to offer open auditions and try to get new cast members. I've got forty-eight hours to get the show back on track or we're cancelled and I'm canned." He yanked on his hair. "I don't want to be canned. I've got too much riding on this show." He paused in front of me. "You know people."

I blinked. "Yes, I suppose that's true."

"Can you offer me a serious contender to take Chef Thomas's place?" He started pacing again. "I need someone here ASAP."

"You're in luck," Frances said. "You happen to be in the fudge capital of the world. Pick any fudge-shop owner and you have a well-qualified host and judge."

"No, no, no." His expression looked as if he ate something nasty. "I can't take a nobody island hick and create a new host. I need polish, I need panache, I need Chef Thomas!"

"How about if you get a new 'guest host' each week until Peter comes back?" Jenn walked into the fray. She put her arm around Brian's shoulder. "Imagine a shocking new guest host every week."

"Shocking? How?"

"Who would the contestants not want to see as host?" I asked.

"I don't know," Brian said. "Who?"

"How about the voted-off contestants?" Jenn asked. "They're here, right? They're qualified and they're under contract. It's a great twist. Now they'll be judged by the very people they beat off the show."

"They'll be judged by the competition . . ." He crossed his left arm, held his right elbow, and rubbed his chin with his right hand. "This might work."

"Of course it will work," I said. "Jenn is great. Jennifer Christensen meet Brian Bere. Brian's my associate producer and Jenn is my partner this summer."

Jenn smiled and stuck her hand out. Brian shook it

without thought. "Remember, your judges are already here on island."

"And under contract. Brilliant! Sometimes I amaze myself." Brian hit the door running. "Where's my assistant . . ."

"You're welcome," Jenn called after him. She rolled her eyes. "People behind the scenes never get any credit." She put her hands on her hips. Today Jenn had on a McMurphy pink polo and a pair of tan cargo pants.

"Maybe you'll get a line in the credits," I teased.

"Money would be nice," she muttered.

"Ha! I wish they paid us." I said and went to get a cup of coffee.

"Wait, they aren't paying you?" Jenn looked horrified. "No wonder you're trying to kill them all."

"Oh, please, I didn't try to kill anyone." I poured half-and-half into my coffee cup, stirred it, and took a swig. "There is only do or do not, there is no try," I quoted.

"Then why is my baby wearing an ankle bracelet?"

I froze, then looked over to see my mother coming through the back door with Mr. Devaney. "Mom?"

"She was out in the alley claiming she was part of the family," Mr. Devaney said and shrugged.

"Ann?" Frances said. "My goodness, it's been a while." Frances stopped Mom and gave her a big hug, allowing me a moment to get ahold of myself.

"Hi, Frances," Mom said as she patted Frances's back. Her gaze never left me. "All right, young lady. Why is there a horde of reporter outside and my daughter on lockdown inside? Come clean or I'm sending your father up here."

"Oh, geez," I muttered, then plastered a big smile on my face. "Hi, Mom! Welcome to the McMurphy."

CHAPTER 27

"All right, spill," my mother ordered. I had managed to get her upstairs and on the couch in my apartment. Jenn made her a cup of tea. "And don't leave anything out."

"It started when Mal found bones in the mulch by the *Town Crier.*"

"Who's Mal?" She asked.

As if on cue, Frances opened the door, and Mal came charging into the apartment. In one leap she was in my lap, licked my cheek, turned to my mom, and held out her paw for a shake.

"This is Mal," I said and wiped off her kiss with the back of my hand. "Frances bought her to keep me company."

"Well, aren't you just the cutest thing?" Mom softened. She shook Mal's paw and then gathered her up as if she were her own baby child and petted and cuddled the pup. "Yes, you are the cutest little thing." Mom looked up at me. "Why on earth did you name this sweet thing *Mal*?"

"Her full name is Marshmallow" I said. "Because she's fluffy and white and lives in a fudge shop."

Mom pulled Mal up to stand her face to face, holding her under her front paws. "What a big mean girl your mommy is," my mother said in a baby-talk voice. "Who calls a cute little thing like you Marshmallow? You look more like a Brigitte to me." She looked at me from around the dog. "Why didn't you name her Brittany or Bridget or something as sweet and cute as her?"

"She prefers Mal," I pointed out and took the cup of tea Jenn handed me. "Thanks," I said to my bestie.

"Well, then, that's fine if that is what you like. Is that what you like, pretty girl? Who's a good girl? Hmm?" Mom let go and Mal circled her lap twice and then curled up and went to sleep.

"Traitor," I muttered.

Mal grinned in her sleep.

"Now, where were we? Oh, yes, why is my baby under house arrest? What were you thinking when you did whatever they arrested you for?"

"It's murder," I said with a sigh. "Some people drive you to it," I mumbled and sipped my tea.

Jenn heard me and stifled a laugh behind her coffee cup.

"Mom, why are you here? I thought you hated Mackinac Island."

"I don't hate it . . . per se," she said. "I wanted to come and check on you. This being your first season all alone."

"She's not alone, Mrs. McMurphy," Jenn said. "She has me and Frances and Mr. Devaney and a part-time chocolatier who makes marvelous sculptures."

"Well, sounds like you have assembled quite the team."

"I have, Mom, we're working well together. We made

lilac-infused fudge and are holding two teas. The first one was just this afternoon and was amazing."

"I'm sure it was." She took a sip. "Was that before or after they arrested you?" Mom raised a delicate eyebrow.

I loved my mom to death. She was a fantastic teacher and a great mom. But I was twenty-seven now and a full-fledged adult. She was always welcome to visit, but I didn't need her supervising my life anymore. "It was before."

"What was this entire hullabaloo about murder? Why would anyone think—let alone have enough evidence to arrest you—that you murdered someone?"

"I was the last person to see a rival fudge-shop contestant alive."

"Is that all?" Mom shook her head. "Why, that happens all the time to people in Detroit and the police don't go around willy-nilly arresting people. There are laws and procedures that must be followed." Mom pursed her mouth in obvious impatience. "Come morning, I'm going down to that police station and have a word with this Officer Rex Manning. Who does he think he is?"

"Mom."

"See, dear, this is what I hate about island life—everyone is quick to judge and put you in your place. I bet they still call you a fudgie, don't they?"

"Mom."

"Just like a place this small. Why, even though your father was a McMurphy, they still called me a foreigner/fudgie. No matter what I did I was never accepted—"

We all waited for her to wind down.

"Mom, I'm tired. I bet you're tired as well. Did the porter bring up your bag?"

"I carried my own, thank you. It's not that far, you know."

"I know. Come on. I'll change the sheets on my bed. You can have my room. Jenn has the spare."

She got up, snuggling Mal, and put her mug on the kitchen counter. "If I sleep in your bed, where will you sleep?" She paused. "You don't already have a boyfriend, do you?"

"No." My voice rose sharply.

"No, of course not." She patted my cheek. "What was I thinking? This is you we're talking about. You always were all about this dreary little hotel in this . . . island."

"I love my work and my decision to keep up the family business." I followed her back to my room.

"We're doing very well," Jenn added as she came with us. "The last six weeks we've been fully booked and our extras like a cocktail party and the two teas have brought positive results for charity."

"Yes, yes." Mom carried Mal and absently patted her head. "I'm sure you feel as if you'll be just fine. But it's still early in the season. And what are your plans for after the season? Hmm? I don't see two vibrant young women like you living full-time on the island." Mom turned to me and put Mal down on the bed. "We are fully expecting you to leave after this season and spend the winter in Detroit. I've got your old room cleaned and ready." She patted my cheek. "You were in Chicago long enough. And now you're playing innkeeper in your grandparents' home. As I said, I understand the appeal, but trust me. It wears off quickly when your entire life is about fudge and island festivals."

"Sheets are in here." I opened the linen closet that was built into the wall at the end of the hall next to my bedroom. "I hung them out on the line like you like." I pulled fresh sheets out of the closet and buried my nose in them. "They smell sunshine fresh."

"Wonderful."

While I helped Mom make up the bed, Frances stuck her head into the room.

"I'm going home. Mr. Devaney's going to accompany me. Good night all."

"Good night, Frances," Mom said. "It was wonderful seeing you. Please tell Mr. Devaney I said good night. I'm sure I'll see you both in the morning."

"Good night, Frances, thanks for your help today."

"It was my pleasure." She nodded toward the heavy bracelet on my ankle. "Are you going to be okay?"

"I'm fine," I said with a reassuring smile.

"Goodnight, then." Frances waved and left.

Mom went to the bedroom door and closed it. "Now that we're alone,"—she picked up Mal absently and petted the soft puppy fur—"what is really going on with you?"

"Nothing," I said.

"That is not nothing," she said.

"Fine, I'm doing Officer Manning a favor."

"You're doing a man who investigated you for murder earlier and who has clearly arrested you in a second—different—case a favor? Why?"

"He's trying to catch the real killer and he thinks they might get bolder when they think I'm taking the blame for their crime."

"That's ridiculous." Mom frowned. "At best they are going to take the next ferry off island, if they haven't already, and let you take the fall for the entire affair."

"Mom, why did you come?" I sat down on the bed.

She handed me Mal and dusted off her hands. "No reason."

"No reason?"

"Why can't a mother simply want to check in with her daughter—especially when her daughter has just been saddled with a monstrosity like the historic McMurphy?"

"So that's it? You came all the way up here—to a place you do not like—to *check on* me?"

"I never said I disliked Mackinac Island." Mom put her suitcase on the cedar chest at the end of my bed and opened it up. "I never felt welcome here." She straightened and put her hands on her hips. "I was always the foreigner. I hope and pray you never have to live in a place where—no matter how long you've lived there—you are treated as the odd man out."

"Oh, Mom, I'm so sorry." I gave her a big hug. "I always thought you hated it here. But I never knew why—thanks for clearing that up."

She sniffed. "They don't treat you like a fudgie, do they?"

"Well . . ."

"Oh, that makes me so mad. Who treats you like that? I swear I will go straight to them and give them a piece of my mind. After all, every single white peon on this island is a tourist and half the Natives as well."

I started laughing at her outburst.

"What?"

"You are so funny. You know you didn't have to come all this way. I'm a grown-up now and fully capable of fighting my own battles."

"Well," she said and sat down with her nightgown in hand. "I hope you don't expect me to leave tomorrow."

"No," I said and hugged her again. "You're always welcome to come and spend all the time you want for a nice visit. Lilac Festival is one of my favorite times. The entire island smells so lovely and the air has that soft quality where it caresses your skin."

"You say that now." She sighed long and hard. "The first time your father brought me on island I thought it was so lovely—all lake breezes and perfectly manicured gardens. The charm of the horses and carriages and if you are up early or out late you can see all the maids and groundskeepers in their uniforms heading to and from the big Victorian cottages. It could be one hundred years ago when the houses were grand and the people who lived in them during the season were even grander."

She grew quiet. "Then you are one of those maids and gardeners. You are the shop keepers and artists. Never quite one with the island. Never quite belonging in the beautiful cottages." Mom looked off into space for a moment. Then she came back and shrugged. "I like Detroit. It has its good and its bad but there is a feeling of accomplishment when I go home at night."

I sat down with her and patted her hand. "I'm all right, Mom. I'm building my life here. That has to be magic enough for me."

"Yes, well, it certainly has been a long day for you." She stood up and bustled about. "Why don't you go and get ready for bed. I'm sure you have to get up at some ungodly hour."

"Good night, Mom."

"Good night."

Heather's English Toffee Fudge

4 cups milk chocolate chips
2 tablespoons butter
1 can sweetened condensed milk
1 teaspoon vanilla
2 cups English toffee chips

Butter an 8" x 8" x 2" pan. Line with wax paper. In a double boiler melt milk chocolate, butter, and sweetened condensed milk until smooth. Be careful not to burn. Remove from heat. Add vanilla and toffee chips. Pour into pan. Refrigerate overnight. Remove from pan. Cut into pieces. Store in a covered container.

CHAPTER 28

"Well, this certainly is not going to help us with the investigation," Jenn said. She came out of the bathroom in her pink-and-white-striped pajamas, brushing her teeth.

I punched my pillow and adjusted my legs into the couch. "What investigation?"

She stopped with the brush in her hand. "Oh, come on, we were on the case to find out about the bones and poor Chef Thomas."

"I'm under house arrest." I waved to the ankle bracelet that stuck out from under my nightgown.

"Is there any way to undo that thing?" She wandered back into the bathroom and spit, then rinsed. "Allie?"

"Oh, please," I said and rolled my eyes. "Better criminals than us have tried to outsmart these things."

"Why did you agree to wear that thing anyway?"

"I have no idea . . ." I stared at the ceiling. "That's a lie. He looked at me with those pretty blue eyes with long black lashes and asked for my help."

"HA!" Jenn ran in. "You like him."

"Rex is just a friend." I waved it off.

"Oh, I don't know—there's something that works between a girl who finds dead bodies and a lawman whose job it is to figure out who did it." Jenn crossed her arms.

"Let's not talk about my nonexistent love life," I said.

"Didn't I see Trent stop in yesterday? What's up with the handsome stable guy?"

"He's certain that the body wasn't in his mulch. He came to let me know."

"He stopped by to see you to tell you that you don't need to investigate him this time?"

"Yes, something like that." I rolled on my side and sighed at the clock that read 10:52 PM. Five AM came quick when you were up after ten.

"Did you offer him a coffee? A Danish? Dinner and a movie with some snuggles after?"

"You have love on the brain," I said. "How is it going between you and sexy scientist?"

Jenn grabbed a spare pillow and crashed on the floor next to the sofa. "Slumber party!"

"Oh, Good Lord, I have to work in the morning—and my mother is here." I waved toward my closed bedroom door.

"What is that all about anyway?"

"I have no idea."

"Well, what did she say?"

"She said she came to spend some time with me."

"But I thought she hated this place." Jenn stretched out on a blanket she had put on the floor. "I guess she sucked it up for you."

"Right. When my mom says that she's always got some other agenda in mind."

"I find it hilarious that she took your dog in with her," Jenn grabbed the edge of the blanket and rolled up in it.

"She certainly has taken to Mal."

"Better watch that she doesn't stick your puppy in her suitcase and take her home with her."

"We can't have that," I said and crossed my arms. "Who would solve this murder mystery?"

"Ha! We need to get her some Scooby Snax." Jenn laughed.

"Stop it." I rolled my eyes, and Jenn giggled like a schoolgirl. "Shhh, Mom needs her sleep."

"It's really terrible about poor Heather," Jenn said.

"I know. Wait, if she interviewed for the Grander, she couldn't have been dead that long."

"It's only been a few weeks since people last saw her," Jenn said. "Shane says it has to do with the increased level of decomposition in the compost pile. He was so excited—you should have seen him get his geek on."

"Okay, so that's creepy. Do they have any idea what she died of? Was it something horrible like falling into a mulcher?"

"I certainly hope not." Jenn shuttered. "I'd rather be poisoned by fudge."

"That was not my fudge and Rex knows it."

"Then why the ankle bracelet and all the fuss?"

"He thinks when the show runs auditions for the new cast members, the killer will be among the auditions."

"Hey, here's an idea, since you are housebound for the foreseeable future, how about if I audition for one of those parts?"

"Why?"

"Well, to help catch the killer."

"But you don't have any candy-making experience."

"So?" She shrugged. I'll get an earpiece and you can talk me through it. Look, it will be awesome. We'll still get publicity for the McMurphy and possibly flush out whoever hurt your friend." She paused, her eyes glittering in the late-night light. "That way, we have a mole on the inside looking out for a killer."

"I don't want you to end up like Peter or like Cathy."

"No worries, I'll be really careful. So is it a go?"

I chewed on my bottom lip. "What if Rex says no?"

"Then we won't do it." Jenn shrugged.

"Okay, if you're sure."

"I'm sure." Jenn's eyes lit up, and she clapped her hands. "Great! I've always wanted to do one of those cooking reality shows."

"Good night, Jenn."

"What time are the auditions?"

"I have no idea. They'll post the notice tonight. Go down to the administration building in the morning. They usually post them on the bulletin board."

"Cool."

Monday morning I was up and making fudge by five AM. At seven AM, Jenn came down fresh as a daisy in white pedal pushers, a turquoise blouse, and turquoise wedges.

She poured herself some coffee while I tossed fudge in the air to cool it.

"You're up early and dressed to kill," Frances said as she came in the back way.

"They're posting auditions for replacements on Allie's reality show. I want to be there and try out."

"But you don't know how to make fudge," Frances pointed out.

"You don't have to know." Jenn eyed Frances over the

top of her coffee. "I read online that all you need to do is come in for a video test to see if you record well and have the ability to read from a script. I have both!"

"No wonder they murdered Cathy. If you don't need to know how to make fudge, then what's the show about?"

"Personality, Frances." Jenn patted her on the back. "Something I have buckets of. Okay, I'm off, wish me luck."

"Good luck."

"You should call that producer guy you talked to yesterday. Tell him to hire Jenn. Having a second pair of eyes in the competition is a good idea."

I made rocky-road fudge, sprinkling the dark chocolate base with mini-marshmallows and peanuts and lacing it with caramel, then I carefully folded the ingredients in so that ribbons of caramel ran through the fudge and didn't just combine with the chocolate.

"I think we should ask Rex before we go any further in our own investigation."

"Why? So he can have Jenn under house arrest, as well as you?"

"I'm his best suspect," I said. "With the ferries coming and going at all hours, plus airplanes, he wanted to ensure I didn't leave the island." I shrugged. "It's okay. I'm used to it by now."

Frances shook her head and poured herself a large cup of coffee. "Poor Heather Karus. She still had so much life to live. I don't know what is going on. They won't specify the how and why of her death. Mr. Karus must be devastated. You know his wife died in January."

"No, I didn't know. I don't believe I've ever met Heather or Mr. Karus. Did you know them well?"

Frances shrugged her shoulders. "They're islanders. I

know them as well as anyone knows a neighbor. Steven is your father's age and Heather is around your age—was—around your age. Darn shame." She took her seat at the reception computer and muttered, "Darn shame."

"Wait," I tilted my head. "Do you think that she committed suicide?"

"It hadn't occurred to me," Frances frowned. "She didn't seem suicidal. I mean, I told you I thought she was in Paris with Fred. Would a girl who has a boyfriend in Paris be suicidal?"

"What if Fred broke up with her from Paris," I spit balled.

"I hadn't thought of that" Frances tapped her chin. "Combine that with her mom recently dying she might have . . ."

"Sometimes when people can't live with their grief, they feel hopeless and helpless. It's a vicious circle."

"How do you know so much about it?" Frances studied me.

"I had a friend who attempted to take her life when I was in college. Her brother died in a car wreck. She was in the wreck as well, but she survived. The guilt of surviving and the pain of grief took her to the edge. Luckily, someone noticed and the authorities intervened and saved her life." I cut one-pound portions of fudge and plated them on a long tray with a paper doily on the bottom to keep the fudge from sticking.

"Are you the one who intervened?"

I winced. "Is it that obvious?"

"No." Frances sent me a soft smile. "It was a good guess on my part."

"We should send flowers," I said. "Does the *Town Crier* have the obit up yet?"

"It's going in tomorrow."

"What a sad thing to learn during the Lilac Festival."

"It's kind of historical," Frances said. "In Victorian times a person in grief moved from black to lilac/lavender when six months passed to signal a new stage of grief and to let everyone know they were grieving."

"Huh, that's a weird and random connection." I bit my bottom lip as I put the tray into the candy counter. "Do you know how they identified her?"

"There was a bit of bridgework on a part of the jawbone recovered. It was enough to identify the person who owned the jaw. Unless there is more than one person in the mulch, it's safe to assume that all of the bones belong to Heather."

"Please tell me she had a sense of humor or at the very least liked dogs . . ." I winced at the idea of Daisy or Mal with my jawbone in their mouth.

"I have no idea. The girl didn't talk to anyone. She thought she was too good for the locals, remember?"

"Too good for everyone, but Fred, I suppose since she was dating him." My eyes grew wide. "You don't think Fred did it, do you?"

"As far as I know he's been in Paris the entire time. If Fred is a suspect, no one's saying, I imagine they'll question Fred when he comes in for the funeral."

"I don't envy Rex having to do that." I turned and pulled out the ingredients to make Snicker's Bar fudge. Starting with a milk chocolate base, I would fold into the fudge a layer of peanut nougat, caramel, peanuts, and chocolate ships. It was the first of my candy-bar fudges.

"Poor Fred—to lose his girlfriend and then be interrogated," Frances said. She sat on one of the stainless-steel stools and huddled around her coffee.

"I don't see how he could have come to Mackinac, killed her and left unnoticed," I said. "Do we even know who saw her last? Wasn't she up for the pastry chef position at the Grander Hotel?"

"Yes, she was," Frances said. "Tammy Gooseworthy beat her out for that job about a month ago."

"That's what you told me." I stirred the base ingredients for Sneaker's Fudge—a smooth milk chocolate fudge. Milk chocolate is lighter and creamier than dark chocolate. It's also sweeter. "Tammy's not the nicest person, is she?"

"Like I said, she can be competitive." Frances chuckled and sipped her coffee.

"I bet she is in line ahead of Jenn for the new cast member for the show." I pursed my lips as the fudge pot started boiling nicely. "You don't think she'd kill for her position—do you?"

Frances's expression grew solemn. "I certainly hope not."

"What if Heather and Tammy got into a fight over the job and Tammy pushed her into the shredder?" I shuddered at the thought that someone might be alive when they fell into the massive shredder.

"Oh, surely not." Frances looked like she tasted something bad.

"Pretty darn convenient that Heather went away and Tammy got the job."

"It could be coincidental," Frances said.

"I'll call Jenn and have her find out from her science beau which shredder had evidence of human DNA. If it's Gooseworthy's then we should seriously consider Tammy our prime suspect."

Mal uncurled herself from the dog bed by the fireplace where she slept while I was making fudge. She stretched leisurely, wagged her little tail, and came over to Frances. She jumped up and stretched against Frances's leg.

That was Mal's typical sign for "take me out please." Frances patted her on the head and scratched behind her ears.

Mal sat down and waited for Frances to realize it was time to go out. Mal had us well trained.

"Okay, little one." Frances stood, putting her coffee cup behind the reception desk. "Let's get your leash."

Mal popped up and ran to the hall tree that held her halter and leash.

Frances helped Mal into her star-studded halter and leash. Straightening, Frances looked at me.

"What?"

"What will we do if it's the Jessops' shredder that holds evidence of murder?"

I winced. "Um . . . look for a killer?"

Frances blew out a long sigh. Mal pulled and tugged on the leash, dragging Frances toward the back door. "Motive," Frances said over her shoulder as they headed down the hallway to the back door. "We need motive."

I tested the fudge for what stage it was in. Still not the soft-ball stage. I didn't like to stir too much—it kept the fudge cooler and meant a longer cook time and more likelihood of sugaring.

"Motive," I muttered. "That's what we need in all three incidents—Heather, Cathy, and Peter." Wait—were they all related? Cathy and Peter were easy to see a motive for—the $100,000 grand prize. But what did Heather have to do with the competition? Anything? I put a sugar dispenser on the countertop. It represented Heather. Next was a salt and pepper shaker—pairing for Cathy and Peter? "Some murder board," I muttered. I took a lemon-juice dispenser and called it Tammy. She circled around Heather due to their competition for the job. Plus Heather was dating Tammy's brother, so they fit on two connections.

I pulled the lemon-juice dispenser to the salt and pepper shaker. Tammy also had reason not to like Cathy. For two reasons: 1) Cathy wasn't a real chef, 2) Tammy wanted a spot on the cast. Then there was the fact that Cathy was poisoned with fudge—something easy for Tammy to re-create.

I rocked back on my heels and studied my murder board. It seemed pretty straightforward. Tammy was the connection in all three crimes. I frowned. Did Rex already think the same thing?

CHAPTER 29

"That would have been more fun if it weren't for the crew being all weepy," Jenn grabbed a flowered mug and made herself a cup of tea. It was near dinnertime, and Jenn had been gone twelve hours. "The cast seemed happy to all be working. I made some friends with my suggestion that they use tossed-out candidates as judges."

"So what is it now? Survivor of the fudge contest?" Frances asked. She turned and looked at Jenn over the top of her pink-with-white polka dotted reading glasses.

"They thought that might not be the best title for the episodes considering that Cathy didn't survive." She dunked her tea bag in hot water a few times.

"Who was at the audition?" I asked as I inventoried the kitchen ingredients. My baking-supply driver would be in in the morning, and I needed to know what I should stock up on before he got here.

"Your friend Tammy Gooseworthy was there." Jenn sat down in one of the winged-back chairs near the fireplace. "She almost beat me to my place in line."

"Almost?" I teased Jenn.

"I ran faster." Jenn grinned. "There might have been a tiny bit of shoving and possibly some hair pulling."

"Jenn!" My mom piped up from her position in the winged-back chair across from Jenn. Mom worked her crochet needle, the pink-and-white yarn she used twisted and looped into a lovely flower-pattern afghan. "I thought better of you than to pull another woman's hair."

"Hey, all bets are off, Mrs. M, when a position becomes open for a cast member in a reality show." She took another sip, her eyes twinkling in the firelight. "I wanted the producers to see that I could play the mean girl if they needed me to."

"What about this Tammy person? What is her excuse?"

"She thinks she's a better fudge maker." Jenn shrugged. "She may be better than me, but she's not better than Allie."

"Thanks for the endorsement," I called from my corner of the lobby.

"Anytime, dear, anytime." Jenn kicked out her legs, and Mal took the opportunity to jump up in her lap. "Hey, hot beverage." Jenn held her cup up high, and some of the contents splashed on the chair as Jenn juggled her drink, trying to stay dry while Mal made a bed of her lap.

"You shouldn't let her climb up on you without permission," Frances pointed out.

"Aw, she's fine." Jenn settled in with her tea and ran her free hand over Mal's soft curls.

"So what did the producers say about your screen test?" I asked as I marked the last of the inventory and closed the cupboards.

"It was okay." Jenn shrugged. "I was one of three callbacks."

"That's fabulous," I said as I came out of the fudge shop. I took the inventory page over and pinned it up to the bulletin board where notes were left for people coming and going. "Way to bury the lead."

"Speaking of leads, your reporter friend was there."

"Liz?" I pulled off the apron I wore. "Was she trying for a position?"

"She went through the process with us, but she made it clear to everyone that she simply wanted a firsthand account of what it was like in order to enrich her exposé."

"Speaking of exposés"—I sat down on the settee and rested my tired feet—"what does your science guy say about the investigation? Did they figure out which mulching machine was used to disperse the body?"

"Yes." Jenn grew solemn. "It was Jessops'."

"What! Really." I sat up. "I would not have bet the farm on that."

"Why?"

"Because Tammy Gooseworthy was my pick for having motive and means to fight with Heather and push her into the shredder."

"Wow, that would have been horrible." Jenn shuddered, and we all gave a moment of silence for the woman, each praying she had been dead already when she was shredded.

"I know you think that Tammy is an aggressive person," Frances said. "But just because a person has a prickly personality doesn't mean they're a killer. How many times have you seen on the news that a serial killer was that nice, quiet man next-door?"

"True," I said, my expression clearly registering my

idea of what a terrible fact that was. "Too bad, it would be so much easier if all killers were terrible, pushing meanies."

"Right." Jenn chuckled. "They should all be followed by a neon sign that flashes *killer*!"

"Oh, no," I said when it hit me.

"What?"

"I saw Trent the other day and he asked me if I suspected him again."

"You said no, right?" Jenn sipped her tea.

"Of course I said no." I frowned. "Now he's going to think I lied to him."

"No, he's not." Frances shook her head.

"Do the police have any idea who at Jessop's might have been involved?" I asked Jenn.

"The thing is that the business is open to the public so it could be anyone."

"So how are the police going to figure it out?"

"Shane thinks that they will try to re-create Heather's last hours."

"That makes more sense than interviewing anyone who bought mulch or had a gardener who used Jessop mulch."

"The real question is"—Frances interjected—"who killed Cathy? Were they the same person who hurt Peter?"

"And are they even slightly related to Heather's death?" Jenn asked.

"That's where Tammy worked as a suspect," I said and ran a hand over my face. "She is connected to Heather— her brother was dating Heather and if they found her DNA on the shredder at the Gooseworthy's place that would put a neat little bow on that."

"Then you could connect her to Cathy and Peter, as

well," Jenn said with a nod of her head. "We were all here when she came storming in to pounce on Peter about how she should have had a chance to be on the fudge show."

"Three crimes, one perpetrator," Mom said as she crocheted in a soothing rhythm. "That would have been a hat trick."

"Unfortunately," Frances said, "life is rarely a neat little bow."

"How much longer do I need to wear the ankle bracelet?" I asked Rex the next morning. I had broken protocol and walked over to the police station. Really, it was a small island. Where was I going to go that I needed to be tracked anyway? "I hate the fact that I have to stop and think before I take my dog for a walk or open the door to go for groceries or the post office."

"I appreciate your patience." Rex sat behind his desk and had that trust-me-I'm-a-cop look in his pretty blue eyes. "It's only been thirty hours."

I made a face and slumped into my chair. "It's putting a crimp in my daily activities."

"You have a date I'm keeping you from?" He raised one eyebrow.

"No." I didn't want to admit I hadn't had a date in months, but it was a small island. I'm sure people had already noticed I wasn't exactly on the party scene at night. "But that doesn't mean I don't want one." I lifted my leg. Today I wore my standard uniform of black slacks and pink polo. "This is one giant buzzkill, if you know what I mean."

Rex chuckled. "You have some fudgie you have your eye on?"

"Oh, Good Lord, no," I said and covered my ankle. "I want to stay on island, remember?"

"That doesn't seem to be a popular notion." Rex sobered. "Most kids from here can't wait to get off the island and drive in fast cars and shop in big malls."

"Whoa now, don't lump all women together like that." I put out my hands. "There are plenty of lovely women who settle down on island and are happy to do it."

"Like who? You? You haven't ever wintered here."

"Yet. And I was thinking of women like Liz MacElroy and Frances and my Grammy Alice and your mom and—"

"Okay, okay, I regret I made an assumption." He waved me off. "One should never argue with a woman."

"That's right." I crossed my arms. "So, what's the word on my bracelet removal?"

"I have a person in the auditions right now," he said. "I'm hoping that they can figure this out undercover."

"Good, then I can—"

"I need you to wear it until shooting on the regular show returns," he finished my sentence for me.

"Wait, that wasn't part of the deal." I put my feet down and stood. "This was supposed to be a temporary thing. It is temporary, right? This arrest doesn't go on my permanent record, does it?"

That got him chuckling. "I'll make sure it doesn't go on your permanent record. Unless you want it to say you did this in the fullest cooperation with the law."

"Wow, that sounds nice and all." I crossed my arms. "But I'd prefer you kind of don't mention it at all. The last thing I need is to have trouble getting a loan or hiring good people because they did a background check and found that I was arrested on suspicion of murder."

"Is he harassing you?"

I whipped my head around to see Mrs. Finch standing in the doorway with her legs spread wide and her arms crossed as if she were the Jolly Green Giant. "No, this ankle bracelet is." I pointed to my bracelet.

"What did you do to have to wear that?" The old woman stepped in closer to get a look at the equipment.

"I've been arrested for the murders of Heather Karus and Cathy Unger."

"I don't know who Cathy Unger is, but that Heather was nothing but a troublemaker."

"How so?" I asked and turned my body to face the old woman in the doorway.

"She used to take a broom to my Daisy. Why, just a couple of weeks ago she got out a gun and threatened to shoot my baby."

"Wow, that's a bit extreme," I said.

"I know." Mrs. Finch nodded. "How would you feel if someone tried to shoot your little white puppy?"

"I'm taking a chance saying this in front of a police officer, but it has to be said. If anyone hurt my puppy, I'd have to hurt them."

"Exactly." She nodded. "And if they put your innocent doggie in jail, then what would you do?"

Oh, boy, she was leading the witness, and that witness was me—stuck between Mrs. Finch's honest question and loyalty to my friend Rex Manning, who was only looking out for the dog's best interests.

"Well?"

I swallowed hard. "I would stage a protest."

"Exactly." Mrs. Finch pointed with her finger to emphasize the point. "Daisy might be a bit scruffy at times, but she is my baby. My baby loves this island and so do I. I know I can let her outside without worry that she'll be hit by a car."

"I put Daisy in that cell because we are currently sifting through mulch across the island, looking for the remains of Heather Karus," Rex said as he sat back. "I need to see how many—if any—bones Daisy passes and to keep her out of any other crime scenes."

"It's been a week. She's passed what she's going to pass and you know that."

"I'm still sifting mulch," Rex said calmly.

"And just how long is that going to take?" Mrs. Finch demanded.

"Another two days tops," Rex replied.

"That awful girl never did like my Daisy," Mrs. Finch muttered. "We need a law against torturing pets."

"What did Heather do to Daisy that you think means she didn't like her? Besides the broom, which I'm here to say I can't see how it would discourage a dog as big as Daisy."

"That girl used to chase Daisy around island with a BB gun in her hands. The day I find BBs in my Daisy is the day I start a petition to outlaw weapons of all kinds from this island."

"Heather hasn't had a BB gun since she was nine years old," Rex frowned. "That was twenty years ago."

"So you think." Mrs. Finch put her hands on her hips. "Why, just the other day I caught her lying in wait for Daisy with a BB gun in her hands."

"Were you walking Daisy?" I asked, aghast at the idea of someone shooting you as you walk by.

"No, I saw it in a vision." Mrs. Finch was serious. "I

was deep into Transcendental Meditation when the vision of that girl being cruel to my Daisy came through the cosmic vibrations."

"Really?" I was stunned—surely she was pulling my leg.

"Yes, of course," Mrs. Finch said. "My guru has taught me how to use my third eye. I use it frequently to ensure Daisy is safe."

"Okay, what did you do when you had the vision?" I asked.

"I commanded Daisy to watch out and come straight home."

"And did she?"

"Of course." She looked at me as if I was an idiot for even questioning her.

"Okay." I didn't understand, but I wasn't about to quibble with the woman.

"Officer Manning, you're lucky my lawyer is in Cancun. I've contacted him psychically and let him know he's to come straight here when he gets back."

"I'll keep a light on for him," Rex said with a straight face.

"You may think you're funny but I intend to sue you and the entire Island Police Department for kidnapping and unlawfully restraining Daisy."

"There is a city leash law," Rex said. "If you've got a dog running loose, it's a ticket and a fine of one hundred and ten dollars. This is the third time I've written a ticket for Daisy."

"And I've paid them." She countered. "There is no need to hold my Daisy hostage and I'm certain the city council will agree."

"Feel free to take this up with them when they meet next week," Rex said. "Until then, Daisy will remain in lockup until we are finished with the mulch and you produce a leash to keep her under your control. There are leash laws for a reason."

"That reason is not applicable to Daisy. She would never hurt a soul." She nodded. Her mouth was a straight line of tightened skin. "Now, for the last time, Officer Manning, I've come to collect my baby from your jail cell."

"Daisy is not supposed to go outside without being on a leash," Officer Manning said.

"Fine, I'll get her leash," Mrs. Finch said. "When I get back I expect my Daisy to be released into my company." She walked off in a bit of a huff.

"If I catch her off leash again, I will have animal control ban her from the island," he called after her.

She waved him an obscene gesture as she continued out the door.

"Wow." I turned back to Rex. "Are you ready to chase that dog around some more?"

He shook his head and moved some papers from one pile to another, stamping the pages as he went. "No." He shook his head. "If I had it my way that dog would be taken off the island until this entire murder investigation or investigations—however it turns out—was solved."

"Can't you do something about Mrs. Finch interfering with a police investigation?" I asked hopefully.

"If I wanted to do that—which I don't—I can only hold her forty-eight hours. I unlocked the cell after that and the old bat moved herself into the hall outside Daisy's door and won't budge. She's already been under my care a week and she's been in my office at precisely ten AM every day." He looked at his watch. "Huh, she's later than usual today."

"What was all the business about Transcendental Meditation?"

Rex shrugged. "Mrs. Finch is part of a group of old hippies. I guess back in the late sixties they had an entire cult up here for a while, communing with nature in the state park. Most of them have moved on. Mrs. Finch is one of a handful of people left. She's harmless."

"Except for Daisy." I chuckled at him.

"Except for Daisy," he replied.

"All right, I'm heading back to the McMurphy. You've got twenty-four hours to find your killer. Don't blow it."

His grin grew cocky. "I always get my man."

"Just like Dudley Do-Right."

That made him laugh harder. I shook my head and left the building, warmed by his laughter following me out.

The sun was bright, and I blinked as I stepped out onto Market Street. It was a busy, bustling day as many of the stores were running specials for the Lilac Festival. There was art displayed on the sidewalk and busy crowds in shorts and flip-flops roaming the streets and sidewalks, only parting when a group of bicycles or a horse and carriage came through.

I scanned the crowd, looking for the easiest way to navigate it and get back to the McMurphy, when I caught Mrs. Finch out of the corner of my eye. What was she doing going in the opposite direction of her home? I thought she was going to get Daisy's leash. As if a 120-pound Saint Bernard could be controlled by an 80-pound elderly woman with a leash.

Out of instinct more than common sense, I followed Mrs. Finch down the street. She never even bothered to look around as she focused on wherever she was going.

Luckily, there were large crowds and I was able to remain unseen as I tracked her down Market Street.

The street ended at the opening to the wide picnic lawn below the bluff that held the fort. She walked with purpose through the park and passed the art museum, the marina, and the Island House Hotel.

Main Street flowed around the southern end of the island. She hurried past a church and into a neighborhood filled with apartments and condos where the summer help lived or the regulars stayed.

Where was she going?

I followed her up away from the lake and into the state park. The crowds thinned out so that it was only me and her weaving through the streets. My heartbeat sped up, and I became more and more certain she would catch me at any moment.

At one point she stopped and glanced around. I managed to hide near the front porch of a painted-lady cottage. She moved on after that, even more laser focused. She hurried right by the Jessop Compost and Mulch Service to a patch of woods where she melted into the shadows.

I chewed my bottom lip. Should I go in and try to keep following? I'd come so far, I simply had to see where she was going. Should I take a detour that could possibly get me arrested for no reason because I was so far from my ankle bracelet's home?

Sucking up my fear, I stepped into the dark shade of thick woods. Mrs. Finch was not difficult to see. Her short white hair gleamed in the shadows. She moved through the woods as if she had been there so much she could traverse it in her sleep.

"Hey, Allie. What are you doing so far from the McMurphy?"

I clamped a hand over my mouth to keep from squealing in surprise. I whipped around to see Trent Jessop striding toward me. He wore jeans and a black T-shirt that did nothing to hide the breadth of his shoulders. He had rubber boots on that covered his lower legs. "Oh, hi, you startled me," I said, trying to sound normal and failing.

I had a tree between me and Mrs. Finch at the moment. Would she hear Trent and figure out I'd been following her?

"What are you doing skulking around in the woods?" He put his hands on his hips, his legs spread wide. He was either intimidating or attractive or maybe both. Should I come clean and say I was following a wacky old woman?

"I heard that the tests came back positive on your equipment for human blood and tissue." I hugged myself.

He frowned. "We have safeguards in place when it comes to working around such dangerous equipment. I have no idea how or when it happened." He ran his hand through his hair. "There's a six-foot fence enclosing the equipment. We keep the gate locked. None of it makes sense. But I've got a stop-work order on my entire crew."

"Oh, ouch." I cringed. "Spring is prime time for gardening."

"Gooseworthy is rubbing his hands in glee." Trent shook his head. "I've got to bury the entire pile of mulch and compost. People won't buy it if there is even a hint that body parts will be found in it. Not to mention Heather's family's grief. It's a mess."

"Wow, I hadn't thought of that. Do you have any idea how it happened?"

"That's what I'm doing now, walking the property and trying to figure out if the threat came from the outside or if one of my crew is a murderer." He scanned the woods behind me. "Speaking of murder, I thought you were supposed to be under house arrest over the death of the fudge maker."

The heat of embarrassment crawled up my neck and into my cheeks. "Um, right. I sort of got off track."

He tilted his head and studied me. "You came out to see if you could find clues to Heather's death, didn't you?"

"Okay, sure."

"The only reason you would be out here is if you think your fudge maker and Heather's deaths are related."

"Wouldn't that be awful?"

"And wildly convenient." Trent crossed his arms. "Did you find anything?"

"No." I let my shoulders slump. By now Mrs. Finch either realized I was following her or hadn't heard Trent and had continued on to wherever she was going. Either way, the jig was up. "I thought perhaps Tammy Gooseworthy was involved, but there is no proof. In fact, there is even less proof because your equipment was the murder weapon and Gooseworthy's wasn't."

Trent rubbed his chin. "Why did you suspect Tammy?"

"She and Heather were both up for the pastry chef position at the Grander Hotel." I walked back toward town. "Plus she's been hounding Peter and the producers to get on the reality show they're filming at the Grand Hotel."

Trent walked with me. "So she could possibly be the link for both murders."

"Right?"

"You might still have something to look into," he said

as we walked back to the road that leads to town and was the edge of the Jessop property.

"How so?"

"Gooseworthy stands to profit hugely from Heather's death. I've lost an entire year of profits."

"So Heather's disposal might have been intentionally done on your property."

"I'd hate to think anyone would be motivated enough to put a person—dead or, worse, alive—through one of our shredders. Turns my stomach to even contemplate it."

"I agree. Whoever did this needs to be found and found fast before anyone else gets hurt."

CHAPTER 30

"So," Jenn said, disgust on her face. "Tammy Gooseworthy is still our best suspect."

I stood in the hallway of my apartment in my white fluffy bathrobe and towel dried my hair. "Weird, right? Who has the kind of mind that would put a body through a shredder in the first place? But to think further and put it in your competitor's shredder? That's just creepier than I want to contemplate. It's why I had to come home and shower. The mere thought of that act had me feeling dirty all over."

"Are you sure that's what it is?" Jenn raised her right eyebrow and smiled knowingly. "Or did you and hunky Trent Jessop get a little too close in the woods?"

"Oh, stop it!" I shook my head.

"What? You're both healthy adults. He's hot and you've been celibate what . . . four months? Five? Shoot, if I were you, I would have seized the moment."

"Oh, right, I'm so sexy in my work clothes with an ankle bracelet marking me as a convict."

Jenn shrugged. "It marks you as a wild child—even more attractive and . . ."

"And what?"

"And"—she wiggled her eyebrows—"the idea that Rex Manning could come looking for you at any moment adds to the excitement."

"Oh, my goodness." I walked into my bedroom. "You read far too many novels."

"Well, did he at least ask you out?"

"No." I picked up a wide-toothed comb from my dresser top and ran it through my wet locks. "We were talking about the murder and mutilation of a young woman. Not exactly a time to be romantic."

Jenn plopped down on the edge of my bed, her long legs stretched out in front of her. She wore a pair of blue shorts and a white see-through blouse with small blue flowers printed on it. Under that she wore a blue tank top. Her skin was a lovely early tan color. Mine, in contrast, was still northern winter pale. "You are going to have to get up the nerve to ask someone out. These island guys are a bit slow. At this rate you could be dateless for a year before one of them worked up the nerve."

"What if it's not nerve they need to work up?" I grabbed a clean pair of black slacks out of my closet, slipped them on, and hung up my robe so that I stood in my bra. "What if they're seriously not interested?"

"What do you mean 'not interested'?" Jenn frowned at me. "I happen to know Trent and you . . ."

"That was for show." I grabbed a clean polo out of my dresser drawer and pulled it over my head. "Besides, my priority right now is the McMurphy."

"Right, that's why you're wearing an ankle bracelet and wandering through the Jessops' woods." She sat up straight. "Which, by the way, you never did tell me how you ended up out there."

"I was following Mrs. Finch."

"The old lady with the Saint Bernard?"

"Daisy, yes." I squeezed the ends of my hair with the towel one last time. "Mrs. Finch told Rex she was going to go home and get Daisy's leash and come back and rescue her baby."

"Okay." Jenn shrugged. "So how did you end up all the way on the other side of the island?"

"When I left the administration building I noticed that Mrs. Finch was walking in the opposite direction from her house."

"So you followed her."

I shrugged. "She was acting weird. Do you know she was part of a cult group that met on the island back in the early seventies?"

"What? Really? Like Scientology or something?"

"Something," I said and twisted my damp hair into a bun at the back of my neck. Then I sat down to put on makeup. It was three PM in the afternoon, and I had two fudge demonstrations scheduled for four and five PM, respectively. "She said that she doesn't need a leash to control Daisy. She commands her by her thoughts while in Transcendental Meditation."

"What? That's so weird. So she goes into a trance and orders Daisy home."

"Yes."

"Okay, now that is really bizarre. Does she wear like flowy clothes and mood rings and such?" Jenn's eyes lit up.

"No. She had on brown trousers and a white printed T-shirt."

"Oh, sad, then she's not outwardly like a Wiccan or psychic or any of that?"

"I don't know. Why—do Wiccans dress in a certain way?"

Jenn shrugged. "Some do. Some are just regular people who believe in the earth and the seasons and cycles of nature."

"Papa Liam used to love to tell ghost stories when we would sit around a bonfire. Did you know about the drowning pool?"

"No, what is that?"

"It's between Mission Point and downtown . . ." I paused in putting on foundation. "I hadn't thought of it in years but now that I mention it I realize that Mrs. Finch was headed in that direction."

"What direction? What drowning pool? You've been holding out on me."

I shook my head. "Back in the late 1700s, early 1800s, there was a hysteria movement on Mackinac and something like seven women were accused of being witches."

"No!"

"Right? Yep. Rocks were tied around their ankles and they were tossed into the drowning pool. Supposedly, if they sank they were innocent—if they floated they were witches and were to be hanged."

"Gruesome." Jenn shook her head.

"Right? Either way you were a dead person." I leaned into my mirror and put on mascara.

"Why were they accused?"

"Supposedly they were enticing unsuspecting soldiers, fur traders, and—get this—husbands into their houses."

"Oh my gosh." Jenn rolled her eyes. "So they killed off prostitutes by drowning them?"

"If they were even prostitutes," I said and put on a touch of lip gloss. "They might have simply been single women in a time when single women were not tolerated. Like you said, unless you take a vow of celibacy, you aren't going to abstain from sex."

"Okay, that's crazy."

I stood. "I can see it. Can't you? The so-called respectable women of the island had to get rid of this threat to their families. Or worse, one of the girls might have spurned an important member of the community and they cried witch."

"Creepy." Jenn stood with me. "So glad we live in the twenty-first century."

"Yeah, we only murder our rivals and shove their bodies in a chipper-shredder."

"Well, okay, if you put it that way, we really haven't advanced all that much, have we?"

"It's crazy." I shook my head. "What's on your plate? How are the plans for the second tea?"

"Plans are great," Jenn said and followed me out to the kitchen. "I've billed it as exclusive seating and now we could be double booked if we wanted."

"Great! How's Sandy doing with her sculptures?"

"She has created these wonderful horse-and-carriage pieces and is giving each table its own float design with samples of fudge inside."

"I'm glad she decided to work here," I said as we moved down the stairs. "I have no idea how good a chef Tammy Gooseworthy is, but my guess would be she can't beat the raw talent Sandy has."

"I'm glad you hired her, she's a real asset. What do you think about my going into business with Sandy? Between my party-planning skills, your hotel, and Sandy's chocolate sculptures, we could corner the wedding market."

"That may help our niche," I said. "What about the reality-television show?"

"Oh, I didn't get in." She waved her hand as if it was no big deal. "Which is fine, I don't want to have to pretend I can make fudge and worse, I didn't want to become a persona."

"Right?" I reached the bottom of the stairs. "What if we added another floor to the McMurphy? We could make it a ballroom here and we could host receptions, etc."

"It could really expand the business," Jenn said. "Can you afford it and will the historical society allow you to build it?"

"I could ask Mom and Dad if they want to invest in the McMurphy."

"Where is your mom?" Jenn asked. "I keep missing her today."

"She went to visit her old friends. She told me not to worry or wait up."

"Don't wait up—that sounds as if she has more than meeting friends in mind."

"What? No, this is my mother we're talking about." I shook my head. "She would never cheat on my father."

"Hmmm," Jenn said.

"What?"

"Why come all the way up here if she didn't have an agenda in mind?"

"That's what I asked her."

"What was her reply?" Jenn leaned in closer, and I lowered my voice.

"She thinks we're doing an okay job but she also thinks the McMurphy is simply a money pit."

"What? No!"

"Yes." I nodded.

"Well, then I wouldn't spring your new plans on her."

"What new plans?" My mom came in through the back door of the McMurphy. She had Mal on her leash. Mal ran to me.

I picked her up and gave her pets, then removed her halter and leash and hung them on the hall coat-tree. "Hi, Mom. Did you have a good time?"

"Yes."

"How were your friends?" Jenn asked.

"They were good," Mom said. "Now tell me what these plans are?"

"I don't have a full-fledged plan yet," I said. "I'll let you know when I decide I'm going to do it."

"Do what?"

I rolled my eyes. "It's not important."

"How can you say that? I thought you loved the McMurphy."

"I do love the McMurphy." I shook my head. "That's why I'm looking at all the options before I make my decision."

"Am I one of your options?" Mom asked. Today she wore old blue jeans and a soft striped blouse with the front ends tucked into her jeans.

"We're holding another tea the last day of the Lilac Festival," Jenn said. "Do you want to come? We can save you a seat. It's a dressy occasion and Sandy is making sculpted chocolate centerpieces. These works of candy art will be for sale the night of the event."

"Frances is making lilac-infused tea and I'll serve cucumber sandwiches and my lilac fudge."

"Sounds cute," Mom said. "Where are you holding this tea?"

"We've reserved space on the lawn at the base of the fort," I said.

"That seems a little awkward," Mom said and put her hands on her hips. "It's too bad the McMurphy doesn't have a ballroom or meeting rooms."

Jenn turned to me and gestured with her eyes for me to tell Mom. I shook my head no. "Yes, Mrs. McMurphy, it is a shame. There are a lot of events I could plan in a ballroom."

"Allie"—my mom touched my arm—"you should really consider adding on to the McMurphy. Perhaps after this first season."

"Mom, I already remodeled. I need to be in the black before I spend any more money."

"I can get your dad to pay for any additions you might want."

"No," I said and realized my tone was a tad sharp. "I already owe you and Dad for the remodel fees."

"Oh, please, honey," Mom said. "We have the money to help you. Why don't you let us?"

"Yes, Allie, why don't you let them?" Jenn echoed, and I gave her the stink eye.

"Because family loans come with expectations that a bank doesn't have."

"Like what?" Mom put her hands on her hips, and I inhaled sharply. I knew that look. She was about to fight to the death.

"I already owe you and Dad from my start-up costs," I said.

"You're paying us back."

"By mandatory visits and winters off island. How can I create a life here if I'm always off somewhere to please you?"

"This place is a family business," Mom said, waving her hands in the air. "That means the family is responsible—not just you."

"The more money you and Dad pour into the McMurphy, the bigger say you have in its fate."

"So?"

Jenn leaned over and stage-whispered, "If I were you, I'd quit while I'm ahead."

I did the grown-up thing and stuck my tongue out at her.

"Allie, really," Mom said. "Your father and I are as invested in the McMurphy as you are. We never would have sold it."

"But you don't want to live here and run it."

"That's right. I prefer my friends around me, but that doesn't mean we expect you to keep it going without family support. You have to think of it as family support."

"Tell her what you want to do next year," Jenn pushed.

"Fine, I was thinking about adding another floor. It would be set up as a ballroom and possibly have movable walls so that we can split it up into salons."

"That's interesting," Mom said. "Why not move the apartment up and turn the current apartment into a ballroom. Don't you want to keep the customers separate from you?"

"But that would destroy Grammy and Papa's home."

"You can't think of it like that," Mom said. "We'll get your father involved. He can come up here and get some measurements and look at the foundation. We have to ensure first that the foundation will take the weight of another floor."

"Then there's the historical society." I sat down in

front of the fireplace. "I'm certain any changes to the building will have to go through them."

"Of course." Mom tapped her mouth in thought. "You'll have to work with the society until they agree. I'm still considered a foreigner. I'll call your father and schedule for him to come up and take a look."

"Thanks, Mom," I said and put on the clean apron that hung from the coat hooks. "I've got to do a demonstration . . . Oh, wait, Mom?"

"Yes, dear?"

"Do you remember a cult on the island in the late sixties?"

"A cult? No. There was a group that tried to start a commune but the island zoning board would not zone the property they wanted."

"Why?"

"They would have had to clear-cut the woods to grow the gardens they talked about and then they wanted to raise goats and chickens and—I'll never forget this—the marina club put their considerable weight and cash behind leash laws and animal control. They couched everything as conservation. Also, they put a limit on the number of people per dwelling. I think it was something like only two people per every one bedroom in a home or business."

"Crazy."

"Funny, I hadn't thought of that in years." Mom shrugged. "I think there was another group that tried to get Wiccans to come up for the solstices and celebrate. But I'm not certain if that ever came together. Why all the questions?"

"Mrs. Finch said she doesn't need a leash to control her

Saint Bernard, Daisy. She uses Transcendental Meditation and thought control."

"Oh . . . dear."

"Right?" I shook my head. "Rex . . . er, Officer Manning, told me that Mrs. Finch used to be a member of a group of hippies. Do you remember if that's true?"

Mom shrugged. "That was a very long time ago. And most of the commune people were from off the island. I remember they held a sit-in protest, but soon found themselves sitting in on the ferry that carried them back to St. Ignace, where they found less resistance in the Upper Peninsula."

"Do you know where they wanted to put their commune?" I asked as I took off the dirty apron and put on a chef's coat then gathered the ingredients I would need for today's candy-bar fudge. This time I was making Almond Joy and Mounds fudge. The first would have a milk chocolate base and coconut and almonds. The other would have dark chocolate base fudge and contain only coconut.

"I think it was on the Lake Huron side between Mission Point and downtown. Why?"

"I followed Mrs. Finch from town, but lost her in some deep woods on the other side of Jessop's Compost and Mulch. I'll have to see if there is a building there or not."

"If there is, then it has been registered to the island planning authority."

"I can't leave the building. At least not until this bracelet is off."

"I'll go," Jenn said. "I want to see Shane anyway."

"Okay." I measured out the chocolate, the cream, and the sugar.

"What am I looking for?"

"Anything that might explain where Mrs. Finch was going and what she was going to do."

"That's a tall order from some dry zoning papers."

"I suppose I could try Zillow, but they only list what properties are for sale and what their list price is . . . I'm not certain that information will help."

"You make fudge." Jenn swept the air toward me. "I'll go dig around in the public records. I promise to let you know the minute I find anything that might suggest what Mrs. Finch is up to."

"Thanks!"

CHAPTER 31

"You are very good at that," Mom said. It was Wednesday and the shop had emptied of the crowd that always gathered when I did a demonstration.

"Thanks," I said as I scrubbed dishes. "A good demonstration can draw them in to buy like a carnival barker. Only, I don't think I'm selling snake oil." I shrugged. "Half the draw is to see how the candy is made."

"I remember how your grandfather loved to do a demonstration because he could get quite a crowd to form while he told his stories." Mom sat on one of the stools just inside the tiled area that separated the fudge shop from the hotel. "Your father says that that kind of storytelling is classically Irish."

I laughed at that. "You know, sometimes I feel as if I'm channeling Papa Liam. I'll start off talking about the fudge and before I know it, I'm telling one Mackinac Island story after another. Thank goodness the fudge cools at a certain rate. It gives me a natural timer. When the fudge is done and samples are ready to go out, the story is over."

"Your Papa was quite the character." Mom shook her

head. "I'll never forget the first time I met him. He was all gruff and bushy but underneath was this warm teddy-bear heart."

"How are you and Dad doing?" I asked as I rinsed the copper kettle I'd been scrubbing.

"What do you mean?"

"It can't have been easy for Dad to lose his dad and you to lose Papa as well. We never talked about it. I was all caught up in getting my stuff together to open the place in time for the season. I didn't think of you and Dad."

Mom smiled. "There's the woman I raised."

I gave her a quizzical look.

"The woman I raised thinks about her family and her friends and sees beyond the end of her nose."

I felt the heat of a blush rush up my neck. I tried to cover it by concentrating on the dishes.

"Your father has his moments," Mom said. "Grief may have stages but everyone experiences them in different ways and in different order."

"What about you?" I asked as I wiped down the counters and the marble cooling block.

"I underestimated Liam's role in my life," she said. "When my parents died, he was right there taking up the space in my life, lessening my grief."

A thought occurred to me. "Your parents died the summer I was ten. I remember Papa and Grammy coming to the funeral and whisking me away to stay the summer with them. That was the year I decided I wanted to keep up the McMurphy tradition. I guess I thought by taking on the McMurphy I could keep my grandparents always with me."

"That's how family traditions get started," Mom said.

"They are created to heal the grief we experience when we lose someone so close to us."

"Why are you here, Mom? Are you and Dad okay?"

"Your father needed some time alone." She ran her manicured fingers along the edge of the class counter, then looked up. "You're the only person I have to go to."

My stomach lurched into my throat. I dropped my dishcloth and went straight to her and hugged her tight. "I love you, Mommy."

She put her head on my shoulder, and tears welled up and spilled over. I held her and patted her back. I noticed that people looked in the windows with concern. "Come on," I said. "Let's go upstairs."

I kept my arm around her slender shoulders and sent Frances a look that asked her to cover the fudge shop. She nodded and mouthed, "Is everything okay?"

I nodded and bundled Mom into the elevator.

"I'm sorry, I didn't mean to do this," Mom said when we got off the elevator and I opened the apartment door. I headed straight to the tissue box and pulled her out a couple of tissues.

She took them and blew her nose. "I don't know what came over me."

"How about grief?" I asked. "Please have a seat. I'll get us some water." I hurried into the kitchen, pulled down two tall glasses, and filled them with ice and filtered water. I turned to see Mom had taken a seat on the barstools that went with the breakfast bar that separated the kitchen from the living area.

"Here." I passed her a glass of water, keeping the bar between us to give her some space. She sipped the water and dabbed at her cheeks with a clean tissue from the box.

"Well, I had no idea that was going to happen," Mom said when she had gotten control of herself. "I know you think I didn't like Liam or the McMurphy or even the island. But that's simply not true."

"I believe you," I said, my heart squeezing. "What's going on with Dad?"

"He's really taking Liam's passing hard." Mom paused and played with the condensation on her glass. She looked at me. "He regrets not doing what you're doing and being a part of Liam's day-to-day life."

"But Dad always wanted to be an architect, right?"

"Yes," Mom said. "It was a point of contention with them. Your father felt so much guilt in disappointing Liam. I made the decision to help them figure out their relationship."

It hit me then what had really happened. "You told Dad you didn't like the island."

"Yes." Mom blew out a long breath. "I took away the decision. As long as I was the bad guy, your father could accept the great job in Detroit and your grandfather could accept that his son wasn't going to go into the family business."

"Oh, Mom." I went around and hugged her. "You know you don't have to keep up the ruse anymore."

"I know, but your father's at the stage of grief when he's blaming me. He feels that if he only took on the fudge shop Liam would have had less stress and would be here today."

"But that's not true—"

"We know." Mom patted my hand. "He knows. He simply needed some room to work out the feelings. We all know that emotions take time to settle."

"That's why you jumped on putting money into the

McMurphy. Here I thought you and Dad didn't trust me to make good decisions."

"Life isn't always all about you," Mom said. "It's something I need to remind myself of every now and then."

"As long as you don't want me to build a second apartment for you to move into, I think we'll be all right," I teased.

"What? You don't want me in your hip pocket telling you how best to run your life?"

"Um, no, thanks. I love you but . . . no."

We both laughed, and I suddenly understood that sometimes you need each other even when you want to be independent. Family is a tricky thing to navigate, but that's a universal thing.

CHAPTER 32

"Allie McMurphy?"

"Yes?"

"Peter Thomas is awake."

"Really? I'll be right there." I dropped everything and left the McMurphy in Frances's capable hands, the fudge shop in Sandy's more than capable hands, and I caught the first ferry off the island.

I stood on the top deck and watched the mainland grow bigger and bigger. Rex Manning stood beside me. "You know he has to speak to the authorities first," he said. "Usually when they wake up from a coma they get tired very quickly. You may be going all this way and not get to see him."

"That's a chance I'll take," I said and tightened my hands on the guardrail. It was one of those perfect days when the sun is brilliant, the lake is calm, and the air is that combination of summer warmth, low humidity, and soft breeze caused by the movement of the boat. It smelled of fresh water and clean ozone. The sound of the motor roared behind us as we danced along the top of the surf.

"Thanks for taking off the bracelet," I said. I'd met Rex at the pier, and he'd removed my ankle bracelet before I'd gotten on the boat. Thankfully, he'd agreed that I no longer needed to wear it.

"I've noticed that since they cast Tammy as a replacement the assaults stopped," Rex said. "It doesn't make any sense to have you as a suspect. I've got permission from the judge to drop the charges."

"Great, but that still doesn't prove Tammy had anything to do with Cathy's death," I said. I hadn't had any time to change, so I wore my usual uniform of black slacks and pink polo with the McMurphy logo embroidered on the front left.

"My hope is that Peter will remember something that will help me bring the perpetrator to justice."

"What about Heather's death? Do you know anything more?"

"I can't discuss an ongoing investigation with you, Allie. You know that, right?"

"Yes," I said and looked away from his pretty blue gaze. "I know, I just forget."

"Hey, you two," Liz came up the steps to the top deck. "I guess we all got the call about Chef Thomas."

"I've put in a strict order that no press be allowed near Chef Thomas."

"Oh, Rex, you are such a buzzkill." Liz shook her head. Her dark curls blew riotously in the wind. "I'm not going to interview the man. I'm going to interview the hospital staff and his family. A girl has to do her job."

At the Mackinaw City docks Rex had a ride waiting for him in the form of the local police cruiser. I had paused to call a cab.

"Do you want a ride?" Liz asked as she approached a

dark blue Ford truck. The truck looked like it had been in use for almost twenty years and had seen the very worst the weather and the lake could throw at it.

"Sure."

She unlocked the passenger door with her key and then ran around the front to climb in the driver's seat as I climbed inside. It smelled of old vinyl and dust. The interior was done in dark gray. A hula girl bobble figure sat on the dash swinging her hips. Liz started the truck up and put it into reverse. "It's not pretty but it's functional," Liz said as she peeled out and followed the police cruiser. "I wanted a brand-new car, but my father wanted to know why. So I said what any teen would say because, you know, I knew better. I wanted the coolest shiny sports car because it was awesome and everyone would be my friend and look twice when I drove around."

"Was it a little red sports car?"

"Close—it was an awesome blue Camaro. I worked for four years to save up my money for a down payment. I bought it, paid my insurance, and then parked it in the lot and took the ferry back to the island. I felt so amazingly proud of my accomplishment. A week later I caught the ferry back to the mainland to do some shopping and generally bum around in my cool ride."

"Let me guess—someone had scratched it." Parking lots were notorious for scratching cars.

"Even better, I got there and the car was gone."

"Gone? As in stolen?"

"Stolen. You see, I used up all my money on gas and insurance. I didn't pay the extra to park the car in a locked parking space. Someone else had seen my cool ride and decided to make it theirs."

"What did you do?" I asked.

"I filed a report and my insurance covered a third of the money I'd invested." She turned the car right, keeping a respectful distance from the cop car. "I kept checking the police blotter for any word on my stolen car. A week or two went by and I knew my car was most likely gone for good. That's when I put my money down on old Bertha here." Liz patted her dash. "She runs like a nice quiet top, but no one would know that looking at her. She's so old there isn't even a need for parts from her."

"I get it. No one wants to steal the old battered Ford."

"Exactly. If they need parts that bad they simply drive through the country and pick one that the owner has sitting out in the field." She turned again, and the hospital came into view. "Lesson learned. I never again asked Angus for a brand-new car."

"I haven't had a car since I left Detroit. In Chicago there was public transportation. Between the 'L' and the Metra and the bus system, it simply wasn't worth paying the extra for parking."

"And now you live on the island, which has a no-car rule."

"Exactly." I nodded. "I don't miss it. Although I do make sure I drive at least forty hours every six months. I need to keep my skills up. You simply never know when you may need a vehicle."

"You should get a truck like Bertha here." She patted the dash. "All I keep on her is liability insurance. She's so old that if she ever got hit she would be totaled. If she got stolen there wouldn't be that much to replace."

"Good idea," I said. We turned into the hospital parking lot. The car Rex was in stopped at the entrance, and he hopped out. I waited for Liz to park before I tore off my seat belt and hurried to the door.

"Whoa, little lady." A man in a security uniform stopped me. "Where are you going in such a big hurry?"

"I'm here to visit my friend," I said. "I was told he finally woke up from a coma. Please, I need to see him."

"Let me see your ID," he demanded. I caught a glimpse of Rex and another officer turning down a hallway.

"Here, it's me," I said as I produced my driver's license.

"Are you wearing glasses?"

"I have contacts now," I said as he compared the bad picture to my face.

"You look like you've gained some weight," the security guard said and bared his teeth. "Are you still living in Chicago?"

"No, I live on Mackinac Island. I haven't had the opportunity to change my address yet."

"Come on, what's the hold up?" Liz asked. She had her press ID on a lanyard around her neck.

"My ID is out of date."

"Oh, for goodness sake." Liz rolled her eyes, snagging my ID out of the security guard's hand. "She's also press," she said as she hung an ID around my neck. "Now let us go through."

"Okay," he said, "but I've got my eye on you."

"Look—no weapons." Liz held my hands up and pushed me through the security weapons detector. She then raised up her hands and grinned as she walked through the metal detector.

"Wow, that was interesting," I said as she dragged me down the hall.

"My sources said he was in room 226."

I followed Liz down the hall and to the right and up a

half a flight of stairs. We ended up in a large open foyer that was mostly empty. We didn't stop when we approached the nurse's desk.

"Peter Thomas wanted to see us," Liz said.

"He's in 226 around the corner," the nurse said.

We rushed on by the nurses' station to find a room with a policeman stationed at the door.

"Peter Thomas?" I asked the officer.

"Yes," he looked at me suspiciously. "Are you related?"

"He's a very dear friend. The nurses contacted me to let me know he was awake."

"According to his daughter he is not supposed to see anyone but her."

"What's your name? Officer Mede? Why are you here?" Liz took out her recorder and asked him point-blank: "Is Mr. Thomas under arrest or is this police protection because you fear for his life?"

The officer stiffened at the verbal onslaught. "I'm here to guard Mr. Thomas's door to ensure that no one but police and family members go inside. If that means I'm protecting him from a killer then that's what it means. If it means Mr. Thomas is a suspect and I'm here to ensure he does not leave, then that's what it means."

"Nice vague answer."

"Who's your boss? Where can I speak to him?" I asked and crossed my arms.

"Here's my card," he said and took two business cards out of his breast pocket. "You can call that number and they might be able to help you."

"Huh, a cop with a business card," Liz said and read it front and back. "I've got a phone call to make." She took off down the hall so that she could use her cell phone in the stairwell.

"Look, I got a phone call from the nursing staff letting me know Peter was asking for me."

"That is new information to me and contradicts what I've been told. I can't help you. Right now it's hearsay that they called you. If you can provide me with proof . . ."

The door to the room opened, and Rex popped his head out. "Good, you're here, come inside." He grabbed me by the arm and pulled me past the officer. I gave the guard the stink eye and went inside with Rex.

Inside was a cool, antiseptic room with white sheets and blankets on the bed. Machines surrounded Peter with the whirring sounds of pumps as they dialed up dosages of painkiller and IV fluid. There was a heart monitor beeping. Peter looked ten years older, and my heart broke.

His short black hair was flat on one side and stuck up on the other. His face was misshapen from the beating he took. The bruises had spread out to cover nearly every inch of exposed skin. He wore a standard hospital gown with multicolored polka dots on the material. He faced away from the door.

"Talk to him," Rex suggested in a low voice. "He's not responsive to me. Perhaps he'll be better with you."

"Is he awake?" I asked, my eyebrows drawn together in concern.

"Yes," Rex said, "but not responsive."

There was a young woman in the room. She had Peter's blue eyes and thick black hair She wore jeans and a pale peach blouse that showed off her beautiful even-toned skin. She had high cheekbones that would be the envy of models all over the world.

"Hi, I'm Allie McMurphy." I held out my hand.

"I'm Constance Thomas," she said and shook my hand. Both of us spoke in low tones. "Thanks for having them call me the day they found him."

"You're welcome," I said, at a loss for words. "I knew you were important to him and he would want you here. Is your mom here?"

"They're separated. She's off with her new boyfriend in Belize."

"Oh, I didn't know."

She shrugged. "He doesn't talk about it."

"How's Peter doing?"

"He comes and goes still," she said. "I'm hoping that your visit will help to pull him back into the world."

"I'll see what I can do." I went over to the side of the bed and reached down to touch Peter's hand. "Hey, it's me, Allie. You gave us quite a scare."

Peter slowly turned his head and winced at the movement. I lightly stroked his hand in comfort. "Allie," he said, his voice raw and whispery. "You came."

"The minute they told me you were awake," I said and squeezed his hand gently.

"You called Connie."

"Yes, I knew you would want her here and she would want to be here." I grew silent when he closed his eyes. His fingers loosened slightly, and I didn't want him to slip back. "Peter," I said his name and squeezed his hand.

He opened his eyes. "I'm so tired."

"It's because you're healing and they have you on pain medication."

He licked his lips and swallowed. "What happened? Was it a car accident?"

"You don't remember?" I glanced at Rex, who frowned.

"You were on Mackinac Island. You stayed at the Grand along with the cast and crew of your . . ."

"Reality series," he finished weakly. "Yes, now I remember that part. Can't be a car accident. There are no cars on Mackinac."

"Right." I smiled, encouraging him. "We were shooting until midnight."

"Was it a final episode?"

"No." I shook my head. "No—remember, they had us shoot another contest with only you as judge?"

"Cathy . . . Cathy Unger is dead."

"Yes," I said, relieved that some of his memory returned. "We had thought they were going to do a hometown shoot for each remaining candidate, but they decided to get one more contest shoot in."

"I remember thinking you were brilliant," he said. "I went to the producers about changing the story line so that you could remain."

That surprised me. I blinked fast. "I told you I didn't want to do a full season."

He closed his eyes for a moment. "You deserve the title and the prize money."

I felt him drift off again, and for the second time I squeezed his hand. "Peter, who hurt you?"

"What?" he croaked, his eyes rolling open.

"Who did this to you?"

"I don't know. It was dark. I stumbled into them. They covered my head with something. I fought to breathe. They had a bat."

"They? Were there more than one?"

"Yes," he said so soft I had to lean in to hear him. "Front and back."

"That's enough for now." A young female in a doctor's

jacket walked into the room. "He needs to rest. There's coffee in the waiting area down the hall."

I looked at Rex. "There was more than one attacker."

"I got that." His mouth was a thin line. His gaze flat. "His wounds are consistent with a bat. He's short but solid. It had to be at least two to take him down."

"Any idea who it is?" I asked.

"Can't say."

"Can't say or won't say?" I asked as we walked out, leaving Constance with Peter.

Rex turned his angry gaze on me. "Either way, I don't like to see this kind of abuse on my island. If you'll excuse me, I've got some phone calls to make."

I watched him storm off. Liz came down the hall and stopped by me, her gaze on the hard expression on Rex's face. "Whoever did this is going to be in a world of hurt."

"When he's done with them it will be my turn."

"Is that a fact?" Liz asked, her pen and paper ready.

"That is a fact."

CHAPTER 33

"You're contractually obligated to finish shooting the reality show," Caroline said on the phone. "So get your bum over here."

"Peter is awake. I promised I'd stay with him."

"Look, it's great he's awake and such but that doesn't mean you can skate out of your shoot. If I have to, I will call our lawyers. This time they won't be defending you."

"What about the new cast? Haven't you been shooting with new people?"

"The producers hated the reshoot. We have to go with the cast we have and that means you."

I glanced at my phone for the time. "It's seven PM."

"And the ferries are making a couple more runs. Get your lovely self back here or you will be fined ten thousand dollars per episode delayed."

"Fine," I frowned. "When does shooting start?"

"Nine—and this time don't be late. I don't care if your mom is dying or your right hand needs stitches. Am I making myself clear?"

"Clear as crystal," I said and hit END. I had been sitting on the chair in the corner of Peter's room so that I would be there if he woke up asking for me again. When my phone rang, I'd stepped out. The scowls from the nursing staff and the points to the posted sign regarding cell phones had pushed me out into the stairwell.

I walked back to the room's doorway and looked inside. Constance sat in the seat closest to Peter. She looked exhausted. I had thought I could sit with Peter while she took a nap, but it wasn't meant to be. She glanced up, and I waved her out to the hall.

"Is everything all right?" she asked.

"I have to go. Caroline called me back to do the next shoot and threatened to sue me if I don't show."

"Caroline is a jerk."

"Can I do anything for you before I go?"

"No, go. Dad's most likely to sleep through the night. I'll call you if he remembers anything."

"I hate that I can't stay."

She gave me a weak smile. "Go find out who did this to him. Okay?"

"I trust Officer Manning." I patted her. "If anyone can figure this out, he can."

"That's something, right?"

"Right. If he remembers anything, please call, okay?"

"I will." She hugged me, and I left her standing in the hall, cold artificial light flickering above her. The policeman who had stopped us earlier now stood beside her, his expression flat. There was no telling what he really thought. Not that it mattered. What mattered now was that Peter got well and no one got past the cops to hurt him.

Krispy Krunchy Fudge

3 cups of sugar
Dash of salt
⅔ cup of cocoa powder
1½ cups of milk
¼ cup butter
1 teaspoon vanilla
2 cups crisp rice cereal

Prepare an 8" x 8" x 2" pan—butter pan, cover the inside
with parchment paper or wax paper. Butter the paper and
set the pan aside.

In a large, heavy saucepan mix sugar, salt, cocoa powder,
and milk. Stir over medium heat until the ingredients
reach a full boil. Let boil unstirred until a candy thermometer reads 125°F or the soft-ball stage is reached.
Remove from heat.

Add butter and vanilla—do not mix. Cool until the thermometer reads 110°F, then beat until fudge thickens
and just begins to lose its gloss. Quickly add cereal, mix,
and pour into prepared pan. Cool completely. Cut into
1" pieces. Enjoy!

CHAPTER 34

"You talked to Chef Thomas?" Austin, my stylist, asked as he handed me my clothes for the episode.

"Yes," I said and went behind the curtain to change. I had ten minutes for hair and makeup before I would be expected to be on my X and ready for another crazy episode.

"How is he?"

"He looks like a bad banana. I've never seen a human being so bruised." I pulled on the jean skirt and shoved my arms into the pale pink camp shirt. I stepped out while I buttoned it.

"Did he tell you anything?" Austin asked. "Do you know who did it?"

"Yeah, I can't say. That would hurt the investigation."

"Oh, right, of course." He walked me over to hair and makeup. "Let's give her a ponytail and sweetheart makeup. She's very close to winning this thing and we want viewers to want her to win."

"I thought they liked to champion underdogs," I said as I sat in the black chair in front of a mirror surrounded by lights so bright I could see every pore on my skin.

"They do," he said. "And who better than a girl wrongly accused of murder? We're going to add some biting comments about you being let back into the competition. While you were under house arrest we shot some confession scenes."

"Wait until you see tonight's helpers," Justine, my makeup artist, said. "It will be shocking."

"Okay." I felt confused. "Why would I be shocked?"

She stopped with her hands full of makeup and brushes. "If I told you that you wouldn't give them a proper reaction."

Fabulous, I thought. Who could possibly be a shocking helper? I suppose my mother would be one. That thought made me laugh.

"Hold still," she scolded. "I need to get your eyeliner right."

I schooled my expression and concentrated on sending Peter good thoughts. Five minutes later I was pushed through the hall to the kitchen set where I took my mark behind the fudge cooling tables.

"What are you doing here?" Erin hissed at me.

I looked around to see it was only me, Erin, and Tim. "Where is everyone else?"

"This is it," she stage-whispered. "This is the final show."

"What?"

"While you took your house-arrest break we shot two episodes."

"Wait." I raised my hand. "Excuse me. Am I supposed to be here?"

The director turned toward me. "Yes. Take your mark."

I watched as the cameras panned the group. Clearly

the remaining contestants were not happy to see me standing beside them.

"For the finale, you will have an hour to make four original fudges and create a display for tonight's fund-raiser for the Women and Children's Center," the director read from a paper. We stood and listened as if the host were narrating. "To aid you in this endeavor, each of you will be given a team of three."

The teams were sent in. They consisted of the voted-off contestants. I was given the two men who were voted off the same day I was berated for being late. They did not look happy being a part of my team. Tony had his arms folded, and Jabar stared at me through narrowed eyes.

"What?" I stage-whispered.

"You killed Cathy," Tony stated. "You should know she was practically a sister to us."

"I did not kill Cathy," I said and got hushed by the director's assistant.

"Right. Don't expect to win this," came the rumbled threat from Tony.

"Each team will be given a handyman to create the appropriate displays."

At this point three handsome men in plaid shirts, jeans, and work boots entered. They wore tool belts on their hips. It was then that I noticed one of the handymen looked familiar. He had sun-streaked hair, brilliant blue eyes, and that I-can-do-push-ups-with-one-hand physique. Officer Polaski gave his head a short shake indicating to me not to say anything.

He took his place as my team's handyman.

"Contestants, sixty minutes has been put on the clock. On your mark, get set, go!"

The other two teams sprang into action. I turned to the first of the big guys. "Tony, Cathy told me you made the Swiss cheese garnish. Can you make fudge?"

"I'm not doing anything for you."

I swung to Jabar. "Can you make a fudge base?"

He stared at me in sullen silence. "Okay," I said as the camera was shoved in my face. "Looks like it's just me making fudge." I went to work quickly preparing a dark chocolate base that I would use to create three classic candy-bar flavors.

"Can I give you design details while I make the fudge base?" I asked Brent. His shirt had the name "Mike" embroidered on it. "Um, Mike?"

"Yeah, okay." Officer Polaski picked up a pad of paper and pulled a pencil out from behind his ear. "What do you want?"

"The fund-raiser is for the women and children's center on island," I spoke out loud while I measured sugar, dark cocoa, and water into the largest copper kettle I could find. "What makes Mackinac Island special is the beautiful parks, the bicycle trails, and horse carriages," I muttered. "Can you make an old-fashioned bike with the superlarge wheel in the front? You know the kind from the 1800s?"

"Okay—like this?" He dashed off a few lines and the image of an old-fashioned big-wheeled bike became visible on the pad.

"Wow, you're good." I met his gaze, and he let me know that I wasn't supposed to know who he was. "But you're a handyman, so you should be good. Yes, that's perfect. Can we get maybe a couple of baskets on the sides so we can fill the display with fudge and lilacs?"

"Got it." He put the pencil back behind his ear. "I'll get started on it right away."

"Great, thanks." Brent went off stage to make the display. I stirred my fudge until it boiled long enough to reach soft-ball stage.

I noticed that the other two contestants had people making three separate fudge bases on my right and cutting up add-in ingredients on the left.

Meanwhile, my two "helpers" stood grim watch over me like a pair of angry genies.

"I thought Cathy said you two were nice guys," I muttered.

"Did you hear something?" Jabar asked Tony.

"Something buzzing like a mosquito," Tony replied.

"We should squish it if it gets too close."

"Really?" I put my hands on my hips. "Really? This is how you're going to play this?"

Neither said a word.

I shook my head and poured the chocolate base on the cooling table and started talking as I folded and cooled it. "My Papa Liam McMurphy made fudge demonstrations a true entertainer's art. He would fold the fudge in long streams and create art outlines in the air as he told his story. One of my favorite stories was a take on the old Henny Penny story. Do you know that story?"

I glanced up, but all I saw were folded arms and unsmiling faces. "I see that you need to hear this story. There once was a little rabbit who said to her friends, 'Wouldn't it be wonderful if we shared carrot fudge?'"

I tossed the cooling fudge in the air and created the outline of bunny ears that fell back to the table as I talked and scraped and folded. "'Who's going to get the carrots?' Little bunny asked." I tossed the outline of a carrot. "All of bunny's friends had things to do and were too busy to gather carrots. So little bunny did. 'Who's going to peel the carrots?' bunny asked. Again all her friends were busy. So little bunny peeled the carrots." Again I tossed the outline of a carrot. "'Who is going to get the cocoa and the sugar and the milk?' bunny asked. Again every one of her friends was too busy to gather the other ingredients. So little bunny did."

I noticed how the cameras were focused on me and Papa's story. "Little bunny was getting tired of doing everything herself. So she asked her friends, 'Who is going to cook the fudge?' But no one had the time to cook the fudge. So little bunny did." I outlined a spoon with the twist of my wrist. The fudge was growing thicker, and I hurried my story. "When the fudge was cooked, little bunny asked, 'Who is going to cool the fudge?' Again no one had the time to cool the fudge. Finally, a sad little bunny added carrots to her fudge."

I separated the base into three parts. For the first part I sprinkled crispy rice and caramel pieces on the top of the cooling fudge and carefully folded it in to create a crunch-bar fudge. On the middle piece I added peanuts and caramel for a Snickers-bar fudge, and on the third part I added coconuts and almonds for an Almond Joy fudge.

"Finally, it came time to cut and serve the fudge. Little bunny asked, 'Who will cut and serve the fudge?' No one volunteered, and so bunny cut and plated her own fudge."

I sliced up the fudge into the appropriate piece count and placed each piece in a tiny paper cup the color of a Reese's candy holder. I kept talking as I worked quickly. "When little bunny's friends gathered to eat the fudge she reminded them, 'Who gathered the carrots?' 'You did, little bunny.' 'And who cut the pieces?' 'You did, little bunny.' 'Who gathered the other ingredients and cooked the fudge and cooled the fudge and folded and cut the fudge?' 'You did, little bunny.' 'Ah yes, so I did. And who is going to eat the fudge?'"

I paused and let the silence draw out. "'That's right,' said little bunny. 'I am going to eat the fudge.' And so she did, giving none to anyone who didn't want to help."

"That's a stupid story," said Jabar. "There's no way you can eat all that fudge."

"In the end," I said, "all the viewers will know who deserved to win the fudge challenge."

For the final type of fudge I created pourable chocolate fudge and used it to coat fresh popped popcorn, then added peanuts to the mix and cut it up into a chocolate version of Cracker Jack fudge.

By this time Brent came in pushing the bicycle display. He stayed to help me fill the display with plated fudge as the audience started the countdown of "Five . . . four . . . three . . . two . . . one."

"Time's up."

I put my last piece of fudge on the display and put my hands in the air. A quick look around showed everyone on set with their hands in the air.

"Team members, thank you for your help. You may now leave the kitchen."

My team was the first to leave. I noted that Brent hung back and watched as the team helpers left the studio to go to the greenroom and await word of the winner.

The other two finalists explained their fudge choices and displays. The man had a baseball diamond display and made classic ball-game fudges—including a hot dog–inspired fudge and a nacho-inspired fudge. I gave the guy points for originality. The other woman had a big birthday cake display with balloons. Her fudges included vanilla cake batter flavored with sprinkles, red-velvet fudge, and German chocolate fudge with pecan and co-conut frosting. My teeth hurt looking at her sweets.

It came time for me to explain my fudges. "I created an old-fashioned bicycle display because bicycles are iconic to Mackinac Island."

"Why the big-wheel bike?" the director asked.

"Because it recalls nostalgic Victorian times, also a hallmark of Mackinac Island. I then chose to create candy-bar fudges because candy bars and Cracker Jacks are all served on the boardwalks where summer and bi-cycles meet."

The director dismissed me so that he could have the surprise judge do the taste test and judge on presentation, variety, and taste.

I walked to the greenroom, where they had a camera set up to capture us waiting and sweating out our final judgment.

"Good job, you two," I said and shook their hands. "Your displays and fudge varieties were truly lovely."

"Thanks," Mark said.

"How do you feel?" I asked Erin.

"I think I could win," she said and sat back. "My fudges speak of the wonder of childhood."

"And you?" I asked Mark.

"There's nothing more iconic than baseball on a summer afternoon," he said. "With my savory fudges I'm pretty sure I won this hands down."

"Wait, savory fudge is not something little kids will eat," Erin said. "I think mine is better."

"I disagree," Mark said. They stood and went toe-to-toe for a while. The camera guy ate it up, sticking the camera into their faces to show the emotion on their faces as fingers pointed back and forth and faces turned red and arguments turned heated.

I moved away from the fight scene, disappointed with what they called good television these days. While I was scooting away from the other two finalists and the camera guy, something caught my eye as out of place.

Tilting my head, I looked again and saw what looked like the handle of a baseball bat sticking out from the skirt of a table that was set up with food and beverages for the cast and crew. Was I seeing things? Was Peter's story going through my mind? I mean, who would bring a bat on set? And who would be silly enough to leave it lying around if they used it on someone?

I went over and got down on the floor to take a closer look. Lifting the skirt to the table, I saw there were a number of boxes under there containing a croquet set, a volleyball set, and bats and gloves for softball.

"What are you doing?" Brian asked.

"Oh." My heart rate picked up. It was a bit like being caught with your hand in the cookie jar. "I dropped . . ."

"What? Did you lose a contact or something?"

"That's it," I said and pretended to feel around on the floor near the table. "Don't move."

"Surely you wear disposables." He tapped his toe.

"Wait! Found it." I sat back on my heels and pretended to put in the contact. I batted my eyes a couple of times and then stood. "Much better. Strange how contacts still pop out sometimes."

He gave me a narrow-eyed stare. "Go sit down on your mark."

"Right." I scurried over and took my seat on the waiting

couch where we pretended to be on pins and needles over who would be the winner. For a moment I contemplated whether it would be Mark or Erin who won. Neither one had made friends or real enemies on set so I guess it didn't matter who won.

"The judge will see you now," the call went out, and we rose and shuffled out the door. I paused at the open door and asked Caroline, the ever-vigilant director's assistant, a question. "What's with all the sports equipment under the table?"

"Oh, the producers wanted to hold a wrap picnic instead of a party. They felt it would be great for the show to highlight the lawns and atmosphere on the island."

"Huh, nice idea."

"Thanks," she nodded. "It was mine."

"Of course it was," I muttered, then asked, "has that equipment always been under there?"

"I've been adding to it every day I get to the mainland."

"Did you get bocce ball?" I added when she appeared to wonder at my questions. "I understand it's a great lawn game."

"Thanks, I'll look for it."

"Allie McMurphy is wanted on set ASAP!" The call came down the hallway, and I scurried off to find out my reality-show fate.

CHAPTER 35

"So, who won?" Jenn asked when I dragged myself home at two AM . . . Thursday.

"What are you doing up at this time of night?"

"Couldn't sleep." Jenn stood in my galley kitchen and stirred a small pot of hot cocoa. She wore a silky night-shirt and matching robe.

"Is that real cocoa?" I sat my weary bum on the barstool and leaned against the counter.

"Yes, I saw you hadn't come home yet. I figured we could both use something to help us sleep."

"You are awesome." I leaned my elbows on the counter-top and rested my chin in my hands.

"Did you win?"

"I can't tell you that," I chided. "By contract, I can't say a word. But I can tell you that I spoke to Peter today."

"How is he?"

"He looks horrible and doesn't remember a whole lot, but other than that, he's alive and mending."

"Did he remember who did it?" She poured the cocoa into two cups and passed a steaming cup on to me.

"No." I sipped. "He remembers having his head covered

and then being beaten. He thinks it was two men and he said it felt like they hit him with wood—like a baseball bat."

"Ouch." Jenn leaned against the counter and hugged her cocoa. "Two men? If they had a bat they could have killed him. Why didn't they finish the job?"

"That's a good question. I think whoever beat Peter wanted him out of the job, but not necessarily dead."

"Someone he knows then. Only someone who cared would say when to stop."

"Something else," I said. "I discovered a series of lawn games in the greenroom under the table. Among the things were baseball bats, softballs, and gloves."

"Did you tell Rex?" she asked. "They could test the bats for residue or something, couldn't they?"

"I don't know. You're the one dating the science guy."

"I'll ask Shane in the morning."

I sipped my warm chocolate. "How's the work going for the last Lilac Festival tea?"

"We're ready to make it quite the bash. I've got tents to be set up in the park at the foot of the fort. We've asked everyone to wear eighteen-nineties dress. I even have costumes from the Old Tyme Photography shop for those who don't have a costume."

"Wow, sounds great. Is there music?"

"Yes, I've scored a three-piece orchestra to play classical pieces. You should see Sandy's centerpieces. They're works of art. I asked her if we could auction them off."

"Wait." I drew my eyebrows together. "Won't an auction disrupt the genteel tea setting you described?"

"A silent auction, silly. It will benefit the women and children's center and I think it will help Sandy get her chocolatier company going."

"I am proud to say the McMurphy sponsored you and Sandy with your new businesses. Just promise me you will never get involved in these reality shows. Deal?"

"Wait, what? But I'm ready for my close-up . . ." She framed her face in the old Vogue manner.

We both giggled. "Oh, now, it's so late we're getting slap-happy." I got off the stool and put my cup in the sink. "I've got to get up in a couple hours."

"I don't know how you are doing this," Jenn said. "You have to sleep sometime. Why don't you text Sandy and have her come in in the morning and take care of the fudge?"

"Yes," came my mom's voice from the hallway. She stepped out into the low light from the lamp over the kitchen sink. "You can't make fudge on this little sleep. . . . You're asking for disaster." Mom wore a silky housecoat in a floral pattern. Her face was bare from makeup and her hair was brushed back and hung to her shoulders.

She was a beautiful woman, one of those women who look better every year. My dad used to tease that she aged like a fine wine—better the longer it lived.

"I asked Sandy to cover me yesterday when I went to visit Peter. She's making centerpieces. She doesn't have time to cover for me."

"And if you get hurt then who will cover for you?" Mom hugged her waist. "Liam would have a fit if he knew you were making fudge on so little sleep."

I cringed. "Okay. Fine." I hated the idea of giving up control of the McMurphy even for a day or two. But Mom was right. The last thing I needed was to be so tired I caused an accident. Burns from boiling sugar were nothing to mess with.

"Good," Mom said. "You go to bed and get eight hours of steady sleep. I will contact Sandy at seven AM and open the fudge shop. You have enough fudge made that things will last until nine AM. I can handle the customers while Sandy makes the first two batches of fudge."

"Thanks, Mom," I said and kissed her cheek. "I'm lucky to have you still looking out for me."

"I'll remind you that you said that the next time you get mad at me for interfering."

Nine hours later I was up and dressed and drinking my first cup of coffee. The problem with getting a good night's sleep after surviving on only a few hours a night was that your brain didn't want to wake up. I stood groggy and crabby and clung to my cup of coffee as if it were the only lifeline to sanity.

There was a knocking at the back door. "Oh," I exclaimed as the sound startled me out of my groggy stupor. The apartment was four floors up, and the only way to get to the apartment's back door was to climb up the fire escape. I went to the door and moved the tiny linen curtain that covered the face-high square window.

"Hi, Allie, can I come in?" Rex stood in front of the window. The man was wearing his official uniform. Somehow it made him even more attractive.

I opened the door. "Why are you knocking on the back door?" I asked as he stepped in. A quick look out behind him showed the metal ladder for the fire escape was lowered. No one else was in the alley.

"I wanted to talk to you without the entire town knowing," he said. "Coffee smells good."

"Would you like a cup?"

"Thanks!"

I pulled a thick blue mug out of the cupboard and poured him the last cup from my French press. "We have fancy coffee downstairs in the coffee bar."

"This is great, thanks." He took the mug from me.

"What's up?" I asked.

"Where's your puppy?" He wandered into the living room.

"She's downstairs with Frances and my mother."

"Your mother's on the island?" He tilted his shaved head, his blue eyes laser bright. "I don't think I've met her."

"Please, I might be tired, but I'm not so tired to smell a redirect when one comes along. Why are you here, Rex?"

"I got word that you saw some yard games being stored on set that may—and I stress, may—have something to do with Peter Thomas's assault."

"Yes, it was the weirdest thing. I saw a bat shape sticking out from under the catering table in the greenroom. When I checked it out, I saw that there were three baseball bats, some gloves, and softballs. There were also more lawn games like croquet and horseshoes. When I asked about them I was told they were being gathered to hold an end-of-show picnic."

"Okay." He sat down on a stool and sipped his coffee.

"Peter said he was beaten by baseball bats . . ."

"That's correct. Is there any evidence that these were the bats used on him?"

"What do you mean by evidence?"

"Did you see blood on them? Smell bleach that could have been used to get rid of blood?"

My shoulders slumped in disappointment. "No. I thought you could get a warrant and check them out yourself."

His right eye twitched. "I wish it were that simple but we have to have just cause and a judge who believes that cause. If Mr. Thomas's wounds are indicative of a blunt instrument such as baseball bats, then if I find a bat near where he was wounded or in the possession of a suspect, then I can get my warrant and have Shane do his magic."

"If his wounds look like a blunt instrument? Did you see Peter?" I put my hands on my hips. "He didn't exactly run into a door."

"The medical examiner is going over the photos of his wounds along with the X-rays to make that determination."

"But Peter told you he was hit with baseball bats."

"Mr. Thomas said that they covered his head and then beat him with what he thought were baseball bats. Witnesses can be wrong."

"Okay, so if the medical examiner says Peter's wounds are consistent with his story, then will you check out the bats?"

Rex stuck his hands in his pockets. "It's never that easy. Just because you saw baseball bats under a table the same day that your friend said he thought he was attacked by baseball bats is not enough to get a warrant. I need a person attached to the bats and a motive attached to a person."

"Fine." I frowned. "Why did you stop by here? I know the McMurphy isn't on your usual route."

"I wanted to talk to you about the show," he said. "I hope you realize that Brent wasn't on there to be a carpenter."

"He did very well with the display piece," I said.

"It's a hobby of his. My condolences, by the way. These things never turn out the way you hope."

"Thanks." I sent him a partial smile. "It's nice that you know the outcome. I hate that we have to wait until the show airs before we can talk about it."

"Are you doing any promotion for the show?" he asked. "I understand that they connect you all with *Ellen* or *The Tonight Show* or one of those talk shows."

"That's up to the PR staff. Right now they're trying to book all the losers."

"Make sure they pay you well."

"Oh, I will," I said. "Did you ever figure out what was going on with Mrs. Finch?"

"What about Mrs. Finch? She finally gave up and came in with a leash and bailed out Daisy."

"Oh, um, good. Well, then that takes care of that."

He narrowed his eyes. "There's more to this story. Spill or I may have to ask Mrs. Finch what you know about her."

I cringed. "It's just that when she left the other day she said she was going home to get Daisy's leash."

"That's right. She came back later and picked Daisy up. I gave her the leash-law talk and told her she would be fined triple if I find Daisy off her leash again." He crossed his arms and widened his stance. "I also threatened to deport that animal off the island if I found her messing with one more crime scene."

"What did she say to that?"

"She said it was a free country and Daisy had every right to roam about it. Then she said she'd never been fined so much before and if I fine her again or deport Daisy, she'd be in the Island city council meetings faster than I could see her coming."

"She tried to intimidate you." I laughed.

"It's not funny," he said. "I'm done chasing that dog down and wrestling with it to get the evidence I need."

"Do you think that Daisy could be motive for murder?" I asked.

"What? Where did that thought come from?"

"Well, surely you can't be the only person put out by a Saint Bernard that has free run on the island."

He raised one of his eyebrows. "So you think that Daisy had something to do with the poisoning?"

"No." I shook my head. "But she might have something to do with Heather's death."

"How so?"

I shrugged. "Maybe Daisy pushed Heather into the Jessops' shredder."

Rex laughed. "That's reaching, don't you think? That mutt doesn't have a mean bone in her body. She's as likely to lick Heather's face off as she is to push her into a chipper-shredder. And even more ridiculous is to think Heather would be alone with Daisy at Jessop's Compost and Mulch."

"Wow, when you say it like that, it does sound silly."

"Let's forget about Daisy for a moment." He put down his coffee cup and crossed his arms. "What Brent learned while on set was there's a strong camaraderie among the cast."

"I know, right?" I said. "They all know each other and have worked other reality shows."

"Which means either no one had a motive to kill Cathy or perhaps someone was holding a grudge from a previous show?"

"Or, Tammy Gooseworthy poisoned my fudge so that she could get her face on television."

"Yes, I heard that they cast new contestants."

"Jenn said that Tammy was first in line to try out for the replacement cast."

"But she didn't end up on television, did she?"

"No." I shook my head. "The producers spent a day looking at the episodes with the new cast members and then decided there was more drama in the old cast. So they shot some extra scenes to up the story line and then brought us all back for the final show. I think they hoped by bringing us all in one room they could solve the mystery. You know, like the old mystery books do."

"Don't we wish we had Sherlock Holmes to piece together all the clues?"

"Is this all you came by for?" I tilted my head and drew my eyebrows together.

"No," he said quietly. "There is one other thing." Then he leaned forward and kissed me.

CHAPTER 36

"Oh," was all I could say after his kiss.

"I've been wanting to do that for some time, but I thought you had something going with Jessop." He had his arms around me, and I could feel his heart beat under my palm.

"I've been busy building my fudge shop and I know that Trent's been busy with salvaging his mulch business."

It was Rex's turn to say, "Oh." He dropped his hands and took a step back. "I'm sorry if I stepped out of line."

"No." I put my hand back on his chest. "No, not out of line at all." I hugged myself. "I meant to say that I'm not dating anyone."

Jenn walked into the apartment in the middle of my sentence. "Amen. Allie's love life is dead. In fact, I think you'll find it buried in a casket in the basement."

"No," I said quickly. "There are no caskets buried in the basement."

"That you know of," Jenn said with a wink. "Don't mind me. I came in to get a sweater." She dutifully walked into her room and then back out, sweater in hand.

"Continue." She waved her hand and closed the door behind her.

There was a knock on the apartment door at the same time that Rex got a call on his walkie-talkie. I left him to talk to Charlene and opened my door to find Trent standing there. Jenn was a few feet away, rubbing her hands together with glee. I gave her the stink eye.

"Hi, Allie, are you busy?" Trent asked.

"Um, I was just talking to Rex about the television show . . ."

Trent looked over my shoulder and drew himself up straight. "I didn't mean to interrupt."

"You didn't," Rex said and stepped to the door. "I've got a call I need to tend to." He kissed me on the cheek as he went by. "We'll talk more about this later."

"What was that all about?" Trent asked as he stepped into my apartment.

"I'm not quite sure," I said and closed the door. "What can I do for you, Trent?"

"I'm sure there is a lot you can do." He sat down on the arm of Papa Liam's chair and crossed his arms. "My question is, what do you want to do?"

"You know what? I need a cup of coffee." I bustled into the kitchen. "Can I get you something to drink?"

He got up and took a barstool and sat down at the breakfast bar that separated the kitchen from the living area.

"Coffee's great, thanks."

I rinsed out my French press and went through the steps to make a fresh pot then poured him a thick black cup in a red mug. I noticed Rex's mug still on the counter. I picked it up and put it in the sink, then refreshed my coffee. "I have half-and-half and sugar if you need it."

"I'm good." His brown gaze studied me thoughtfully. "How'd the taping of the television show go?"

"It was okay." I shook my head. "I'm not allowed to say anything about it until it airs."

"I wasn't asking about the outcome." He looked at me over the top of his cup. "I was hoping you'd have more clues into that cast member's death."

"Oh, you should have asked Rex, he's working on the case."

"Manning wouldn't tell me anything. He's still investigating Jessop Compost and Mulch for a suspect in Heather's murder."

"Oh. You know, I think there has to be a way that these two deaths are connected."

"I don't see how."

"I keep coming back to Tammy Gooseworthy. She was in competition with Heather for the pastry chef job at the new Grander Hotel. Her father owns the Island Compost and Mulch, which stands to gain over your shutdown. If it had been their shredder that had evidence on it, I would have said it was her right away."

"What about the other girl? What was her name?"

"Her name was Cathy and she ate what looked like my fudge and was poisoned. Maybe it wasn't Cathy the poisoner was trying to kill." I paused, letting my thoughts settle. "Tammy wanted an in to the television show. She came into the McMurphy and tried to get Peter to taste her fudge."

"It makes sense in a weird sort of way," Trent said. "Jessop Compost and Mulch was set to leverage Island out of business. I was in talks with Gooseworthy to buy him out before he went bankrupt."

"So, you think your business was sabotaged by the murderer?"

"It was an efficient way of shutting me down." Trent had that smooth, thoughtful look of a man in charge.

"Plus, Tammy's been busy. When she's not at work, she's been skulking around the show set," I said. "Jenn can corroborate that." I frowned. "I don't see how she had the time—or frankly the intelligence—to not only murder two people but to frame you and me in the process."

"Maybe it wasn't Tammy. Maybe it was someone who loves Tammy and wants to see her succeed at all costs," I pointed out.

"Like who? Her father?"

"Maybe." I winced. "Frankly, I don't know Ed Goose-worthy."

"Yeah, well, I do, and I can't see Ed killing Heather and then disposing of her body on my property."

"And they say it's women who use poison to kill." I bit my bottom lip. "Still, Peter said he was pretty sure there were two people who attacked him with baseball bats. That's a lot of anger."

"What if the two aren't connected?"

"Which two?"

"Your friend's beating and Cathy's murder."

"Then I would believe that Cathy's murder and Heather's murder are connected and Tammy Gooseworthy is the key."

"It's an interesting idea."

I leaned against the breakfast bar. "I have a question."

"Okay."

"What's behind your property? I saw Mrs. Finch

disappear back into the woods behind the compost and mulch yard. What would she be doing back there?"

He shrugged. "Looking for her dog, maybe?"

"No, Daisy was in jail—literally. Rex had her behind bars to keep her out of his crime scene."

"I haven't been through those woods back there in a couple of years. There was a cabin back there at one time. When I was a kid we pretended it belonged to pirates."

"Okay, now I have to know what Mrs. Finch was doing." I put my cup in the sink and grabbed my jacket. "Want to come?"

"I thought you'd never ask."

CHAPTER 37

The walk was faster when I wasn't following someone. Trent knew the shortcuts to his property, and we were there in less than ten minutes.

To keep things from looking too suspicious, I put Mal on her leash and took her with us. If anyone asked, we were walking the dog . . . to the compost area . . . through the woods. Okay, so it was suspicious.

When we reached the compost yard, I was shocked by how different it looked. "Wow, you got rid of all the mulch." The two-story-high piles had been leveled, and the earth was bare and smooth where the piles once were.

"I had to—the family was horrified. I received permission to respectfully dig a deep hole in St. Ann's Cemetery. We buried the mulch and compost and planted two trees. The family intends to place a bench between them with a placard with Heather's name."

"Oh, what a nice thing you did. Heather's family is lucky to have someone like you."

"I'm not all that nice," he said with a pirate's smile. "I couldn't sell any of it with human body parts in it.

Placing it in the cemetery saved me from having to get a permit to bury human remains."

I shook my head. "I guess, then, congratulations on making the best of a bad situation."

Mal had her nose to the ground and pulled on the leash.

"She smells something," Trent said and shoved his hands in his pockets. "Let's hope it's not any more body parts."

"She's tugging me in the same direction Mrs. Finch took the other day."

I loosened my grip on the leash, and Mal started to run, nose to the ground. Trent and I jogged behind her as she edged the woods behind the Jessop property.

"I haven't been back here in years," Trent said as he held up a branch so I could duck under it. Mal followed a path only she could see through the ferns and sumac and old growth of cedar and beech trees. After about one hundred yards the woods opened up into a small clearing. Daisy bounded out of a small shack and greeted Mal with a hearty "woof."

"Hi, Daisy," I said when the big dog came over to sniff her welcome. "What are you doing out here?" I let go of Mal's leash and patted Daisy on the head.

"Hey, girl," Trent said as he gave her a welcome scratch on the back of her neck. "Is Mrs. Finch inside?"

Mal barked, and I realized that she was nowhere to be seen. "Mal?" Panic rose in my body, going from my heart to my neck to my throat. "Mal, come here now."

Mal popped out of the half-opened door. Relief washed over me. "Come here, you little sneak."

Mal barked once and disappeared into the shack.

"Oh, for goodness sake," I muttered and peered in the door. "Mrs. Finch, are you here?"

There was no answer, so I opened the door to let the light in and called, "Hello?"

"Mrs. Finch?" Trent called from directly behind me. "We're coming in." He motioned for me to stay put while he moved around me and put himself between me and whoever or whatever was in the shack.

The building was smaller than a one-car garage, with a sloping roof made up of cedar shingles. There were two windows, both so small they didn't let much light inside. To the left was a small stone hearth and a potbelly stove with a chimney that vented outside through a hole in the wall.

"Mal? Come, Mal." I ordered and snapped my fingers. Mal came out from under a wooden cot. Her normally white, fluffy fur was streaked with black. She turned and faced the underside of the bed and barked, her little stubbed tail wagging wildly.

I got down on all fours and looked under the bed with Mal. "What is it?" It was so dark there was no way I could see anything. I grabbed my cell phone out of the pocket of my jacket and turned it on to use it as a flashlight.

"Oh," was all I said as I sat up on my knees.

"What is it?" Trent was beside me in a moment.

"Um, not a what, but a who," I said, and Mal barked and wagged her stubby tail.

"What?" Trent got down on all fours and looked under the bed. "It's pitch-black."

"Here." I handed him my cell phone to use as a flashlight.

He shone the light under the bed, jerked back, bumped his head on the bedframe, and scooted three feet behind me.

"Was that a . . . ?"

"Mummy," I replied. Mal jumped up and kissed my cheek. I grabbed her and held her fluffy body next to mine and let her kiss me.

"You're so darn calm," Trent said as he stood with my cell phone still in his hand.

"I know, right? So weird. I mean, on television everyone goes running and screaming when faced with a dead person."

"Everyone, that is, but you." He brushed his hair out of his eyes.

"It makes me look suspicious," I said and sat.

"I was going to say brave," Trent said. "Who do you think that is?"

"I don't know," I shrugged. "Are you missing anyone?"

"No," he replied. "And that body is all bones in a T-shirt and jeans."

"We should phone someone," I said from my position on the floor in the middle of the dusty shack. I noticed that there was little inside but the potbelly stove, the old fashioned rope-strung twin bed, a small table, and two chairs.

"Right." Trent used my phone to call 9-1-1. "Hi, Charlene, no, this is Trent Jessop. Yes, I'm using Ms. McMurphy's cell phone. No, this is not a prank. Yes, she seems to be fine." He glanced my way. I held Mal tight and watched him deal with Charlene like a pro. "We need Officer Manning and his team to come out here. We've found another body."

Sneaker's Fudge Bars

3 cups of sugar
Dash of salt
⅔ cup of cocoa powder
1½ cups of milk
¼ cup butter
1 teaspoon vanilla
2 cups peanuts
2 cups caramel chips
Nougat—see recipe below.

Prepare an 8" x 8" x 2" pan—butter the pan, cover the inside with parchment paper or wax paper. Butter the paper and set the pan aside.

In a large, heavy saucepan mix sugar, salt, cocoa powder, and milk. Stir over medium heat until the ingredients reach a full boil. Let boil unstirred until a candy thermometer reads 125°F or the soft-ball stage is reached. Remove from heat.

Add butter and vanilla—do not mix. Cool until the thermometer reads 110°F, then beat until fudge thickens and just begins to lose its gloss. Quickly pour half the fudge in the pan and spread to cover the bottom. Layer nougat (see recipe below), peanuts, and caramel chips. Top with remainder of fudge. Cool completely. Cut into 1" pieces. Enjoy!

Nougat

2 cups powdered sugar
1 teaspoon corn syrup

> 2 tablespoons honey
> 2 tablespoons water
> 1 egg white

Place first four ingredients in a saucepan—stir over low heat until it reaches the soft-crack stage (about 3–4 minutes) or a candy thermometer reads 275°F; remove from heat.

Whisk egg white until stiff—drizzle in the cooling sugar mixture until egg white is glossy and stiff.

Add to fudge for Sneaker's fudge.

CHAPTER 38

"Don't let Daisy in the house," Rex ordered as he moved toward me. I waited in the shack's doorway. "I don't want to have to arrest her for tampering with evidence."

"I've made sure she stayed outside," I said as he walked by me. I still clutched Mal to my chest. She had long ago given up squirming and had snuggled in for the long haul.

"Keep her there," Rex said and narrowed his pretty blue eyes. Then he walked into the shack like a lawman, with careful, deliberate steps. "Jessop, what happened?"

"We were out walking when Mal went nuts, so Allie gave her her lead and she led us to the shack. Daisy was inside guarding something."

"Let me see," he said and nodded to the plainclothes policemen at the head and the foot of the old-fashioned bed. I watched from my perch near the door as they carefully lifted the bed and moved it across the shack.

The faint scent of decay filled the air. Rex squatted down to examine the body. He pulled out a pen and carefully looked under the shirt collar. "This is the first mummy I've ever seen," he said. He touched a white substance on the shirt. "Someone used lye to cut the smell."

"How long has he been under there?" I asked in a stage whisper, not quite sure why I was whispering except it felt like I should keep my voice low. Something about reverence for the dead.

"Hard to tell," Rex said. He looked up at Officer Polaski. "Find out who the shack belongs to and canvass the neighbors. See if anyone knows anything."

"Yes, sir," Brent said, his sun-streaked hair giving him a boyish charm. He had the looks and charm to get a whole lot of story out of the neighbors.

"It might be Mrs. Finch," I said.

Rex narrowed his eyes and looked at me. "What makes you say that?"

"Well, Daisy was here . . ."

"That dog is everywhere. There's more, isn't there?"

I swallowed hard. "I followed Mrs. Finch out this way the other day." I held out my hand in a stop gesture when he scowled. "I didn't get any farther than the Jessop property. Seriously, I ran into Trent."

"I'll vouch for her," Trent said, his voice low as well. "It was day before yesterday. I was out here measuring the cubic footage of the contaminated mulch and compost."

"Did you see Mrs. Finch?" Rex asked Trent.

"No, in fact, I didn't know that Allie was following anyone." Both men turned to me.

I shrugged. "She had said she was going to get Daisy's leash and when I left the police station I noticed that she was walking in the opposite direction of her cottage."

"So you followed her."

"Yes," I nodded.

"Without any backup or anyone knowing where you were or what you were doing?" Rex crossed his arms, disappointment and a note of fear on his face.

Trent cursed under his breath. "What were you thinking going into the woods alone?"

I hugged Mal to my chest. "I was thinking I was following an old lady and I had my ankle bracelet on. What could have possibly happened?"

Both men waved toward the mummy at the same time. Their reply to my question was self-evident.

"Oh," I said. "Right."

"Wouldn't Mrs. Finch be in trouble, too? I imagine she passed right by here," I said.

"I'm having Lasko go check on her," Rex said. "The last thing I need right now is another body."

"Do you think this is all related?" Trent asked.

"Wouldn't that be easy," Rex said. "I'd guess this guy's been here for at least a year."

"Was it foul play?"

Rex ran his big, square hand over his face. "Hard to tell. I don't see any bullet holes or obvious stab wounds."

"His head seems intact," I interjected.

"It's up to the ME and Carpenter to figure out how this fits in the big picture."

"Who's using my name in vain?" Shane asked as he stepped inside the tiny cottage with his big, black evidence kit in his hands. He wore a black Windbreaker that had CSU embroidered on the pocket. It hung open, showing the light blue shirt and black slacks he wore underneath.

"I told Jessop you were the guy to ask about COD. This one is beyond my scope." Rex straightened. "Come on, Allie. Let's get out of this man's way so he can do his job."

We stepped outside, and Mal wiggled until I put her down. I made sure I had a good hold on her leash this time. She wandered around with her nose to the ground.

"We have to stop meeting over dead bodies," Rex said. His pretty blue eyes zeroed in on me long enough for me to become aware of my heart beating. "What made you come back out this way?"

"I was walking Mal," I said, but we both knew it wasn't entirely accurate. "Okay, I wanted to see where Mrs. Finch might have gone. We should look and see if there's a leash for Daisy in the shack."

"Noted," Rex said.

"Do you think Mrs. Finch killed him?" I nodded toward the mummy in the shack.

"More likely he died of natural causes and for some reason his family didn't want to bury him, so they hid him here."

I wrinkled my nose and scrunched my brow. "Why wouldn't you bury someone?"

"There are as many reasons as there are families," Rex said as he eyed the terrain. "Sometimes grief causes a person to do strange things. Then there's the fraud aspect."

"What fraud aspect?"

"Someone in the family might be receiving social security or pension checks and would rather store the body here than declare him dead and lose those monthly checks."

"That's pretty creepy," I said.

Liz came striding out of the woods with her camera

hanging from around her neck. "Hey kids, I heard we have another body."

"This one's a mummy," I said. "It looks like he's been in the shack for some time now."

"Too bad—it would be really great for sales if there was a serial killer on the loose."

"Ugh, I don't want to think about serial killers," I said.

"Is that because you're busy spending your grand prize winnings?"

I put my hands on my hips. "Now you're just fishing. None of us see a cent in earnings if the beans are spilled before the last episode is shown."

"When's that?" she asked.

"In about eight weeks."

Mal went over and sniffed Liz's leg and nudged her until she bent down and petted her. "Hello, little dog," Liz said. "Did you find yet another body? Maybe we should change your name to Sherlock—"

Mal looked offended and sneezed her opinion of the name change. We laughed.

Liz caught movement behind us and lifted her camera and got off a shot or two before Rex pushed her camera down. "Have some respect for the guy."

"Do you have any idea who owns the shack?" I asked Liz.

"Angus says it belongs to the Finch family. They used to use it as a camp. A place where they could come and warm themselves if they were out hunting."

"That explains the potbelly stove."

"As far as we know, no one has used it in years," Liz said and got off a couple of shots before Rex put his hand over her lens. "Hey."

"No photos of my crime scene."

"So this was a murder?" Liz and I asked the question at the same time.

"Looks like natural causes to me." Shane walked out, escorting the body bag on the stretcher to the ambulance. It always struck me as odd to see the modern vehicle. Emergency services was the exception to the no-car rule.

"Oh, thank goodness," I said. "I think we've had enough murder and mayhem."

"Let me take a guess, that's Mr. Finch," Liz said.

"We don't have an ID at this time," Rex said.

"No worries." Liz snapped couple more pictures then danced away when Rex tried to grab her camera. "I'll find out when was the last time anyone saw Hector Finch. Tootles." She waved her fingers and strode back into the woods.

"Are you going to let her do that?" I asked Rex.

He sent me a miniscowl. "The First Amendment gives her the right. Let's just hope she doesn't mess up my investigation."

"Maybe she'll help." I tried to put a positive spin on it, but Rex glared.

"Are you ready to go?" Trent came up behind me. He put his hand on my elbow.

"Yes," I said. "You know where to find me if you need me." I directed that comment to Rex. "I doubt there's anything I can do to help."

"You've done enough," Rex said and stalked off.

Trent and I walked in silence until we were out of reach of the police.

"Was that Liz MacElroy?"

"Yes," I replied and ducked to avoid a branch as Mal tugged me back to the sidewalk.

"She's a good resource," Trent said.

"For what?"

"Mackinac is a small island," Trent said. "News travels fast and the press travels faster. Maybe this was the break Manning was looking for."

"How so?"

Trent shrugged. "I don't know, it's a gut feeling I have."

"You think all of these murders are related? Like there's a serial killer on the loose?"

"More like an opportunity killer," Trent said and took my hand as we walked down the sidewalk. "Do you ever have time for a movie or dinner?"

"I eat," I replied. "Movies, not so much. I prefer to watch the old black-and-whites."

"Even better." Trent winked at me. "They have a black-and-white movie night in the park once a week. I don't know what's playing but I'd like to take you."

"Oh." I was surprised. "Sure. I think that would be fun."

"Great." His eyes lit up. "I'll stop by at eight." He left me at the back door to the McMurphy with a kiss on my cheek. All I could do was stand there and watch him walk away.

"Nice view."

I turned to find Jenn half out of the door. "He asked me out."

"Score!" Jenn smiled. "It's about time you started scoring."

"Who's scoring?" My mom asked as she too popped her head out the door.

"No one," I muttered and sent Jenn a dirty look for catching Mom's interest. "Hey," I changed the subject. "Guess what Mal found on our walk today?"

"Oh, no, let me guess . . ." Jenn started.

"Another dead body," Mom finished.

Chocolate Ways Fudge

4 cups milk chocolate chips
1 can sweetened condensed milk
4 tablespoons butter
1 teaspoon vanilla
1 recipe of chocolate nougat
1 bag of caramel chips

Butter an 8" x 8" x 2" pan. Then line with wax paper or parchment.

In a double boiler melt milk chocolate, sweetened condensed milk, and butter until smooth and thick.

Remove from heat. Add vanilla and stir. Pour half of the fudge into pan. Layer chocolate nougat, then caramel chips, and cover with remainder of fudge. Cool. Remove from pan. Cut into pieces. Store in a covered container.

Chocolate Nougat

2 cups powdered sugar
2 tablespoons cocoa powder
1 teaspoon corn syrup
2 tablespoons honey
2 tablespoons water
1 egg white

Place first five ingredients in a saucepan—stir over low heat until it reaches the soft-crack stage (about 3–4 minutes) or a candy thermometer reads 275°F; remove from heat.

Whisk egg white until stiff—drizzle in the cooling sugar mixture until egg white is glossy and stiff.

Add to fudge for Chocolate Ways Fudge.

CHAPTER 39

"That dog needs to be deputized," Mr. Devaney said. "She's doing better work than our esteemed police department."

"At the very least she should be on the payroll," Frances added.

"I bet they could pay her in dog biscuits," Mom said. She petted Mal, who was curled up on her lap. We all sat around in the apartment living room after a nice dinner. Mr. Devaney had changed his shirt and washed up. Frances wore a lilac printed skirt and a white blouse. Mom had on a pair of tailored slacks in navy and a crisp navy and white blouse.

I had changed into jean shorts and a McMurphy T-shirt.

Jenn passed out beverages, using a wooden tray from Grammy Alice's things and five matching tea cups and saucers with a carnation print. Mal got down from Mom's lap as soon as the drinks were brought out.

"And of course, everyone knows the real news story for today," Jenn said.

"What news?" I asked, confused.

Jenn curled up on the couch and sipped her cup of tea. "The fact that you have a date with one Trent Jessop."

"Really?" Frances asked, her expression perking up.

"*The* Trent Jessop of the Jessop Stables and the Jessop Compost and Mulch and the Jessop manor house and the—"

"Okay, we get it." I cut Jenn off and put my hand up in a stop sign. "Yes, Trent Jessop asked me to go to the black-and-white movies in the park."

"Well, good for you," Mom said. "It's not healthy for a girl your age to do nothing but work and walk her dog."

"Really, Mom, you're concerned about my love life?"

Mom sipped her coffee and took her time settling the cup into the saucer. "I do want to have grandchildren one day."

I shook my head. "It's just a movie, Mom. Don't start saving for your grandkids' college."

Mom raised her right eyebrow. "Who says I don't already have said savings account?"

I rolled my eyes. Mal came over with her leash in her mouth. "Looks like someone needs to go out. I'll be right back." I put Mal's harness and leash on, then turned to the family assembled. "No discussing me or my love life while I'm gone."

"Why would we talk about you when you aren't here?" Jenn batted her lashes at me.

I narrowed my eyes as Mal tugged me to the door. "I mean it. Remember, I know your secrets."

We went down the stairs to the back of the McMurphy. I opened the door and stepped out to a perfect cool summer night. The sky was clear and filled with twinkling stars. Mal and I moved across the alley and to her favorite potty spot.

"I've been waiting for you."

I started as Mrs. Finch emerged from the shadows under the fire escape. "Oh, hello, Mrs. Finch. You gave me quite a scare." I put my hand on my heart.

"I plan to do more than scare you," she said, her voice oddly tight.

"I'm sorry? What?" Mal finished her squat and went over to the older woman, who wore a Windbreaker jacket, black slacks, and a pale pink T-shirt.

"You ruined everything," she said and jerked Mal's leash from me. Mal growled. "Don't worry, little doggie. I know it's not your fault." She turned back to me, her dark eyes a void of blackness in the soft summer air.

"Give me my dog back," I said with as much authority as I could muster and held out my hand.

Mal sat at my tone, knowing that I was all business.

Mrs. Finch acted as if I hadn't spoken. "First you discover Heather, then Cathy, and now, the worst thing of all, you have taken my Hector from me."

"Wait—what? You knew your husband was under the bed?"

"He asked me to stuff him and stand him in the corner but my taxidermy skills are rudimentary, so I did the next best thing and mummified him."

"Why?"

"They were his last wishes."

"Okay, so why not get a mortician to help you? Why hide him under the bed?"

"No mortician would stuff him. The taxidermists recoiled in horror at the thought. Then one busybody started asking questions. She said she was going to the authorities as it seems there are laws against keeping a dead body. She forced me to hide Hector. The shack was the perfect place until you came along."

She drew her arms up and revealed a long, slender knife in her free hand. "You have been such a bother," she said, as if discussing the weather. "If you hadn't made a fuss about the mulch, Heather would be resting in peace."

"Wait, what do you know about Heather?"

"She was a nuisance. Poor girl thought she could win my nephew's heart and acquire his fortune."

Mal wandered around, bored, at her feet. The whole encounter seemed as if it were a bad dream. "Fred Gooseworthy is your nephew?"

"Yes." She waved away my question. "Everyone knows that I married well and brought the Finch fortune to the island."

My mind clicked through the clues. "You're Tammy's aunt."

"Of course." She tilted her head and studied me like a bug. "Are you putting the pieces together?"

"Heather was up for the same job as Tammy."

"Another reason to get rid of her." The old woman grinned, sending chills down my back. "I tried to buy her off, but she simply laughed at me and called me an old bat. She wasn't laughing when I stabbed her. I have a good idea where the arteries are, you know. We used to butcher our own pigs and chickens. Although a human's neck is not as easily snapped as a chicken's." She shrugged. "Nonetheless, she bled out quickly."

Mal had her nose to the ground and sniffed, following a trail I couldn't see. Mrs. Finch had dropped Mal's leash and to my relief my puppy hurried off into the shadows.

"But Heather was shredded," I pointed out. It occurred to me that Mrs. Finch might be hallucinating or grandstanding. There was no way this little old woman could kill a grown woman. Was there? At least I needed to believe she couldn't.

"That was brilliant, right?" Her eyes glittered in the street light. "She followed me out to the cabin after I told her that I would pay her fifty grand to move off island and never return. Unfortunate for her, Heather declined my good offer," she cackled. "Really, what kind of stupid are you to give up that kind of money?"

"You look cold, Mrs. Finch. Why don't you come in by the fireplace and put your feet up?" I offered, my thoughts circling as I tried to figure out how to handle a crazy woman. With any luck Mal would stay away from Mrs. Finch, although I believed the crazy old woman was a pet lover and would rather stab herself than hurt my pup.

"No!" She pointed the knife at me. "I'm here to kill you." She circled me and I turned with her, keeping my gaze on her as we shuffled around in the alley.

"I don't want to be killed," I said and gauged how far I was from the back door. The McMurphy back door was locked at eight PM, when the fudge shop closed. I kept a key card in my pocket.

"If you insist on being a problem, it will only hurt more when I miss." She shook her head. "Trust me, you want it to be clean and fast."

Okay, I wasn't playing anymore. We had rotated so that my back was in the alley and my face to the back door of the McMurphy. I had dog-walking shoes on, but I had no problem screaming and running. I could outrun an old woman, right? "You don't really want to hurt me. My family will find you and then all this will be for nothing."

She laughed a strange and gargled sound. "This isn't about you or your family, dear." She snapped her fingers, and two men stepped out of the shadows. It was Jabar and Tony from the reality show. They flanked Mrs. Finch and crossed their arms over their massive chests, spreading their legs wide as if preparing for a fight.

"Wait." I decided to play clueless. "Why are you two involved?"

"Surprising, right?" Mrs. Finch said with a nod. "You see, the joke is on Heather. I really did have fifty thousand dollars to give away. The boys were smart enough to take it and in return are doing me a few favors."

"By beating up Chef Thomas?"

"Well, yes, that did go a bit far, but the boys were tired with the whole charade. Chef Thomas was the main reason they weren't casting new contestants. And then taking out cast members gave my Tammy a chance to be cast."

"But they didn't recast."

"That little man who decided that is next on my list." She sighed long and hard. "So many bothersome people to take care of, so little time. Boys"—she gestured toward me, but I had been watching her every move, waiting for her to give them a signal.

I bolted. I wasn't sure if they could catch me, so I screamed, "Fire! Fire!" as I ran. I could feel Jabar catching up, so I turned and ran toward him, ducking under his arm before he could think.

There was a problem with my brilliant plan. Tony was far enough behind Jabar to stand between me and freedom.

I made him work as I went left and tried to climb the fence that lined the alley. He caught my right ankle as I flung myself over the fence. He was strong. Strong enough to jam me back against the chain-link fence. I was slammed so hard against the metal chain link it took my breath away. So much for screaming.

"Come on now." Jabar grabbed me by the waist and pulled me back toward the alley. "Take your consequences like a good girl."

I struggled against him and screamed out, "Mal! Mal!"

Mal popped out of the darkness and barked at Jabar. We made quite a racket, Mal's barking and my screaming her name. My thought was that Mal had quite a few friends in the neighborhood and one or two of them might look out to see if there was something wrong with the dog.

"I said shut up." Jabar boxed my head so hard I saw stars, but I knew my only chance for survival was to keep screaming.

"Police, freeze!"

Of course, I kept screaming so loud my brain barely registered the words. I had no idea really why Jabar froze on the spot. What I knew was that I got in a lucky elbow shot and he let me go, cursing and doubling over.

The second he let me go, I was off like a shot. I was down the alley and inside the police station before I could even think. Mal was with me the entire way. I pulled the door open, and she and I ran inside, and I shut the door and drew the lock.

"Freeze!"

Okay, see, now *that* I heard. Well, "freeze" and the sound of a lot of guns being cocked. I put my trembling hands up in the air. Mal stayed beside me, not making a sound.

"I'm sorry," my words came out in between huge gasps for air. Really, I needed to find a gym or start running on a regular basis. Especially if I was going to keep running from bad guys.

"Turn around slow."

I did as ordered. "I'm unarmed," I said. "I was attacked in the alley behind the McMurphy and managed to get free."

"So you ran to the police station?" Officer Lasko asked, her gun still pointed at my heart. Why did she not like me?

"It was the safest place I could think of."

Someone tried to open the door behind me. The sound made me squeak and whip around. Rex pounded on the door. "Let me in."

Officer Lasko grabbed my arm as she put her gun away and pulled me away from the door. Officer Heyes moved from behind the reception desk to the area where I stood. Officer Beech unlocked the door.

Rex pushed Jabar through the opened door. The big man had his hands cuffed behind him.

"Did you get her?" I asked.

Rex ignored me and handed Jabar off to Officer Lasko, telling her to put him in an interview room.

Finally he turned to me. "Are you all right?"

"Yes," I said, and then my knees gave out. I fell to the floor with a *woof* of my breath. "Or, maybe not."

Mal climbed up in my lap and licked my face. I started laughing, which only encouraged more licking. I laughed until I cried. I was only partially aware that Rex had left and come back with a blanket and a glass of water.

"Drink this." He handed me the cup. I took it in both hands to keep from trembling as I tried to do as he ordered. Mostly, I got water sloshed on me, which only served to cause another fit of laughter. Seriously, my sides hurt.

Rex squatted beside me and draped the blanket around my shoulders. "Breathe," he ordered. "In . . . and out . . ." I concentrated on him and tried to breathe in time with his words and breath.

We did that three or four times, and he stopped and pushed my hand toward my mouth. "Drink."

I realized that I still held the water glass, and I took a sip. The shaking had slowed down. Mal licked a puddle of water I had splashed on the tile floor.

"Now," Rex said, his pretty eyes serious. "Are you okay?"

"I think so," I said as slowly as he had spoken. "Did you get her?"

"Who?" he asked and motioned for Officer Beech to do something.

"Mrs. Finch," I said as I concentrated on Rex's eyes. "She wanted to kill me."

"Mrs. Finch wants to kill everyone." Rex waved off my comment. "The crazy old bat always has some complaint or another."

"She was in the alley," I said, trying to convey the importance of my words. "She had a knife."

"You saw Mrs. Finch in the alley with a knife," he made it sound as if I were making it up.

"This is not *Clue*," I said, suddenly angry. "Mrs. Finch is Tammy's aunt. She killed Heather when Heather wouldn't take money to go away."

"Mrs. Finch killed Heather."

"Yes, she told me."

"How did she kill her?"

"She stabbed her and let her bleed out. Like a chicken or something."

"Mrs. Finch," he said. *"The* Mrs. Finch who is ninety-two years old if she's a day."

"Yes," I stressed. "Ask Jabar. She paid Jabar and Tony to beat up Peter and to come for me. Didn't you see them in the alleyway?"

He shook his head. "No, I only heard you screaming Mal's name and I turned down the alley in time to see Jabar haul you back over the fence. I pulled my gun and said, 'Police, Freeze.'"

"That's why he let go of me."

"Yes."

"I ran to the police station," I said. "Mal and I came here for safety."

He shot me a look. "Are you okay to stand?"

"Yes, I think so." I stood and wobbled a bit but was able to stand. He walked me to a chair as George Marron came in through the side door.

"Beech called me and said you had a hysterical woman who could be shocky."

"Um, that would be me." I raised my hand and smiled weakly. "How are you doing, George?"

"I'm well." He took my wrist and measured my pulse. "One ten is a little fast." Flashing a light in my eyes, he asked me, "How many fingers am I holding up?"

"Three."

"Anything hurt? There's a bruise on your ankle. It looks fresh. Do you know how you got it?"

"I think Jabar did it when he yanked me over a fence."

George took my hands and tsked as the abrasions on my palms rose up in ugly welts.

"Weird," I muttered. "I didn't see that."

"You could be hurt and not feel it." He calmly listened to my heart, then held my chin in his hand and gently turned my head from side to side. "You have swelling on your right cheek and your left jaw line."

"Jabar hit me."

George shone a light in my eyes. "No concussion, but you're going to hurt tomorrow," he pronounced and cracked open two instant freeze bags. "Put these on your face." He gently showed me where to hold them. "Take a warm bath with Epsom salts tonight. It'll help with the rest of the bruising."

"Okay, thanks."

"My pleasure." He patted my knee and packed up his stuff. "Someone should keep an eye on her tonight," George said to Rex. "To be safe."

I wasn't sure, but I think George winked at Rex.

Before George could leave, my mom and Jenn and Frances came through the door like a mob on fire.

"Is she hurt?"

"Rex, what is going on?"

"Allie, why didn't you call us?"

They all talked at once. The din made my head hurt. Then Mr. Devaney walked in and nodded at George as the EMT left.

"I heard this happened in the alley behind the McMurphy," Mr. Devaney crossed his arms and locked eyes with Rex.

"Allie, what happened?" Mom asked. She took my hand, winced at the abrasions, and pressed my head to her tummy like I was a little kid. "My poor baby."

"Mom, please . . . I can't breathe."

"Oh, sorry." She patted my shoulder. "What happened, dear?"

"Was it terrible?" Jenn squatted down beside my chair. "I heard one of those big guys from the show attacked you."

"I heard he jumped you right outside our back door, didn't you scream? Surely someone would have heard you if you did," Frances said with a frown. "This island is safe, isn't it?" She looked at Mr. D, who nodded. "A girl shouldn't be assaulted taking her dog for a walk."

"Where's Mal?" Jenn asked.

My fearless pup came running out from behind the reception area, where the policemen had been sneaking her treats and telling her what a good and clever girl she was.

"There she is, right as rain." Frances patted Mal's head.

"So what happened?" Mr. D asked Rex.

"I was walking by the alley and heard shouting." He turned to me. "What were you shouting?"

"I tried 'fire'! But no one came. So I called out Mal's name thinking someone would come to check on the pup."

Mal sat at my feet, pretty pleased with her doggie self.

"I witnessed the perpetrator lifting a shouting woman over the chain-link fence. When I heard the dog, I knew it was Allie. I had my gun out and startled the man by identifying myself and shouting for him to freeze. He let go of Allie and she took off running. I had two choices: get the man or go after Allie." Rex shook his head. "I trusted Allie would find a safe place. I chose to bring the man in."

"So you have him?"

"Yes." Rex gave a short nod. "He's cooling his heels in the interview room."

"Jabar wasn't the only one there," I piped up. "It all started with Mrs. Finch. She came out of the shadows as

Mal did her business. Mrs. Finch is crazy. She had a butcher knife and said I was becoming a nuisance and she needed to get rid of me like she did the others."

"Wait—our Mrs. Finch?" Jenn asked. "Daisy's owner?"

"Yes," I said excited to finally get someone to listen to my story. "She's Tammy's aunt. She killed Heather and she poisoned Cathy. Then she enlisted Jabar and Tony to beat up Peter. When none of that got Tammy on the show, she got pretty mad."

"Why did she come after you?" Mom asked.

"Mal found her secret—that she had hidden her dead husband's body. I called the police. When she saw them take Hector away in a black body bag she got Jabar and Tony to help her kill me."

"Why would those two nice boys do such a terrible thing?" Mom asked.

"Mrs. Finch paid them. She had fifty thousand dollars she tried to pay Heather to leave the island."

"Well, fifty thousand dollars is more than they offered those two for the television show," Jenn mused. Mal went over and leaned against Jenn until she reached down and picked Mal up.

"I didn't see Mrs. Finch or the other man you claim was there." Rex had his hands on his hips.

"They were there. Ask Jabar. He'll tell you. Mrs. Finch was so calm. It was weird. She expected me to stand there and let her kill me." I shuddered. "She said it would hurt less if I didn't struggle."

"Oh, poor baby." Mom hugged my head again and, ignoring my wincing, she turned to Rex. "You'd better find that old woman and that other man. If you don't, I will and you don't want to be around for what this old woman can do!" She pointed to herself.

"Yes, ma'am." Rex nodded. "I'll put patrols out to canvass the area and go to the places Mrs. Finch frequents. We'll get it sorted out as soon as possible." He turned to me. "I need you to give a statement to Officer Beech. Once that's done we'll need a couple of pictures of your wounds. Nothing too terrible but the more evidence we can gather the better."

"You believe me about Mrs. Finch, don't you?" I asked.

Rex's mouth became a thin, tight line. "I believe you believe in what you think happened. That's a good start. Now it's up to me to help prove the case."

"Well, then do your job, young man." Mom waved him away.

Rex was a smart man and knew when he was dismissed. I have to admit I hadn't seen my mother in this role before. She was normally so careful about the way people perceived her.

"I'll walk Jenn and Frances home," Mr. Devaney said. "Then I'll come back and walk you ladies back to the McMurphy."

"You don't need to go that far, sir," Officer Beech said as he rounded the counter with a clipboard in hand. "Officer Manning requested a police escort for these ladies and a round-the-clock police presence until things get figured out. We'll keep them safe, sir."

"You'd darn well better," Mr. Devaney said. "Come on, Frances, let's get you home."

Frances gave me a hug, then Jenn handed me Mal and kissed my cheek. They both pulled their jackets around them and let Mr. Devaney corral them through the door.

"How could we not have heard her?" Jenn asked Frances.

It was a fair question. One I had myself. But I never heard the reply as the door shut firmly behind them.

"Are you ready?" Officer Beech gave my mom a chair and pulled another old chair over to sit on himself. "Let's begin at the moment you decided to take the puppy out."

CHAPTER 40

The day of the last McMurphy Lilac Festival tea dawned cool and bright. George Marron was right. I did hurt in places I didn't even know existed. Thankfully, Sandy was able to make the day's fudge, while I took aspirin and moved as little as possible.

"It's all set," Jenn said. "Here's your costume."

She pushed a pink, mutton-leg dress at me.

"What?" I waved her offering away. "I'm not into costumes. I'll wear my chef's coat."

"Oh, no, you don't," Jenn took my hand and closed it around the hanger. "We are all in costume. People want to see *Somewhere in Time* and we are going to give it to them."

"But—"

"It's for a good cause, remember?" She stood with her hands on her hips. "I'm wearing green-and-white striped. I thought you'd be perfect in McMurphy pink and white. Hurry, we only have thirty minutes before we need to be under the tent in the park. In fact, the three-piece orchestra is setting up. So get dressed!"

"Oh, dear, there is no hurrying me today."

"Okay, if you're going to be late the very least you can do is wear the dress."

Oh boy, I fell right into Jenn's plans. I either hurried or I wore the dress. Since there was no way for me to hurry, I was stuck. "Fine."

"Good girl," Jenn said and Mal barked. Jenn laughed and reached down to give the pup a pat on the head. "I meant your mama, little dog."

I looked the dress over. "How am I supposed to do all these buttons?" The dress buttoned in the back.

"Your mom is ready and waiting to help." Jenn waved toward the steps where my mom stood.

"Fine." I moved to the stairs a little slower than usual.

"I've got the bustle and unmentionables upstairs on your bed." Mom locked her arm through mine and helped me up the stairs. Really, it wasn't so much helpful as to ensure I didn't come up with a new reason why I couldn't wear a 1900s costume.

Twenty minutes later I was properly cinched into a 1900s mutton-sleeved gown with a bustle whopping around behind me. At least by 1900 the bustle had started to decrease in both size and fashion.

"You look so lovely," Mom said and clapped her hands. She wore a similar getup in lavender and mint.

"I want the McMurphy to stand out but I hoped that didn't mean I had to."

"Oh, pooh." Mom dismissed my thoughts with a gentle hand motion. "You do two demonstrations a day. You should be used to people looking at you."

"Yes, well, that's different."

"How so?" Mom handed me a parasol and a pair of white lace gloves. She put her gloves on and watched me expectantly.

I put on the gloves. "When I do the fudge demonstrations, I'm showing my talent. This . . ." I waved at the dress, "Is not the same. Everyone will stare."

"That's the point." Mom pushed me toward the door. "Put up your parasol. And here we go . . ." She opened the door, stepped out into the street crowd, and put up her parasol. I took a deep breath and followed her. My parasol was pale pink. My mother's was lilac. The crowd parted around us as we kept our heads up and gently glided—or in my case tripped and tried not to fall—down the sidewalk. Officer Polaski followed a few lengths behind us. We passed the grocery store and had gathered behind us a trail of people interested in what was going on.

We hit the large lawn at the foot of the fort. Thankfully, the tent was set up at the near side of the lawn. First I spotted the tent, and then I saw the small groups of women in costume milling around it.

Relief washed over me. If I were with a crowd in costume, then I was less likely to stand out. The tent front had been tied back so that you could see the ten cloth-covered tables inside. The sound of the orchestra seeped out from the open doorway.

"It's so lovely," Mom said, and I had to agree with her. Jenn stood at the entrance, checking the elegant invitations she had given to each and every person who had bought a ticket. We closed up our parasols as we stepped into the tent.

Jenn had each table covered in white and lilac blue. In the center were more chocolate creations that Sandy had made. Then each plate was garnished with lilac flowers. The sugared lilacs I had made looked lovely on the multicolored petit fours. The chairs had high backs and were also covered in white linen with lilac blue bows in the back. Each table had a teapot with a different lilac theme.

Women filled the tent and took their places. If anyone could host a costume party in a tent in early June, it would be Jenn. Luckily Office Polaski stayed back, hanging out on the corner talking with the carriage drivers as they waited in the street for fares.

The tea party was perfect, and two hours later Jenn and I waved every attendee through the door with a thank-you and a card for one free pound of fudge from the McMurphy.

"That went well," Jenn said when the last lady had left.

"Of course it went well," Mom said. "You girls are very professional. I'm going to go find Sandy and let her know that I have collected orders for her chocolate work."

"Thanks, Mom," I said as she hurried off, her parasol open and the crowds parting on the street.

"We raised five thousand dollars," Jenn said with glee. "I'll be sending the children's clinic a nice check."

"This was a fantastic idea," I said. "It not only showed off what our team could do, but also helped build awareness of the McMurphy."

"I love the Lilac Festival," Jenn said. "What's the next festival?"

"Let's see, there's the yacht race next month and then the festival of the horse in August."

The cannon fired above us and the sound startled us both. We looked at each other, gloved hands on our chests, and we laughed. The cannon went off twice while we were inside with the tea, but with the band playing it didn't have the same effect.

The catering crew came in to clear away the dishes and then take down the tables and linens. "Why don't you go home," Jenn said. "You look worn out. I can handle the teardown."

"Thanks," I said. "I can't wait to get out of this bustle."

Jenn laughed. "Come on, you have to admit that you liked it."

"Yes." I grinned with reluctance. "I did like it." I gave Jenn a quick hug, grabbed my parasol, and strode out of the tent in a hurry to get back to the McMurphy and out of the corset. I was in front of the grocery store when Mrs. Finch emerged out of the crowd.

I could not believe it. In fact, I had to pinch myself to see if it was a dream. She wore the same clothes that she had on last night. Her Windbreaker was torn and her pink T-shirt dirty. This time there was a wild light in her eyes, along with the big butcher knife in her hand. She advanced on me with the knife held high.

The crowd around us screamed and parted as the crazy woman approached, knife held high. I glanced back and forth looking for Officer Polaski in the crowd.

"Stand still and take your punishment," Mrs. Finch said. She had an odd expression on her face as if something inside her had snapped.

"No," I said loudly. "Stop."

She paused for a brief moment as if to process what I said. "I can't, I won't," she said. "You need killing." She slashed at me with the knife. I defended myself with the parasol. The knife missed me but made direct contact with the umbrella. The force of the hit sent a shock wave up my arms.

As she raised her arm again, Rex and Officer Polaski

came running around the corner, guns pulled. "Stop, police!" Rex shouted.

She paused a moment, arm raised, and turned in the direction that Rex ran. "No." She turned back to lower her arm, but I had taken the opportunity to lift my skirts and run out of her reach. "Nooo!" She wailed at the top of her voice when she realized I had bolted. "Come back here, girl. I have to kill you."

By this time I had Rex between me and the crazy old woman. Officer Polaski was on her in a blink and removed the weapon from her hand. She wailed a strange animal-like noise that had the hairs on my arms standing on end.

She was cuffed and hauled off toward Market Street and the police headquarters. Like a huge wave, the crowd parted and then filled in as they passed.

"Are you okay?" Rex asked me.

I was bent in half with my hands on my knees and my head down. I looked up. "Yes, just a little scared." I took a couple of deep breaths—as deep as you could get when wearing a corset—and straightened. "By now I should be used to this."

"Being from Chicago you should be able to handle crime better than this," Rex teased with a wink.

"Are you okay?" Trent appeared from the crowd.

"Yes, I'm good. Rex and Brent were here in good time."

"I got a call that there was a crazy old woman with a knife," Rex said. "The first thing we thought of was Mrs. Finch. I was in the McMurphy when Frances said you were out here in the tent. Brent tells me he didn't see you leave the tent."

"You both got here just in time," I said.

"Why hasn't Mrs. Finch been taken into custody before this?" Trent asked.

"We've been looking for her since last night, but she knows the island well and apparently she can keep out of sight if she wants. In fact, if she hadn't become fixated on Allie, we may never have seen her again."

I put my glove-covered hands on my exaggerated hips. "Do you believe me now?"

"I believed you last night," Rex said. "That said, I have to stay objective."

"Do you have the other guy in custody?" Trent asked.

"Yes, we caught Tony trying to sneak off island." Rex nodded. "Mrs. Finch was the last one found. Her family has contacted a lawyer and are petitioning that she is innocent by insanity."

"Well, she certainly looked insane," I said.

"We need to ensure that she never gets out of treatment," Trent said to Rex. "She's already killed two people. I can tell you this—she's definitely not going to be allowed on island ever again."

"What will happen to Daisy?" I asked, and both men turned to me as if in slow motion.

"That dog is off island as well," Rex declared.

"That's sad. It wasn't the doggie's fault. Daisy's innocent."

"Until proven guilty," Rex muttered. "She's been in police lockup since yesterday. I have a woman from the Saint Bernard rescue service coming in tomorrow to take Daisy and find her a new and better home."

"Thanks, Rex."

He nodded.

"Come on Allie, I'll walk you home." Trent put his

hand on the small of my back and guided me away from Rex. "You look good in pink and white."

I felt the heat of a blush rise up over my face. "Thanks. Jenn and Mom seem to think they will get me to wear this dress again. But a betting man would look his fill now, knowing he may not ever see it again."

Trent threw his head back with a loud laugh. "You are so funny." He sobered. "This is the last day of the festival. The movies start tomorrow. Are we still on?"

I smiled at Trent. "Yes, I believe it'll be safe for you to be with me by then."

"I have a feeling being with you is far from safe. Especially for my heart." He shook his head slightly.

"That's one heck of a line."

He took my hand in his and kissed my cheek. "Did it work?"

"Maybe . . . a little."

"I know a shortcut to your house. One with significantly fewer people."

"You do?" I raised one eyebrow.

"Yes." He winked and kept hold of my hand as his presence parted the crowd until we moved into the alley. There was nothing left but the crunch of our feet on the alley gravel. The scent of lilacs drifted by on the breath of the wind. We walked hand in hand, enjoying the bright blue sky and the company. When we hit the McMurphy's back door, he bent and kissed me properly on the mouth.

"Let's go another month without sleuthing, okay?"

"Okay," I said dreamily.

"I need you safe." He kissed my forehead, opened the door to the McMurphy, and guided me inside. "See you tomorrow."

The door closed behind me as he walked away. The hardest thing to do was to let him go.

Later that evening I sprawled out in the McMurphy lobby wearing jeans and a pale blue T-shirt. Frances sat nearby knitting. Jenn sat next to her, teasing Mal with a dog toy. Mom tapped something on her phone. Sandy lounged on the settee.

"Well, that festival was certainly interesting," Jenn said. "All in all it was a success I think."

"Between the teas, the sugared lilacs, and the chocolate centerpieces," Sandy said, "it was a huge success."

"Don't forget solving a string of murders," Mom said.

"Rex said that Mrs. Finch admitted to killing Heather and putting the body in the nearby shredder," I said.

"Creepy." Jenn shuddered.

"Creepy smart. She snuck into the Jessops' yard to do it. Thus ensuring her brother's competition would have to get rid of an entire season's worth of products."

"That means she is more clever than crazy," Frances mused over her knitting

"I think the judge may agree," I said. "At the bare minimum she'll be in mental health lockup for the rest of her life."

"Good," Mom said. "I can go back home without worrying about you."

"You're going back home?" I tilted my head, not sure how I felt about the news.

"Yes, your father called. He wants me back." She got up, put her phone away, and kissed my cheek. "I'm packed and going to take the last ferry off the island. It was so nice to meet you, Jenn and Sandy. Frances, thanks for all you do for my family."

"We love you, too," I said. "Group hug." We all got up and surrounded my mom with love. I watched with amazement as tears came to her eyes.

"I love you all, too," she said and stepped back to wipe the tears from her eyes.

"Have a safe trip," Frances said.

"Can I walk you to the dock?" I asked.

"Sure," Mom said.

And so it was that I stood on the pier and waved good-bye to my mom.

Refreshed from a good night's sleep, I did two demonstrations the next day, enjoying the art of it. Then Trent came by, took my hand, and escorted me to the black-and-white movie. I realized that at this moment in time all was well. And with the support of my family and friends, running the McMurphy was far from the crazy venture I had held on to for so many years. Perhaps, just perhaps, I was finally and truly home.

Acknowledgments

Special thanks to The Island Bookstore of Mackinac Island for help with the details—all mistakes regarding Mackinac Island life are mine as I've never met an embellishment I didn't like. Thanks to the team members at the day job, USDTL, for taste-testing fudge recipes. Thanks to all the wonderful book lovers who support me by reading, editing, cheering, and suggesting—you know who you are Liz, Joelle, Dru Ann, and all . . . Your time and efforts are truly appreciated. Special thanks to my editor Michaela Hamilton for believing in the series, enjoying the recipes, and bringing Gene with her because he has a talent for taking great pictures that make us look so young. Last but far from least, thanks to my agent Paige Wheeler, who advises, negotiates, supports, and frees me to do what I do best—write.

Join Allie, Mal, and their friends
in the next Candy-Coated Mystery

Oh Say Can You Fudge

Coming from Kensington in 2015
Turn the page for a preview excerpt . . .

CHAPTER 1

I was working on a red, white, and blue striped fudge recipe when I got a call from Rodney Rivers. So, of course, I let the call go to voice mail. I mean, nothing, but perhaps the curtains on fire, interrupted working with hot sugar. I was at the most delicate part of making fudge—the stirring to cool. If you overbeat the fudge while it cools, it sugars. If you underbeat the fudge, it's too soft. Therefore a random phone call from the pyro technician in charge of the Mackinac Island Star-Spangled Fourth firework celebration could be answered later. Right?

Except I got caught up in the fudge.

Three hours later, still not happy with the recipe, I noticed the blinking light on my cell phone and called up the voice mail.

"Allie, we've got a problem. Meet me at the fireworks warehouse as soon as possible." Rodney sounded angry. "The entire program is in ruins."

Oh, man, that was not good. I had had to fight my way onto the Star-Spangled Fourth event committee in the first place. It was only because old man Slauser had died in May that I had been able to join the committee and take over the fireworks program. It was all part of my ongoing plan to become an upstanding member of Mackinac Island society.

Message two came up.

"Allie, answer your phone, will you. This is serious and time sensitive." Rodney's tone had gone from angry to desperate. "The entire back row of fireworks has been tampered with—Hey, you, what are you doing here? Are you responsible for . . ." The phone went eerily dead.

Well, that certainly can't be good. I dialed the callback number, but it went straight to voice mail. I left a message. "Hey, Mr. Rivers, this is Allie McMurphy. I just got your voice mails. I'm headed to the warehouse. Call me if you're no longer there. Otherwise, I'm coming down to see what I can do to help." I hung up my phone and stripped out of my chef's jacket, which was stiff from sugar and candy ingredients that tended to float in the air whenever I was inventing something new. The lobby door to the McMurphy was open to let in the soft, fresh lake air, which blew the summer white linen curtains softly. "Frances, I need to meet Mr. Rivers at the fireworks warehouse. Can you cover for me until Sandy comes in?"

"Sure can," Frances, the historic McMurphy Hotel and Fudge Shoppe reservation manager, whom I inherited with the McMurphy, answered from her perch behind the reservation desk. "What's up?"

"He didn't say exactly, but there may be something wrong with some of the fireworks."

"Do you want me to call the fire department?" Frances looked at me over the top of her dark purple reading glasses. It was hard to tell she was in her seventies. She kept her brunette hair immaculate and her skin glowed in a way I hoped mine would at her age.

"No, I think if it were bad enough for the fire department Mr. Rivers would have called them. He's an expert at that kind of thing and has always stressed safety first."

My bichonpoo puppy, Marshmallow—Mal for short—got up from her comfortable spot in the pink doggie bed beside Frances. She stretched her back legs in a manner I liked to call doggie yoga and trotted over to me, then begged to be picked up. When I ignored the blatant display of cuteness, she poked my leg with her nose—a sign she knew I was going out and she expected me to take her.

"No, Mal, it's too far for you," I said and gathered up my keys and things in a small bag with shoestring handles that went over my shoulders like a backpack. Mal sat, sighed loudly, and turned back to her bed. "I'll call as soon as I find out more." I pulled the bag over my shoulders. "Let Sandy know we're short on the chocolate cherry and the cotton-candy fudge."

"Will do," Frances said and went back to her computer. She had been my Grammy Alice's best friend and a teacher who worked for Papa Liam as his reception desk worker for over forty seasons. When Papa had died this March, she had stayed to help me navigate the ins and outs of running the McMurphy. I made her my hotel manager and we made a great team.

I counted on her to introduce me to our recurring customers. Some had been summering at the McMurphy for generations, others just a season or two—but Frances remembered them all.

I went out the back door of the McMurphy and unchained my bicycle from the stand in the back alley.

Part of the appeal of Mackinac Island—besides the world-famous fudge and the grand Victorian painted-lady cottages—was the fact that motorized vehicles, with the exception of the ambulance, were not allowed on the island. That meant there were three modes of transportation: horse-drawn carriage, bicycle, and on foot. Since the fireworks were stored in a cinder-block warehouse near the airport, I decided to bike it. Two miles on foot might make my current tardiness even worse.

It was a lovely day. I was continually amazed at the laid-back beauty of the island and the large state park in the center. The park offered good hiking, beautiful views, and fresh air to anyone who had had enough of the hustle and bustle of the fort and shops of Main Street. I watched the Grand Hotel's Cessna 421C charter plane land as I drew close to the airport.

The warehouse, just outside the airport, was built to store supplies that were flown in during the winter months when the ferries quit running. We picked it for the fireworks storage because it was cinder block and away from the crowds.

A handful of tourists stepped out of the plane and onto the tarmac. The Grand Hotel was a magnet for the wealthy and offered the charter plane service as a quick and easy way onto the island from Chicago or Detroit.

The three men stepping out of the plane were perfectly groomed and wore aviator sunglasses, stylish jeans, and immaculately pressed linen shirts. Two women wore what appeared to be designer-cut halter dresses with floral patterns. Their long bare legs were made even longer by their gold-toned sandals.

The last to step out of the plane was Sophie Collins, the local pilot. She wore a crisp white shirt with epaulets and tan slacks. Her dark curly hair was pulled back in a low, easy ponytail. I waved at her. She waved back, then turned to escort her clients to the waiting horse-drawn carriage that would take them to the Grand Hotel.

I met Sophie at a dinner party Trent Jessop's sister had given for about twenty of the local island folks. Unlike the others, Sophie had been the only one to treat me like an equal. We had a long discussion about the cliquishness of island society. Sophie was in her early thirties and had been a full-time pilot for the Grand Hotel for ten years. She still occasionally ran up against people treating her like an outsider.

I parked my bike in front of the warehouse and took note that there were two other bikes nearby. One had the look of a rental bike. On Mackinac Island there were many places to rent bikes. Most of the better hotels had bike rental right outside their doors. The second bike was a professional off-roader. It had the used look of a local's.

"Hello?" I said as I opened the door. "Mr. Rivers? It's Allie McMurphy. I'm sorry for the delay. I was in the middle of developing a new fudge recipe. I came as soon as I got your messages."

The overhead fluorescent lights buzzed and hissed above me. "Hello?" The first aisle was quiet. While the shelves were filled with boxes large and small, there wasn't a human to be found. "Mr. Rivers? It's Allie. You left me a message about a problem?"

The second aisle of shelves was also empty. I paused to see if I could hear anyone talking. There were two bikes besides mine, so someone had to be here, didn't they?

The warehouse contained two offices in the back near the bay doors, which were big enough to bring in full pallets of supplies—in this case, fireworks. Maybe

Rodney Rivers was in one of the offices with whoever else was here. It could be that they had closed the door and couldn't hear me.

A quick glance down the third and last aisle didn't reveal anything tragic as his voice mail stated. Perhaps he cleared everything up already. After all, it had been over an hour since the last phone call.

My phone rang. Startled, I jumped what felt like ten feet. Clearly I was on edge in the warehouse. I pulled my phone out of my pocket and saw that the number belonged to Rex Manning, sexy police officer and now my good friend. "Hello?"

"Allie, are you okay? Frances said there may be trouble at the fireworks warehouse."

"I'm good, except my heart is racing from being startled by my phone ringing," I replied and walked toward the two offices. The offices were built with half walls of cinder block and the rest of each wall was a window so that the manager of the warehouse could look out and keep an eye on the workers.

Rex chuckled. "Spooky at the warehouse? Where's Phil Angler? He's usually around there somewhere."

"I have no idea. When I got here there were two bikes parked outside. One looked like a rental, so I assume it belongs to Rodney Rivers, maybe the second belongs to Phil."

"Was it a blue off-roader?"

"I think so," I said and continued toward the darkened office. "I wasn't paying that much attention. I was in a bit of a hurry."

"Hurry for what?"

"I got two voice messages from Rodney Rivers. He's the pyro technician I hired for the two fireworks shows.

The first one said we had a problem at the warehouse and I was to call him back. The second got interrupted, but I think he said something about sabotage."

"I don't like the sound of that, Allie. Get out of the warehouse." His tone of voice brooked no argument. Not that his tone had any effect on me.

"I'm fine. As far as I can tell no one's here." I put my free hand on the glass to break the glare and peered into the dark office. "According to my phone the last call was an hour or so ago. Maybe he resolved things already."

"Allie, I'm serious. Get the hell out of the warehouse. Do it now."

"But—"

"I swear, Allie, sometimes you are too stubborn for your own good. Get out. The place might be rigged and—"

"—could explode," I finished and pursed my mouth as I peered down the aisle. The last office was just a few feet away with only the distance of the bay door between me and it. "I watch TV, too. How often does that happen in real life?"

"Allie—"

"Okay, fine. I'm at the bay door in the back anyway. I'll just stick my head over and take a peek in the second office and I'll leave."

"I'm nearly there," Rex said. "I need you to leave now."

"But it's only a few feet and I'll be careful." I checked for trip wires or anything like what you see in movies that might cause an explosion as I carefully tiptoed across the bay door. "If anyone sees me doing this, they're going to think I'm crazy."

"Allie, I'm very serious—"

"I'm being careful, really. I promise, I won't open the

door or anything. I'm only going to peek inside." I slowly made it across the bay to see there was a light on in the second office. "The light is on. I'm sure it will be fine. Phil's probably inside, unaware that you have me skulking around."

"Darn it, Allie."

I peeked inside the window and stopped cold. "Oh, no."

"What is it? What's going on?"

"There's a man slumped across the desk faceup." I couldn't help the wince in my voice. "He's faceup so I can see his expression and his eyes have the same look that Joe Jessop's did. I'm pretty sure he's dead. Do you want me to go in and see?" I reached out to the office doorknob.

"Freeze!" Rex's voice echoed from both the phone and hall behind me.

I screamed a little and wheeled around to see Rex Manning striding purposefully toward me, dressed in full police uniform, his bike helmet still on his head. He had one hand out in the universal sign of *stop* and the other hand on the butt of the gun on his hip.

"Darn it! You scared me half to death." I scowled at him. "How did you get here so fast?"

"Frances called me the minute you left the McMurphy."

"Figures," I muttered. "Why didn't you tell me you were in the building?"

"Get your hand off that doorknob, Allie." Rex was serious, and his seriousness got to me. It was one thing for him to be authoritative on the phone and quite something different to see him face-to-face in full cop mode. I raised both hands slowly in the air.

"I'm not touching it."

"Good," he said and was beside me. "Hang up your

phone." He looked into the office. "Shoot, you're right. He has the blank stare of a dead man. You need to get out of the building." He put his hand on my arm and gently led me to the entrance door beside the bay door. He stopped and carefully inspected the door, running his hand along the edges. "Feels clean." He cautiously opened the door. Alarms went off, blaring.

I covered my ears and let him lead me outside and a few hundred feet from the building. We stood where the surrounding parking lot gave way to woods.

"Charlene," Rex said into the walkie-talkie on his shoulder. "We need the fire department and the EMTs— and call in a bomb squad from Mackinaw City."

"Bomb squad?"

"That's right." Rex studied me. "Allie McMurphy reported a phone call that someone tampered with the fireworks. I want a bomb squad here to check out the warehouse before anyone goes back in there."

"I've got a call into Mackinaw City," Charlene replied over the crackle of the walkie-talkie. "Do I need to send in Shane?"

"What makes you think we need the assistant ME?"

"Allie McMurphy's there, right?"

"Yes."

"Then there's a ninety-eight percent chance she found another dead body."

Rex's mouth went flat, making a thin line of disgust. "Get the fire department out here."

"Yes, sir." She didn't sound the least bit contrite. "That girl is trouble, Officer Manning. Be careful."

"Allie didn't find a dead body," Rex said sharply. "She called in the bomb threat like a responsible adult."

"I'm sure she did." The communicator went dead as they hung up.

I hugged my arms around my chest. "You're right. He only looked dead. You should have let me go check on him. What if he needed help?"

"Let me hear your phone messages," Rex held out his big hand. I called up the voice mail, tapped in my password, and handed the phone to him. His frown grew darker as he listened. "I'm going to have to keep these. They're evidence."

"What about Mr. Rivers? If you won't let me, shouldn't you at least go and check on him?"

"You recognized the guy in the office?"

"Yes, I think it was Rodney Rivers. He is the lead pyro tech I hired to do the Star-Spangled Fourth fireworks show."

He shook his head. "Dead or not, I can't take the chance that the place isn't rigged to blow. That's a warehouse full of fireworks. If it explodes, he really will be dead, along with anyone else inside."

I heard sirens in the distance. The island was anti motor vehicle except for first responders. Then all rules were broken. It only made sense that we had an ambulance and fire truck. There was a limit to charm when people needed help.

"Stay put!" Rex ordered and stepped out to direct the vehicles.

I stuck my tongue out at his back. He whirled around, but I put my hands up and blinked innocently. "I'm staying right here."

Rex was not much taller than me, but he was a big man with shoulders as wide as a mountain, a thick neck, and a shaved head in the fit manner of an action hero. In the last few months I'd gotten to know him well. He had even asked me out once, but I'd already said yes to my current boyfriend, Trent Jessop. It's not that Rex wasn't attractive, but Trent left me feeling like the luckiest girl alive. Meanwhile, Rex was a bit bossy. If you haven't already noticed.

Thirty minutes later I still didn't have my phone and had finally given up and sat down on the curb of the parking area. I had watched as Sophie had flown out right after the call and came back. Three guys in thick bomb suits, with helmets in hand, strolled around the corner where the fire truck and ambulance sat. I assumed that was who Sophie had collected in her quick flight.

I was far enough away from the vehicles that I couldn't hear what Rex said to the men, but their expressions were deadly serious as they put on the helmets and carefully entered the building through the door Rex had pushed me out.

"First time I ever had to escort a bomb squad on the island," Sophie said as she walked toward me from the far edge of the parking lot. "It must be serious for Rex to call in trolls."

Some people called anyone from the Lower Peninsula *trolls* because they lived under the Mackinac Bridge. The suspension bridge is the longest in the Western Hemisphere and the fifth-longest bridge in the world. People around Mackinac were proud that it was nearly twice as long as the Golden Gate Bridge, but the claim to fame ended there as it was not nearly as wide.

"Frances told him I had phone messages about trouble at the fireworks warehouse," I said as she sat down on the curb next to me. "He got all bossy and practically dragged me out of the warehouse."

"If Rex called the troll bomb squad he had good reason to drag you out," Sophie said. "I've known him for ten years and have never seen him panic."

"In my defense, I didn't see anything to worry about until I peeked into the last office." I hugged my knees to my chest.

"Rumor has it you found yet another dead guy," Sophie said as she stretched her long legs out in front of her. "Kind of got a knack for that, don't you?"

"It's a newfound talent," I sighed. "I'd much rather be making fudge right now."

"I heard you hired Sandy as your assistant. That was good. She's one of the best chocolatiers I've ever met—and living on the island, I've met more than my fair share."

I turned my gaze from the goings-on at the warehouse to Sophie. "Sandy is good. She should have her own shop."

"Well, some of us don't have family businesses to go into."

"Ouch."

She sighed and leaned back on her hands. "Sorry. That didn't come out right." She straightened. "I'm glad you gave her a chance. No one else would."

"I needed the help and she's good—better than me with the chocolate sculpture." I studied the building. "Do you think the warehouse will really blow up?"

"No, not unless the bomb guys come across something they haven't seen before."

I winced. "I hope they don't blow up. I've seen enough death in the last few months."

"I'm sure it's just Rex being overly cautious—"

Sudden movement from the emergency guys caught our attention. They were running and hopping in the vehicles and moving them.

"Where are they going?" I stood and drew my eyebrows together in concern.

Sophie stood with me. "This does not look good." She took my arm and pulled me back to the woods.

Rex sent a quick shout to the last responder and ran at us. "Get back!" He waved his hands and Sophie linked her arm in mine and ran headfirst into the woods.

Panic had my heart racing and my feet pounding over uneven ground. We jumped over fallen logs. Ferns and scrub and wild raspberries ripped at our pants and tore at our shirts. Rex caught up with us and pushed us even faster until we hit the top of a hill and half ran, half slid at least one hundred feet down.

The loudest explosion I'd ever heard erupted from the trees above us. Rex shoved us both into the earth, shielding us with as much of his body as possible as dust and rocks rolled over us. I inhaled dust and dry pine needles and coughed, my eyes watering. Pushing to sit up and get some fresh air, I watched in amazement as fireworks whistled into the air, exploding at low angles; their color and sparkles, lost in the daylight, showered the dry woods.

"Get down!" Rex ordered, dragging me back into the dirt as a second loud explosion rumbled, raining more rocks and dust.

The walkie-talkie on his shoulder squawked. "Rex, what's going on? Are you all right?" It was Charlene.

"Call the forest rangers," Rex barked into the communicator. "We've got potential wild fire at the airport."

"Roger," Charlene said. "The fire department is on it."

"What about the airport?" Sophie asked. Her blue eyes shone in her dirt-covered face. "What about my plane?"

Another explosion filled the air. We ducked. I covered my head with my hands as rocks and branches rained down. We were lucky the small ridge above us sheltered us from most of the blast.

The scent of smoke and dirt and fireworks filled my senses. Falling ash burned my hand, and I shook it off. Rex moved, and I looked up to see him stomping out sparks as they threatened the dry pine needles.

Sophie and I got up. She tore off her shirt, leaving her white athletic T-shirt on, and used the shirt to beat out small fires. I kicked dirt over the sparks that fell near me. The fireworks continued to scream overhead. Their whistles and winding patterns drove them to various heights through the air, showering the area in ear-shattering explosions and sparkles of red, white, and blue.

My first Star-Spangled Fourth had just become the worst disaster Mackinac Island had ever seen. Considering the War of 1812, that was saying a lot.